BATTLE TUPI

THE TUPI FIELD SERIES 2

RONALD C. FISH

ISBN: 978-1-63950-264-6 (hc)
ISBN: 978-1-63950-275-2 (sc)
ISBN: 978-1-63950-265-3 (e)

This publication contains the opinions and ideas of its author. It is intended to provide helpful and informative material on the subjects addressed in the publication. The author and publisher specifically disclaim all responsibility for any liability, loss, or risk, personal or otherwise, which is incurred as a consequence, directly or indirectly, of the use and application of any of the contents of this book.

Gateway Towards Success

8063 MADISON AVE #1252
Indianapolis, IN 46227
+13176596889
www.writersapex.com

CONTENTS

INTRODUCTION

T his is the 2nd book in a two-book series "The Tupi Field Series". The series is kind of like Archer meets TOPGUN. In the first book, three characters, all of whom bring their own special baggage to the story, strive to become Marine Officers, jet pilots, pilots who do the hardest thing a pilot can do land a jet on the pitching deck of a carrier at night and in bad weather, and, finally, TOPGUN Aces. Ricky hates all politicians who have run up a national debt of 34 trillion dollars and delivered a future we all are likely to live through. Carmen hates all Chinese Communists, but especially the ones that machine-gunned her Dad right in front of her as a child. And J.J. hates anybody who can pass his jump serve. The three become fast friends as they endure the rigors of training to become Marine Officers and jet pilots. Along the way, there are many hijinks, some steamy sex, many new friends are made, and love accidentally blooms between two of the main characters. The female readers will love this love story, and they are forgiven for skimming over the technical details of wing loading and thrust-to-weight ratios.

For the exciting conclusion of this story in Book 2 featuring a carrier battle between the U.S. and China over the Tupi Offshore Oil Field, including: the dogfight at Top Gun; the gang of aviators partying in San Francisco; a big dogfight at Red Flag; skiing in Vail with the lovely Amber Wong, consigliere to the mob; President Parry, an honest man with guts who was willing to do what was right for country regardless of the political cost to him personally, stopping payment of interest on the T-bills and U.S. bonds owned by China and the Chinese going apoplectic as a result; the Chinese ambassador to the U.S. being called before the president and lying about China's intentions; mysterious Chinese activity at the underground shipyard at Hainan discovered by KH-11 satellites; the Chinese armada setting sail around the Drake Passage, Cape Horn at the southern tip of South America; the U.S. sending liquid methane powered ramjet Aurora spy planes searching for the Chinese fleet; the nuclear raid on and destruction of the missile launch complex at Xichange Satellite Launch Center in Sichuan Province, China; the targeting and knockdown of Chinese satellites following the Chinese knocking down all our spy and communication satellites; the CIA finding the GinWui rootkit installed the Chinese hacker Wicked Rose on all government computers; the nuking of French and British carriers heading for the battle by a Chinese boomer; U.S. Virginia-class stealth submarines that take out the practically invisible Chinese Kilo-class submarines and the Chinese boomers; FEL laser weapons development to shoot down aircraft and missiles and use of it to melt the arming and ignition system of the 5 kiloton nuclear warhead of the DF-21 ASBM fired at the U.S.S. Nimitz; action by the MARSOC raiders using an insect swarm of drones to find the Chinese ASBM hidden in warehouses in Porto Alegre; a SEAL team taking out the Chinese crew of an offshore oil rig; Ricky getting into hack for telling the brass he would not lead the second raid on the carrier killer missiles; the brass relenting after they figures out that what he was talking about was true; Ricky and J.J. and Carmen figuring out the unique strategy to overcome the unique anti-stealth radar system defense of the missiles and leading the raid that took out the Chinese DF-21 carrier killer missiles; and the rest the action of the gripping battle between China and the U.S. Incidentally, Ricky, after being shot down and going into a coma, recovers and finds the love of his life. All this action and more is found in book 2.

Here is what two readers who read both books said about these books:

"When I read The Tupi Field and really didn't know what to expect. To my surprise and delight, it was a kick ass novel for a first-time writer. It starts with a Chinese missile fired at long range from a stealth jet at one of the Marine pilots flying an a F/A-18 Hornet. He beats the missile after running out of propellant trying to follow his juking. But it gives a close-up look at modern aerial combat and the inventive way of using the F-35 for its 360-degree infra-red search and track system to complement the Hornet. The novel traces the trials and tribulations of three Marine jet pilots, one of which is a woman, in their quest to become jet pilots. The Tupi Field has lots of action in the air and the hotel rooms!!! Ron's characters are well-developed, interesting, exciting, and fun. This futuristic view of the world as we run out of energy and start fighting over what's left is sobering and scary. The jet and weapons technology classes that the pilots attend in the middle of the book are pretty deep for the average person, so you may find yourself skimming over those pages so you can get back to the actual battles, and the steamy relationships!!! Along the way, there is lots of kidding, some steamy sex, a whole lot of hijinks, and a Navy pilot who becomes their best friend. The book revolves around the challenge the pilots face in dealing with the technical superiority of the Su-30KII flankers and the fearsome capability of the Chinese DF-21 "carrier killer" anti-ship ballistic missile. The Chinese put up a clever anti-stealth defense to our raid to take out the missiles resulting in a loss of all our planes on the first raid, but our Marine pilots figured out what the Chinese were doing a devise, a daring raid to take the missiles out. I had a great time reading this book, and you will too."

CHAPTER 1

HORIZON BLACK

JANUARY, ABOUT A YEAR AND A HALF BEFORE THE WAR

CHINESE FLANKER PILOT CHIN WOO INTRODUCED

It was twilight at the Cangzhou Air Base in Hebei Province, China. Captain Chin Woo of the People's Liberation Army Naval Air Force (PLANAF) fighter wing was sitting in a strip club in the city outside the base with his wingman Captain Gang Weng. They were both slightly wasted having come to the club on a Friday night after a hard weeks work of classes and air work practicing their tactics for J-20/Flanker wolfpacks for the upcoming invasion of Brazil and takeover of the Tupi Oil and Gas Field.

Captains Woo and Weng were both top pilots in the PLANAF, and were both former instructors in the PLANAF's equivalent of what used to be called Top Gun in the U.S. Navy fighter community. They were assigned to fly the navalized Su-30MK2 Flankers off one of the new Chinese supercarriers that had been under construction since 2015.

VARYAG REFITTED TO MILITARY USE
AND RENAMED SHI LANG

China had started its carrier program in 2001 when it bought the unfinished Soviet aircraft carry *Varyag* from Ukraine supposedly to turn it into a floating casino. Spy satellite photos of the *Varyag* while in port indicate that the plan to turn it into a casino had been abandoned in 2002 and that work had commenced to retrofit the ship at the Dalian shipyard to maintain its military capabilities. She is now operational and has been renamed the *Shi Lang.*

CHINESE PLANS TO BUILD CARRIERS

The Chinese had also purchased three other retired aircraft carriers from Russia and the Australians: the *Kiev,* the *Minsk* and HMAS *Melbourne.* The *Kiev* and the *Minsk* were turned into floating amusement parks after the Chinese engineers had studied their designs including study of the full set of blueprints they purchased for the *Kiev.* The Chinese has also purchased a full set of blueprints of the *Varyag* design, and those designs underwent intense scrutiny by Chinese engineers. In addition to legitimate efforts at acquisition of designs, spy activities were simultaneously being conducted by China to obtain information on carrier design and operations. In February 2011, the Ukraine courts sentenced a Russian national by the name of Aleksandr Yermakov for being paid by the Chinese to steal military secrets relating to carrier operations from the Land-based Naval Aviation Testing and Training Complex in the Crimea.

In the ultimate irony, it was reported in 2009 that the Brazilian Navy trained PLA naval officers in carrier operations in exchange for assistance on nuclear submarine technology.

In August 2011, China conducted sea trials of its first military aircraft carrier. Earlier, in December 2008, multiple reports surfaced that China would build two conventionally powered aircraft carriers based upon the *Varyag* and displacing about 60,000 tons. Those reports turned out to be true, the ships having been subsequently finished early and launched in 2014.

Reports had also surfaced that the Chinese were building two 93,000 ton Type 085 super carriers and two additional Type 089 *Shi Lang* class carriers. What the West did not know was that China had in fact been secretly building six nuclear powered super carriers at their underground navy base on the island of Hainan out of view of the U.S. spy satellites. Although that base was originally thought to be a major underground base only for nuclear submarines, the Chinese had secretly enlarged the Sanya navy base at the southern tip of Hainan Island to enable super carriers to be built and docked underground there inside Hainan Island.

The carriers and nuclear submarines entered and left the underground port and shipyard via a harbor entrance sized big enough to accommodate super carriers. In addition to the super carriers, the Chinese were confirmed to have five Type 094 nuclear submarines operational in 2010 out of Hainan, each capable of carrying 12 JL-2 nuclear tipped missiles. Two 950 meter long piers and numerous smaller ones visible from the sky outside the caverns dug into the interior of the island are large enough to accommodate two carrier strike groups and a collection of amphibious assault ships. Six more carrier strike groups were built inside Hainan Island's caverns to keep them out of view of the spy satellites.

The U.S. knew something top secret was going on at Hainan Island, but was never able to penetrate the thick veil of Chinese security imposed by the Chinese. The Chinese keep a contingent of Su-27 Flankers based at the Lingshui airfield on Hainan Island. The Chinese also maintain a large signals intelligence facility on Hainan Island to keep track of U.S. activity in the area and to monitor traffic from commercial communication satellites. It was super secret, and the U.S. wanted to know more about it.

In 2001, a U.S. Navy EP-3E ARIES II four engine sub hunter aircraft which had been converted to signals intelligence was dispatched from Kadena Air Force Base on Okinawa to make a fly-by of the secret Hainan Island navy base. While operating about 70 miles away from Hainan Island, the EP-3 was intercepted by two Chinese J-8 fighters, and a midair collision between the EP-3 and one of the J-8 fighters occurred. This caused the J-8 to break up in flight and crash killing the Chinese pilot.

The EP-3 was damaged heavily. The J-8 had made three close passes to harass the EP-3 pilot, and, on the third pass, the J-8 tail fin crashed into the left aileron and left outboard engine ripping its propeller off and forcing the left aileron up into the fully upright deflection. This sent the EP-3 into a 30 degree dive at a bank angle of 130 degrees, which was almost inverted. The EP-3 lost 8000 feet in 30 seconds, and lost another 6000 feet before the pilot got the plane under control. The radome atop the plane was completely ripped off and an antenna tangled itself around the tail. Crippled, the EP-3 had to make a forced, emergency landing on Hainan Island after 15 distress calls were ignored by the Chinese. During the 26 minute flight to Hainan Island, the crewman of the EP-3 frantically destroyed sensitive items such as electronic equipment related to intelligence gathering, documents and data. Thinking fast, they poured freshly brewed hot coffee onto disk drives and motherboards to destroy them.

The Chinese not only ignored the 15 distress calls by the EP-3, but also ignored the internationally recognized emergency code the transponder was squawking. The EP-3 then made an unauthorized emergency landing at 170 knots with no flaps, no trim and a damaged left aileron while the pilot was holding a fully deflected right aileron to counter the effects of the loss of number 3 engine and increased drag from the number 1 prop which could not be feathered. The U.S. pilot landed without a working airspeed indicator and no altimeter. It was a miracle nobody was killed on the landing. The crew continued to destroy sensitive equipment and data for 15 more minutes while on the ground before Chinese soldiers with rifles and bullhorns ordered them out of the plane.

The 24 crewman were detained and interrogated by the Chinese until negotiations between the U.S. and China resulted in their release. The plane was studied intensely by the Chinese and they refused to let the Americans repair it and fly it out. Ultimately, it was torn apart, crated up and flown out on a Soviet cargo plane and was repaired and returned to service.

The Chinese pilot, Commander Wang Wei, who flew the J-8 that collided with the EP-3, was seen to eject, but his body was never recovered and he was declared dead. This was not Commander Wei's first such intercept. Commander Wei had recklessly intercepted other EP-3 recon flights in the past, and, in one incident, he flew so close that his email address on a sign he was holding up in the cockpit was visible and readable to the crew of the EP-3. Presumably they sent him some nasty emails.

U.S. submarines have also operated near Hainan Island and have been aggressively harassed by ships and planes of the Chinese Navy and Air Force.

Weng and Woo were getting pretty wasted by now and the Chinese currency was flowing freely which resulted in about six Chinese strippers hovering around them and giving them continuous lap dances.

In a moment of sanity, Captain Weng offered (from the Mandarin): "You know when we invade Brazil and the Americans figure out the Tupi Field is at risk of being brought under the sole control of China, they are going to send their super carriers down to battle us and keep that from happening."

CAPTAIN WOO'S ARROGANT RANT ON
CONDITION OF US MILITARY AND US

"I know. We have already figured that out. Weren't you listening to General of the Army Comrade Lo Binxiao's presentation? That is why we are bringing our anti-ship ballistic missile truck launchers and our Kilo class submarines over to Brazil with us. And furthermore, we are also bringing a couple of ballistic missile submarines loaded with anti-ship ballistic missiles with one of the carrier strike groups. The Brazilians only have one aircraft carrier operational, and it is not an advanced weapons system having been built in the 60's in France. We will not need these ASBM weapons for the flabby, decrepit Brazilian carrier. The Brazilians had a second carrier built in the 60's, but they decommissioned it in 2001. Amazingly enough, they actually tried to sell it on eBay™. Nobody bought it. We can take the single Brazilian carrier out with anti-ship cruise missiles fired from our Flankers or Kilo class submarines.

As for the American super carriers, we can keep them outside of a 1500 nautical mile bubble around the Tupi Field with the ASBM weapons. If they come in, we will blow them out of the water, and they go home with their tails between their legs." Captain Woo replied.

"The Americans are so arrogant, they think they can still control the high seas and establish air superiority even with their out-of-date fighters. The truth is they have been on a long, slow decline for decades. Their government has been running such high deficits that they cannot even afford to build enough F-22 Raptors and other good planes to counter our stock of Su-30MKK and MK2 Flankers, our J-20 stealth jets or even our older J-11s. Our new J-31 carrier-based stealth jet is without equal in their fleet. And we have many J-10 and J-8s we can throw at them too. They have spent trillions on entitlements for their old people, civil service and military personnel and, more recently, on 28 million illegal aliens that they foolishly let in their country to garner their votes for Democrats. That was money that they did not have and had to borrow by issuing T-bills and government bonds upon which they must pay interest. As a result, their interest payments are rapidly approaching their Gross National Product. They now have a National Debt to Gross Domestic Product ratio of 126%. Others still believe the American debt instrument is a good, safe investment. I am not convinced. When their interest payments on that national debt take over almost their entire income, there won't be enough money for defense and other very important programs.

The F-35 Joint Strike Fighter is carrier-based in one version, but it cannot survive against our Flankers, J-20 or J-31 stealth planes. It is a good ground attack fighter and electronic countermeasures platform, but it is a bad air superiority weapon.

The U.S. has the world's greatest air superiority fighter in the F-22 Raptor, but they do not have enough Raptors to go around, and they do not have enough money to build more. The Navy and Marines who we will be facing do not have any at all. Further, even if they could afford to build more F-22s, there is no navalized design of the Raptor so that it can operate off carriers. All the Raptors are in the hands of their Air Force, so I do not think we will be facing any of them. We will control the Brazilian airfields, and our J-20 Stealth jets will shoot down any U.S. tankers over Brazil, so they will not be able to fly any F-22s in from the U.S. to face us."

Woo took a breath and threw down another shot and continued his rant even though he had a hot Chinese stripper on his lap.

"Their F/A-18's are not as good as our Flankers aerodynamically or in it avionics, and the F/A-18 carries many fewer missiles than our Flankers and J-11s. Our Su-30MK2 Flankers can carry up to 14 air-to-air missiles. The F/A-18 can carry only 4 Sidewinders or 4 AMRAAMs, plus 2 Sparrows or 2 additional AMRAAMs. We will outnumber them in terms of both planes and missiles. Our avionics and sensors on the Flankers are at least equal to the avionics on their F/A-18s, and when we get the new AESA radars next month, they will be better. The

F/A-18s have no Infrared Search and Track system, whereas every Flanker has an Infrared Search and Track System with plus or minus 90 degree azimuth coverage and +60 degrees to −15 degrees elevation coverage and a range of 27 nautical miles. We will be able to see even their stealth F-35s with our IRST.

We will shoot their F-35s and F/A-18s down in droves, and hand their pilots heads back to them on pikes. We will end America and take all their possessions. Once we have America under our control, the first thing we will do is to execute all their bankers. It was their greedy bankers who triggered the 2008 meltdown that put 20% of their people out of work and caused everybody to lose half their retirement savings and much if not all the equity in their houses." Woo wrapped up throwing another shot down and grabbing the stripper's breasts .

Finally he was done Captain Weng thought, relieved. But he knew Woo was dead serious. And he also knew that Captain Woo was telling the truth for a change. Weng had been Woo's wingman for awhile, and he knew Captain Woo was a habitual liar and an arrogant blowhard. Woo always shaded the truth, or ignored it altogether to make himself look better.

"Holy shit, you are such an arrogant prick. If I didn't know you were from Beijing, I would swear that you were from Texas. Except some of the Texans actually tell the truth sometimes. That is how I know you are not from Texas." Weng said smiling. But underneath his smile, Weng was serious. Woo was an arrogant jackass who thought he was invincible. Captain Weng hated him, but put up with him because it was not good politics to do otherwise. For reasons known only to Buddha, Captain Woo had throw-weight in the PLA Naval Air Forces, so it was not good for one's career to cross him.

"The J-20 is a great jet. When our hacker network stole thousands of super secret files on the F-35 design from the dumb ass American defense contractor's computers, we greatly improved its stealth." Captain Woo said.

What Captain Woo did not know was that the American CIA had put thousands of fake F-35 designs that were not actually stealthy at all on their defense contractor's computers and left their defenses weak and easy to hack. The CIA effectively let the Chinese hackers steal these bogus files just to screw up their designs. The J-20 was not as stealthy as they thought. And it was not stealthy at all from the rear.

Having had enough for one night, and having been completely relieved of all their money by the strippers, Captains Woo and Weng staggered out of the nightclub and hailed a taxi.

The next morning dawned clear. They were scheduled for an early morning flight with a pair of Su-30MK2 Flankers to engage in a mock dogfight against a pair of simulated F/A-18s.

Captain Woo was standing at the base of the ladder up to his cockpit when Captain Weng walked by on the way to his jet. Woo's jet had a painting of a red Chinese dragon as its nose art. The dragon was holding a Japanese Samurai sword above its head about to swing it downward on the neck of an American pilot. "How do you feel Woo?" Captain Liu said.

"Like dogshit" Woo replied. "Cover me in case I fuck this up."

"Roger that." Captain Weng said. He hoped Woo did fuck it up.

CHAPTER 2

MELTDOWN

President Richard Parry watched with fascination as the CNN coverage of the food riots in Ghana, Senegal, Shanghai, Sudan, Ethiopia, Beijing, Paris, Rome, Athens, London, New York, Los Angeles and Miami unfolded. People were getting desperate all over the world as the rising cost of gasoline and diesel fuel caused the price of food and pretty much everything else too to go up while their incomes, if they had any, stayed the same. Desperate people took desperate measures. People were battling with armed riot police, smashing store windows, looting, setting cars and buildings on fire and generally running wild in the streets. Lawlessness was rampant.

Especially disturbing were the images of class warfare as poor people invaded rich neighborhoods, broke into homes and looted them of everything of value. Rich people were dragged into the streets and beaten before the news cameras.

People had just had enough and could not take it any more. All the inane government spending and waste and the lack of leaders who were willing to tell the truth and set their ships of state on a proper sustainable course finally came down to this. Civility was in the toilet. It was the law of the jungle now.

President Parry called his Chief of Staff into the Oval Office and said, "Set up a meeting with Joint Chiefs, the Defense Intelligence Agency, the National Reconnaisance Office, the Office of Naval Research, the CIA, the NSA, and the heads of the Congressional Budget Office and the Department of Education please. I would like to meet with everybody tomorrow morning in the Situation Room if we can fit everybody in there. Tell everybody I want to hear their opinions on what they think the reactions of foreign governments are going to be to these food riots, what they think we should do to ameliorate this situation in this country and prepare for reactions by foreign governments, and whether or not we should respond militarily or by passing any emergency relief measures. I also want to hear ideas on revising the tax code to raise more revenue and revising the education system."

"Right away sir." Parry's Chief of Staff said. The President spent the rest of the day thinking and preparing.

"Good morning everybody. I have called you together this morning to discuss the dire situation that is unfolding now with widespread civil unrest in this country and abroad, and the implications for our national security. I would first like to discuss the national security implications of this situation so let us open up the discussion with that. I would like to hear first from the heads of the CIA, the National Reconnaissnace Office and NSA. Mr. Rogers why don't you go first with Mr. Headman." President Parry said.

CIA/NRO BRIEFING ON CHINESE PREP FOR WAR AS FOOD RIOTS BREAK OUT WORLD WIDE

Richard Rogers, Director of the CIA and William Headman, Director of the National Reconnaissance Office rose to speak. Mr. Rogers went to the podium, and Mr. Headman took the control for the overhead projector so he could project some spy satellite imagery to illustrate the points Mr. Rogers was about to make. Rogers began his presentation.

"Mr. President and distinguished colleagues. Good morning. We think the Chinese are about to take some drastic military action to seize energy resources they need to bring the cost of living down in their country and stop the food riots. They have 800 million people in poverty, so their situation is dire with the cost of everything rising as energy costs continue their upward spiral.

CIA and the National Reconnaissance Office been observing an unusually high level of preparation activity at the Chinese PLA Navy Bases at Hainan Island and their South Sea Fleet navy bases at Zhanjiang. Amphibious landing LST ships are undergoing maintenance, sea trials and are being loaded with stores adequate for a long voyage.

Many trucks loaded with supplies have been observed entering the caverns at the secret navy base at the southern tip of Hainan Island and off-loading at ships moored at the piers outside the caverns at Hainan Island. This shot from a Misty KH-13 stealth spy satellite was taken yesterday showing a massive convoy of trucks queuing up at the Hainan Island PLA-N navy base to unload their cargoes of weapons and supplies. Many other trucks have been observed making their way to the navy base at Zhanjiang and off-loading at the ships moored to the piers there as seen in this next shot, also taken yesterday. NSA intercepts and other spy satellite photos indicate all these trucks going to Hainan and Zhanjiang originated at Chinese manufacturing centers for laser guided smart bombs, air-to-air missiles, air-to-surface missiles, depth charges, anti-ship and anti-sub torpedoes, anti-ship cruise missiles. Some of the trucks originated at agricultural centers where food is grown and distributed and others came from refineries where bunker oil for ships and JP-5 jet fuel is refined. The degree of supply activity indicates the Chinese are preparing for a long voyage and an extended campaign somewhere.

The ships moored at the outside piers at Hainan, as seen in this next shot, comprise two full carrier strike groups minus the carriers. We believe the carriers are inside the caverns and we have no overheads for those, but we know they have been built and are there. At Hainan, among the ships docked external to the caverns, there are two Aegis-class guided missile cruisers of the *Ticonderoga* class, each armed with Tomahawk-class cruise missiles and anti-ship cruise missiles. There are also six destroyer squadrons, one for each carrier strike group, each destroyer squadron comprised of two guided missile destroyers of the *Arleigh-Burke* class and a multi-mission surface combatant destroyer for anti-aircraft and anti-submarine warfare. Usually one or two *Los Angeles* class attack submarines accompany each carrier strike group and sometimes a boomer boat with ballistic missiles is also included. No submarines are visible, but it is known that up to twenty nuclear-powered submarines may be hiding inside the caverns at Hainan. A combined ammunition supply ship and oiler for each strike group is also visible moored to the outside docks at Hainan.

The ships moored at the docks at Zhanjiang People's Liberation Army Navy (PLAN) navy base comprise the cruisers, destroyers, submarines and ammunition and oiler supply ships of four carrier strike groups minus the carriers. That is clearly shown in this next shot, taken three days ago by a KH-11. We believe six super carriers have been built by China, and are hiding inside the caverns at Hainan.

At various Peoples Liberation Army Navy bases we have observed intense training activities by 24 different squadrons of navalized Su-30MK2 Flankers, 6 squadrons of AWACS planes, 6 squadrons of helicopters, 6 squadrons of Anti-Submarine Warfare planes that double as tankers like our S-3, 6 squadrons of J-31 stealth planes that double as all weather interceptors/bombers and electronic warfare planes like our E-6Bs and F/A-18 Growlers, and 6 squadrons of J-11 copycat Flankers. Preparations include simulated dogfights, air-to-air refueling, simulated attacks on surface ships, tankers and AWACs, anti-submarine warfare and close air support type missions to support troops on the ground. That many aircraft comprise at least six carrier air wings and then some. A couple of new breed of ships we call helo carriers loaded with helicopters have also been observed, and we believe they will carry the helicopter squadrons.

Satellite imagery has also shown intense activity at PLA Ground Force bases including simulated amphibious assaults by four amphibious assault divisions and two amphibious mechanized divisions headquartered in the Nanjing and Guangzhou military regions. Intense training at the bases of their special operations forces and Chinese marines has also been observed. SIGINT satellites have picked up intelligence indicating increased levels of training activities at the bases of their surface-to-air missile defense units and their electronic warfare units also.

CIA has been analyzing the probable effects on the world of future severe shortages of oil and gas. We anticipate that the first effects will be wars between the have and have-not nations. We think China is preparing for just such a war right now. Where exactly that war will occur is the big question.

China has invested heavily in Africa in the last 10-15 years to secure access to the vast natural resources of Africa. The growing appetites of its burgeoning middle class have outstripped the ability of China to satisfy them from its own natural resources. A third of all China's oil consumption is supplied from sources in Africa. China also buys 70% of all Africa's timber. China has 20% of the world's population, but only 9% of its arable land, so China also needs access to Africa's farmland. Will China invade Africa? We do not know. Perhaps our friends at the NSA can answer that. What we do know is that these ships are loaded for bear, and it seems unlikely that the Chinese would need so many air-to-air and anti-ship missiles and so many carrier strike groups to defeat any opposition to an invasion by the military forces of African countries. They are also preparing submarines for long voyages, and that does not compute for an invasion of Africa to safeguard their investments there unless they are expecting us or the Europeans to come to the aid of Africa if that is their target. That is all we have for right now."

"Thank you Mr. Rogers. Mr. Wilmont, can you shed any light on what NSA thinks the Chinese are preparing for?" President Parry inquired.

Tom Wilmont, Director of the National Security Agency, rose to speak and walked to the podium.

"Good morning ladies and gentlemen. NSA's Central Security Service has been making intercepts of Chinese military and civilian emails, telephone calls, telegrams, telex messages, microwave transmissions, satellite communications, military radio communications and military cyphers for quite some time now. We have cracked their cypher codes. We assume the Chinese know we have cracked at least some of their codes, but the fact is we have actually cracked them all. The encrypted military communications we have intercepted contain quite a bit of chatter about Africa and plans to invade the continent to stabilize the situation there and prevent destruction of facilities the Chinese have invested in or built. We suspect this might be a disinformation campaign similar to the one the Allies used before D-Day to fool the Germans into believing the site of the invasion would be at Calais instead of Normandy. The reason we believe this is disinformation is the same reason Mr. Rogers of the CIA already noted: these ships are loaded for bear and seem to be over-prepared for an invasion of Africa with the anemic military forces there. We have detected no other possible targets in communications we have intercepted and decoded.

It is possible, the Chinese might be planning on invading the U.S. if their aim is to gain control of petroleum resources, but frankly, we do not have the volume of petroleum resources they need, so we do not think the U.S. is the target. We do have significant amounts of farmland, coal and natural gas however, and there are significant amounts of oil and gas in the Bakken and Riobraro and other shale formations which can be reached by horizontal drilling and hydraulic fracking. So we cannot rule out the U.S. as a target just yet. But we think since those formations are not yet under full production, immediate production of large amounts of oil and gas in the quantities they need would not be possible and that tends to negate the U.S. as the target.

We believe that the Chinese need huge quantities of oil and liquefied natural gas immediately and so the target is probably Saudia Arabia, Libya, Qatar, Canada, Brazil or the Arab Emirates all of whom have still have oil reserves remaining, some more than others. The Tupi Oil and Gas field off the coast of Brazil ranks high on the list of possible targets since it is the closest and richest field in terms of remaining reserves.

In the case of Canada, their oil reserves are locked up in the tar sands, but there is quite a bit of oil in those tar sands still waiting to be harvested.

If coal or natural gas is what the Chinese are after, then the U.S. is a probable target since we are the Saudia Arabia of coal and natural gas. But we think that is unlikely since the industrial facilities that are necessary to convert coal to synthentic fuel are not built yet. And the facilities in the U.S. to liquefy natural gas for convenient shipping are not large enough to satisfy China's immediate needs. America's only LNG plant is in Alaska. The other LNG liquefaction plants in the world are in the Emirates, Algeria, Indonesia, Brunei, Tobago, Eqypt, Australia, Libya, Malaysia, Nigeria, Norway, Peru and Qatar and there is one in Russia. That is all we have for now."

President Parry said, "Thank you Mr. Wilmont. I would like to hear next from Mr. Steadman and the DIA about what he thinks we ought to do to prepare militarily for what may be happening."

Tim Steadman, Director of the Defense Intelligence Agency rose to speak and walked to the podium.

"Good morning Ladies and Gentlemen. DIA has been working with CIA, NSA and the National Reconnaissance Office for the last several months in assessing the intelligence being gathered about what is going on in China. We believe that the Chinese are getting ready to attack either Brazil or Saudia Arabia and that they expect the U.S. to come to the aid of the target nation. We believe that is why they have built at least six super carriers, and supporting ships for their carrier strike groups.

They have also built at least six ballistic missile submarines that we know of, and they have also built a potent Anti Ship Ballistic Missile force which they would not need to attack most countries in the world. These ASBMs can sink a carrier at 1500 miles. I will have more on that later. We do not believe they think they need that kind of power to defeat Brazil or Saudia Arabia. They probably think that they need that kind of power to defeat us, and that we will come to the aid of whoever they are planning to attack. We believe that is a good assumption, since the security interests of this country would be gravely impacted by a Chinese takeover of any country having significant oil reserves upon which the U.S. is reliant. We know that is true from the effects on our economy from historical events such as the oil embargo during the Carter administration.

We are fairly certain that a carrier battle between us and China is in our future, probably over Brazil or Saudi Arabian oil fields.

In such a carrier battle, the advantage goes to the Chinese. The Chinese Su-30MK2 Flankers they operate from their carriers carry twice as many air-to-air missiles as our Navy and Marine Corp jets we operate from our carriers. Futher, they have developed a new J-31 carrier-based stealth jet which is better than our F-35 carrier-based low observability jet.

The Chinese have made serious investments in their military over the past twenty years building ICBMs, super carriers, fifth generation fighters, stealth jets and ASBMs. They have been investing heavily in their military because they have the money, and they know that eventually the world is going to be overpopulated and resources will run short. Almost everything is made in China now, and they are loaded with cash. So they chose to spend much of it on weapon system development. They have also been busy making deals all over the world to secure resources such as copper, aluminum, wood, food, water, coal, natural gas, oil and many other things a growing country needs for construction.

We, on the other hand, are broke. This may not end well for us. Pardon my brutal frankness Mr. President.

PRESIDENT IS INFORMED OF PLANAF PLANE SUPERIORITY

Let me be more specific about that. The Chinese have acquired from the Russians a large number of Su-30MKK and navalized Su-30MK2 Flankers that are very high capability fighters. In fact, these fighters have better aerodynamic performance and avionics than our Navy F/A-18s and are substantially better than our F-35s in several respects including wing-loading and thrust-loading. The Chinese Flankers have Infrared Search and Track systems that our F/A-18s do not have and their radars can receive data from their AWACs so that they do not have to turn on their radars to make an intercept. They can find our F/A-18s either by seeing them on their IRSTs or by being vectored from their AWACs by downloading AWACs radar returns into their radars by data links. Of course our AWACs will warn our Hornets of approaching Flankers, but in a one on one dogfight, the edge goes to the Flankers.

Our F-35s are more capable and have the same or better capabilities as the Flankers in terms of avionics, and they have much greater stealth. The problem is the F-35s cannot out-fly the Flankers once they are engaged because of the superior aerodynamic performance of the Flankers.

The Chinese MIGs are not better than our F-22s, but neither the Navy nor the Marines have any F-22 Raptors, and will never get any since that program has been cancelled. Further, there are no F-22s that can land on carriers, and, unless we control the airspace all the way to the battle area, no F-22s can be flown in from U.S. or foreign bases because the tankers needed to fly such a mission would be shot down.

If the attack is on Saudi Arabia, we can use our F-22s like we did in Iraq.

CHINA ACQUIRING SUPER FLANKERS

To further complicate the picture, we believe the Chinese are also acquiring an appreciable number of Su-35 Super Flankers from the Russians. The Su-35 Super Flanker is an improved version of the original Su-27 Flanker which is considered to be the best contemporary fighter in the world other than the F-22. The Super Flanker will have improved manueverability with thrust vectoring and improved avionics which gives it a serious advantage in dogfighting. It has been seen at various airshows doing maneuvers which were previously thought to be impossible such as the 360 degree somersault known as the Frolov Chakra and the Pugachev Cobra. The Su-27 and Su-30MKK and MK2 Flankers can do these maneuvers also.

The F-22 can also do them. An F-22 would be able to take out a Super Flanker, because the F-22 has thrust vectoring in addition to stealth which the Flankers do not have. An infrared search and tracking system was originally included on the F-22, but then it was deleted, and the Navy dropped its plans to make a navalized version of the F-22 in 1992. We really should have built a lot more of those F-22s including a navalized version, but it is too late now to help us in this situation. There may not be any F-22s in this fight anyway.

Thrust vectoring and canards on the Super Flanker make it a deadly adversary. Our F/A-18s and F-35's just don't stand a chance against a Super Flanker unless they outnumber it. Extensive use of high strength composites and aluminum-lithium alloys in the Super Flanker reduces its weight and increases its fuel volume and its payload so it can carry even more missiles than its predecessor jets. This further increase its advantages in a dogfight. The Super Flanker also uses two of the Luylka Al-31FM engines which are each more powerful than the original Flanker engine. It has a pulse doppler radar based fire control system which can track fifteen separate aerial targets and guide up to six missiles toward six of them. In short, it is an impressive weapon system which our F/A-18s will not be able to deal with. The F/A-18s are already going to have a hard enough time dealing with the Su-30MK2 Flankers.

To borrow a metaphor Sir, we are going to need a bigger boat."

The President chuckled a little bit and then said, "That would be really funny if this was not so serious Mr. Steadman. Are you done yet?"

OUR DEFENSES TO ASBM DESCRIBED TO PRESIDENT- THAAD, SM3 AND FREE ELECTRON LASER

"No sir. I need to discuss the status of our defenses to the Chinese ASBM. In addition to our Terminal High Altitude Defense or THAAD system, which is a ground based system, we have our AEGIS Ballistic Missile Defense System built around the SM-3 anti-aircraft missiles deployed on our AEGIS cruisers and destroyers. Neither of these systems has been tested against an ASBM, which is different than a standard ballistic missle. It is an open question as to whether either system will work against an ASBM.

The THAAD systems have had pretty good success in their tests. The problem is having a place from which to launch these missiles. The THAAD system is comprised of 5 elements: launchers, interceptor missiles, a radar, THAAD fire control and communications units and support equipment specific to the system. All this requires ground held by us on which to place the system and which is close enough to the area we want to defend. If, for example, the target is Brazil and our carriers are off-shore, we may be able to use THAAD missiles to defend the carriers, but we would have to have a base on land that is secure from which to fire them. This is problematic if the Chinese invade Brazil and take over the whole country. The same is true if the target is Canada or Saudia Arabia.

In addition, there is the Free Electron Laser weapon system which we hope to have operational very soon and which we hope can shoot down a missile by burning up its re-entry vehicle. The Free Electron Laser is a ship-mounted, 100 kilowatt laser beam which can hit incoming missiles, drones and small planes such as fighters and knock them out of the sky without being dependent upon a supply of missiles. Our first successful test was 2011. The Office of Naval Research working with a private lab in Newport News, Virginia pumped 500 kilovolts into a prototype accelerator and got a 15 kilowatt laser beam out of it. That prototype technology was given to Boeing with an order to turn it into a 100 kilowatt laser weapon system. They did that and successfully shot down a drone in 2009 with their Avenger system. The Avenger system was deployed in 2012 at 100 kilowatt power and is now on all our AEGIS cruisers and destroyers. Development has continued. They got close to the 100 megawatt mark in 2024. Operation at 1000 megawatt levels is expected sometime in 2026 or shortly thereafter, but there is certainly no guarantee of success.

The system is still not perfect and does not work sometimes. We are hoping to deploy the system on each of our super carriers this year, but there is no guarantee it will work, and it has never been successfully tested against a ballistic missile. When it works, the system can be tuned to operate at different frequencies which is advantageous to meet the conditions of the day.

When the Free Electron Laser works, the incoming targets cannot evade the beam even while in clouds since it is a free electron laser and not a solid state laser. MIRVs are useless against it since the beam moves at the speed of light and can rapidly be targeted on each independent re-entry vehicle. Drones and airplanes have little chance against it.

This Free Electron Laser technology is much more sophisticated and will be more effective than our "Star Wars" Anti Ballistic Missile programs which have reached their limits in terms of hitting a piece of metal in the sky with another piece of metal, both of which are travelling faster than a bullet. MIRVs with decoys were a major bugaboo to the ABM programs. The ABM systems could not destroy all the re-entry vehicles without excessive expenditure of resources given the limitations of the intercept process. There was never a 100% success rate guarantee in the ABM systems. This is because of the extreme difficulty of hitting a target screaming in hypersonically from space with a mach 4 missile shot from the ground. It was like hitting a bullet with another bullet except the target was moving faster than a bullet as was the interceptor missile.

PRESIDENT INFORMED OF DF-21C ASBM

The Chinese also have the Dongfeng DF-21C medium range ballistic missile. We believe over 100 of these have been built. It is solid fuel, two-stage rocket originally designed to be launched from an SSBN nuclear submarine, but it has also been developed to be launched from a transporter-erector-launcher vehicle. It carries a 600 kilogram conventional warhead, and is believed to be capable of carrying a single nuclear warhead of 200-300 kiloton yield or Multiple Independent Re-entry Vehicles some of which are nuclear and some of which are dummies to foil our Anti Ballistic Missile defenses.

The U.S. has 75 different varieties of nuclear weapons, and the Chinese have stolen the designs for every single one of them and copied them. Therefore, there is no reason to believe that any DF-21C carried aboard a Chinese boomer will not be nuclear-tipped with Multiple Independent Re-Entry Vehicles (MIRVs) since our Trident

II submarine-launched ballistic missiles are all nuclear-tipped with MIRVs, and the Chinese have the designs for all our warheads.

The Chinese Anti-Ship Ballistic Missiles are based upon this DF-21 airframe and have a range of at least 1200 miles, probably 1500 miles max. One test of a DF-21 that was observed involved a flight over China of about 1300 miles.

SEA SCANNING SATELLITES, DRONES AND AIRCRAFT FEED FIX

The Chinese ASBMs use a C4ISR Command, Control, Communication, Computers, Intelligence, Surveillance and Reconnaissance system for geo-location and tracking of surface ship targets to give the missiles an initial target location. Basically, the ASBM can use satellites or aircraft or drones to give the missiles an initial fix to which it should fly to be in the neighborhood of the target ship. The Chinese are also working on over-the-horizon VHF radar to give the missile an initial target fix also.

HOW ASBM FLIES DESCRIBED TO PRESIDENT

The ASBM starts out by flying ballistically straight up and then, at the edge of space, it turns and flys horizontally parallel to the ocean surface toward the initial fix. The missile then uses on-board Synthetic Aperture Radar for terminal phase guidance as it is flying parallel to the ocean surface. During this phase, the missile is looking down at the ocean with its synthetic aperture radar to find the specific surface ship which is the target. Once it finds its target ship, it starts a vertical death dive and crashes into the ship and detonates its warhead.

Our intelligence indicates the Chinese have launched a constellation of 16 sea scanning satellites, 8 spy satellites for imaging and 8 radar satellites as part of their ASBM C4ISR system. Their radar satellites use Russian-made Synthetic Aperature Radar to create detailed radar images of the ocean's surface to find our ships.

This Chinese ASBM is a nasty weapon system to which we are not sure we have an answer. It was originally designed to keep our carriers at bay and away from any battle over Taiwan. But now, with truck mounted launchers and deployment on their boomers, there is no reason why they cannot take these ASBMs to any remote operation theatre.

CHINESE NUCLEAR BOOMER SUBS

China has been developing a second-generation, nuclear-powered ballistic missile submarine designated the 09-4 at their Hu Lu Dao Shipyard to replace their older Xia-class SSBNs. The second generation SSBN will have 16 tubes and will carry the JL-2 ballistic missile. Russia is believed to have helped them improve the noise insulation of the hull to make the sub quieter and decrease its vulnerability to ASW systems. China is believed to have built at least four and possibly six of these second generation boomers at their secret underground navy base on Hainan Island out of view of our spy satellites.

They are also believed to have developed a second generation attack submarine designated the 09-3 with Russian assistance. These attack boats are quiet and are believed to be armed with the nuclear-tipped Skhval 200 kiloton, rocket-powered torpedo, ASW missiles to attack other submarines and probably submarine-launched cruise missiles such as the Sizzler for attacking surface ships. If a carrier battle develops with China, DIA recommends sending at least six of our attack submarines with six carrier strike groups to find Chinese attack boats, boomers and Kilo class mini subs and take them out.

PREPARATION ORDERS SUGGESTED TO PRESIDENT

Since it takes awhile for a carrier strike group to provision its ships and get all of its personnel ready to ship out, and since it is very likely we are going to have to get involved in whatever the Chinese are planning, I would suggest that orders be given to at least six carrier strike groups to prepare immediately for possible deployments within the next 3-6 months to Brazil or Saudia Arabia. I would also give orders to the First and Second Marine Divisions to prepare for deployment soon for a possible amphibious invasion of territory controlled by the Chinese in Brazil or Saudia Arabia.

I would also order the 101st and 82nd Airborne Divisions of the Army to begin immediate preparations for a deployment to happen very soon. We are going to need to seize control of airfields on land to act as bingo fields for our carrier-based fighters and as bases for operation of F-22s and for tanker operations of the Air Force.

We are also going to need to seize control of an area near the coast off which our carriers are operating to place our THAAD systems. I would suggest ordering the 75th Ranger Regiment to prepare to deploy their three Ranger Battalions on an airborne assault to take and hold an area to set up and operate or THAAD systems on the coast of Brazil or Saudia Arabia. They should start their training now. I am not sure we can seize any ground to put THAAD systems in if the carriers cannot get within 1500 miles of the coastline where ASBMs are stationed on truck mounted launchers. 1500 miles is too far away for carrier-based jets to establish an area of air superiority, and the THAAD batteries would be in trouble without air superiority over their heads.

I would suggest contacting the Air Force First Operations group and ordering it to get the 27th Figher Squadron of F-22s at Langley Air Force Base ready for a long deployment possibly to Brazil or Saudia Arabia within the next 3-6 months and to plan for the contingency that we do not have air superiorty to protect the tankers. I would also order the 7th and 19th Fighter Squadrons at Holloman Air Force Base and Hickam Air Force Base to get their F-22s ready for the same deployment.

This is risky business though. If the Chinese bring their J-20 and J-31 carrier-based Stealth aircraft with them, the F-22s would be at risk since they are not designed to land on carriers and would be heavily dependent on a viable tanker force. The J-20s are long range jets designed to sneak up on our tankers and take them out. Without tankers to gas them up for the trip home, the F-22s will flame out and crash before they ever make it back to base. So seizing control of one or more airfields in or adjacent to whatever country is attacked is imperative for the F-22s to operate. It is also imperative for carrier jets to have a bingo field land if necessary when conditions dictate. Seizure of all the airports in the target country by the Chinese is highly likely since the Chinese are obviously arming for some type of amphibious invasion.

We have to get the First and Second Marine Divisions ready to invade the target country to seize control of the ports and air bases. We will also need to find and take out their boomers and their truck-mounted ASBM launchers. We know they brought truck mounted missile launchers. We are just not sure whether they are DF-21C medium range ballistic missiles or DF-21D ASBMs. I suggest we notify the SEALS and MARSOC Force Recon to start training teams for this mission of finding the truck-based ASBMs.

We should also order the Screaming Eagles of the 101st Army Airborne division to prepare for an aerial assault to wrest control away from the Chinese of one or more airbases for F-22 operations and for bingo fields. That necessity would arise if one or more of our carriers is sunk or if our aerial refueling tankers are shot down and the fighters do not have enough gas to get back to the carriers. It is also necessary if a pilot is having trouble getting back aboard a carrier such as in bad weather.

I suggest that orders be determined and finalized and issued very soon. Also, getting two entire divisions of Marines and the 101st Airborne division embarked and on their way cannot happen overnight. We also need to issue orders the First through Sixth Ranger battalions to prepare for assaults on drilling platforms, oil wells, pumping stations, refineries and oil export ports because we think oil reserves are what the Chinese will be after.

We also need to prepare orders to all the SEAL Teams to prepare to deploy aboard the attack submarines to assist in deploying towed Continuously Active Sonar towed arrays to find the Kilos and to assist in rescuing downed pilots and recapturing oil rigs and drilling ships. We also need to prepare orders to Force Recon teams in 1st and 2nd Marine Divisions to prepare for missions to assist in finding and rescuing downed Navy and Marine Corp pilots that are shot down over land. We need to issue orders to the MARSOC Force Recon teams to prepare for missions to infiltrate and destroy Chinese radar, satellite uplink and downlink and command and control communications facilities.

That is all I have for now."

President Parry stayed seated and spoke in a steady voice despite what he had just heard. "Thank you Mr. Steadman. I would like to hear from Mr. Picket now regarding what the Joint Chiefs think about Mr. Steadman's advice, and I would like to hear from Dr. Bianchi and ONR for more information on the status of development of the Free Electron Laser System." President Parry said.

Roger Picket, Chairman of the Joint Chiefs of Staff stood up and walked to the podium along with Dr. Michele Bianchi, Director of the Office of Naval Research which was working with the Department of Energy on development of the Free Electron Laser. Roger Picket spoke first.

JOINT CHIEFS RECOMMENDATIONS TO PRESIDENT

"Thank you Mr. President and good morning ladies and gentlemen. The Joint Chiefs concurs with Mr. Steadman's assessment and recommendations. We would add that orders should be given the 82nd paratrooper division to get ready for an airborne assault in support of the Marine division's amphibious landings.

Mr. Steadman did not include much detail about the Chinese capability to use small, very quiet Russian-made Kilo class diesel-electric submarines to attack our carrier strike groups. The Chinese are known to have 2 of the original Kilo class submarines and 10 of the improved Kilo boats.

These Kilos are only 230 feet long so they are tiny by sub standards and that makes them hard to find. What makes them even harder to find is the fact that they have anechoic sound absorbing tiles fitted on casings and fins and lining the hull to absorb the sound waves of active sonar systems. This results in reduction in amplitude and distortion of sonar returns thereby making it difficult to detect them with active sonar systems. The anechoic tiles also help absorb the sounds made internally in the submarine, and this greatly reduces the range at which these small subs can be detected by passive sonar systems.

KILOS DESCRIBED TO THE PRESIDENT

These Kilo class subs have a 7500 nautical mile range at 7 knots while snorkeling and 45 days sea endurance. That means they would have to be towed to the area of operations presumably if the target is one of the two areas we think most likely. Kilos are best suited for operating in shallow water as their dive depth is only 250 meters, but they can operate in deeper water also.

The Chinese Kilo class subs are based with their Eastern Fleet at Zhoushan, Zhejiang Province near the Taiwan Strait.

Each Kilo class sub has a combat information system which can track 5 targets simultaneously, 2 automatically and 3 manually. Each boat has launchers for up to 8 Strela-3 or Igla surface-to-air missiles with infrared seeker heads and 2 kilogram warheads with a maximum range of 5-6 kilometers at mach 1.65.

These Kilo subs can also be fitted with the Novator Klub-S Sizzler sea skimming anti-ship cruise missile system which fires 3M-54E1 supersonic missiles with a 220 kilometer range and a 450 kilogram high explosive warhead. These Kilos are designed for anti-submarine and anti-surface-ship warfare, but they are short on countermeasures. Once we find them, they are toast.

CAS AND UNDERWATER DRONES AND SEAL DELIVERY VEHICLES DESCRIBED

Continuous Active Sonar towed arrays are the only thing we have that can detect them. CAS arrays emit a continuous stream of low level acoustic signals the echoes of which provide a continuous stream of data which are integrated by computers running high tech signal processing programs into a single high definition image. This defeats the sound absorbing anechoic tiles that line the hulls of Kilo class boats, because the CAS systems are so sensitive, they can pick up even weak returns in the continuous stream of return data and integrate them into a good image. Testing has been completed for arrays towed from surface ships, and testing for use of CAS arrays either on or towed by underwater drones is almost complete with substantial success. The underwater drones are small vehicles that can be launched from submarines and from rubber boats or dedicated SEAL delivery submarines to cruise a programmable course or search pattern. They are armed in some case also with torpedoes. The SEAL Teams and their delivery submarine can be air dropped into an area or inserted into an area by a sub. The SEAL delivery submarines can also tow the CAS arrays.

Therefore, we would also recommend that orders be issued to supply USNS *Impeccable and* USNS *Able* with Continuous Active Sonar towed arrays and to supply several SEAL Teams with small underwater drones equipped with CAS arrays. We would also recommend the special SEAL teams with SEAL Delivery Vehicles be supplied with towed CAS arrays and trained in their use. We concur with the recommendation that several SEAL teams be deployed with these drones or SEAL Delivery Vehicles and CAS towed arrays onto *Virginia* class fast attack submarines to be deployed to the area quickly to hunt the Kilos. That is all I have to add for now. Dr. Bianchi, the podium is all yours."

Dr. Michele Bianchi took the podium.

FREE ELECTRON LASER WEAPON

"Thank you Mr. Picket. The Office of Naval Research has been working with the Department of Energy's best scientists to develop the Free Electron Laser weapon system. This work has been going on in various labs of the DOE and in universities across the country. We are treating this as a high priority project. Our goals are to increase the power of the system, increase its reliability and decrease its size. We have experts in electron injection, accelerators, electron beam dynamics and photon optics all working on the problem. The problem is very complex. If any one of the components fails, the system will not generate enough power in the beam to destroy the inbound target.

The FEL laser uses a superconducting electron gun powered by a microwave tube and which feeds its output beam into an accelerator. Amplifiers increase the power of the beam. The frequency is tunable and no time between shots is necessary. The FEL can run continuously. We have made substantial progress, but the system has not been perfected yet to run in the megawatt power range. The current shipboard systems are running at 100 kilowatt power and have been successfully been tested against drone targets. This FEL system is not powerful enough yet to shoot down an ASBM coming down from the edge of space, but we think we are getting close. Another couple of years maybe. That will take 1000 megawatt power, and we are not there yet. But we are very close, and we have a Beta test system installed on the USS Enterprise now. A carrier is the ideal vehicle for an FEL weapon since the carrier generates tremendous amounts of power in its engines that we can use.

So for the moment, we will have to rely on THAAD missile interceptors or AEGIS SM-3 missiles to shoot down ASBMs in their terminal phase or Network Centric Airborne Defense Element missile interceptors to shoot down ASBMs in the boost phase.

Alternatively, we can find their truck-mounted launchers and their boomers and destroy them. Before the ASBMs are ever launched.

Still another option is to shoot down their targeting satellites and destroy the over-the-horizon targeting radar that give the ASBMs the initial target location information needed before they launch. However, shooting down their targeting satellites and destroying their over-the-horizon targeting radar is not enough since they can get their initial fix information from drones or aircraft also. That is all I have for now. Do you have any questions Mr. President?"

"Yes. Realistically speaking, no bullshit, how close are you to achieving 1000 megawatt power output on the FEL?" President Parry asked.

"Pretty close. We think we will have it within the next year or two." Dr. Bianchi replied.

"Thank you Dr. Bianchi. Please crack the whip on your troops to perfect that FEL systems. OK Chiefs, I agree with your recommendations. Make it so. Send the orders you draft to me for final review by tomorrow end of day.

I would like to hear from Dr. Handler next on the feasibility of providing direct food aid from the federal government as a disaster response to the people in the U.S. who are rioting for food. I would also like to hear proposals to reform the tax system to generate more revenue for the federal government." President Parry ordered.

DR. HANDLER RANT ON WALL STREET, DEFICIT SPENDING, TAX REFORM, DERIVATIVES

Dr. Lucy Handler, Director of the Congressional Budget Office took the podium and began.

"Thank you Mr. President. Direct food aid to the rioters in the U.S. is not feasible right now unless some drastic measures are taken to cut spending elsewhere. Some of these measures would be quite inflammatory, and I hesitate to recommend them for that reason. Direct food aid to U.S. rioters would cost 450 billion dollars. As you know and stated in your 2017 speech to the public introducing the bill to eliminate funding for Medicare and cut the military budget by 45%, federal spending to service the national debt was 80% of the gross domestic product when you made that speech. It is up to 95% now just 3 years later. The situation is now critical and any further federal deficit spending is not recommended.

The federal budget is on life support. Drastic cuts in spending and reform in the structure and operation of government are absolutely necessary or the United States will soon be a thing of the past. Reform of the tax system to generate more revenue for the federal government is unfortunately also necessary. I would suggest legalizing drugs and taxing them, because we are never going to win that war as long as there is profit in selling drugs.

Like Rome, we will become a civilization that was once great but collapsed if the interest payments on the national debt becomes so high we can no longer afford to pay for critical services. In our case, the cause of our demise as a society will be fiscal mismanagement which has become so severe, that we can no longer afford a strong military to defend us.

I would recommend a flat income tax at 10% which is non voluntary, a national sales tax at 10%, a value added tax of 10% but maintaining depreciations deductions so as to encourage buying of capital equipment needed to form small companies which is where all the major job creation occurs.

I would also recommend eliminating the capital gains tax to encourage investments, especially in small companies, and implementation of a financial transactions tax to tax the big deals Wall Street makes. It is time those investment bankers pay for their reckless excesses. You are going to need major political courage, because Wall Street spreads so much money around the Hill on both sides of the aisle."

"Whoa Dr. Handler, I asked about food aid and tax reform, not your recommendations on how to reform Wall Street and federal deficit spending." the President interrupted.

"Sorry Sir." Dr. Handler was trembling now and quite upset. She lived with the numbers everyday, and she knew what was going to happened to the United States in the not too distant future unless something drastic was done. She had never been invited to a meeting like this and felt morally obligated to do something while she had the President's ear.

"Continue." the President said.

"I would also make most if not all derivatives illegal, and make it a crime to construct CDOs based upon undocumented or stated income 'liar loans' and then peddle them as AAA rated investment grade instruments. They are junk. Wall Street knew it, and sold them anyway without the slightest concern for the well being of their clients.

Nobody went to jail for it. How can that even be? That is what brought the whole world's economy to this sorry state of affairs, destroyed the real estate market, brought 1 in 10 Americans below the poverty line and decimated everybody's stock market investments."

"Dr. Bianchi, did you not hear what I said?"

"Sorry sir. I just feel somebody has to tell you this stuff in case your staff and aids are a bunch of yes men and never tell you what you don't want to hear.

On a more realistic note, here are a couple things we could probably actually get through Congress. I would recommend complete and permanent elimination of the estate tax so families can maintain operations of their farms and companies upon death of the owners as opposed to having to sell them just to pay the death taxes. I would also recommend a stiff tax on oil and gas consumption to drive the market to alternatives, rail and other public transportation and to decrease the amount of greenhouse gases we put into the air every year."

And with that, Dr. Handler briskly walked to her seat and sat down still trembling.

President Parry was visibly upset now. He spoke from his chair without going to the podium.

"OK Dr. Handler, I am suitably chastised now, and you have made some very good points upon which I will direct my staff to draft legislation. But I really want to explore the possibility of giving food aid to our population. Although I am generally a proponent of smaller government, and self-reliance by the people, this seems to be a worldwide meltdown. We seem to be facing the end of the United States as we know it. Something drastic must be done. A whole paradigm shift is needed. What can we do? Do you have any recommendations Dr. Handler on how to implement the changes you suggest and actually get them through the legislature? By the way, I am with you on the derivatives thing and making it a crime to peddle junk as AAA rated instruments. Those Wall Street pricks spread 300 million dollars a year in lobbying money around the Hill and they own Congress. It will be rough sledding to get anything through Congress that adversely impacts the bankers."

Dr. Handler remained seated and spoke quietly but firmly, just loud enough to be heard by all present.

"Mr. President, we simply cannot add any more to the national debt by continued deficit spending. If you insist on giving food aid, you must pay for it by cuts in other spending. I would recommend first cutting off all foreign aid, especially to Pakistan. Those people have been harboring our enemies for years while gladly accepting our aid. And when we have a disaster here, nobody comes to help. What is the point of foreign aid except in countries where we need bases. Next, I would disenfranchise all people receiving government financial benefits of any kind or who does not pay at least a minimum level of taxes. Our system has been hijacked by moochers, and they keep electing anybody who promises them benefits or spending programs. The spending must be drastically cut back. Why should the moochers be allowed to dictate how the taxes collected from producers is spent so they can get more benefits. So as to avoid it becoming one of the biggest consumer frauds in history, I would not impose a means test on people collecting social security, but I would raise the retirment age to 70 and really go after age discrimination. I would impose quotas on companies to require they have a certain percentage of mature workers over 50.

Finally, I would stop paying interest on the T-Bills and Bonds purchased by China. They will go ballistic, but it looks like we are going to war with them anyway. That is what I would do. It's your call. If you introduce such legislation, it will be up to the House of Representative to man up and pass your bill and for the Senate to man up and approve it. It will take big time political guts by you and the Representatives and Senators to finally do what is right for the country and not just right for their own re-election prospects. I am a realist, so I don't think any of this will actually pass. There is just too much influence on the hill by the big money interests.

This should have been done decades ago, but all the previous Congresses kicked the can down the road, and now we are paying the price."

"You've got guts Dr. Handler. I really like that." President Parry said smiling at her.

"The question now sir is do you have the guts to do what needs to be done. I think you do from what I know of you as a man and from your record in California. God help us all if you do not." Dr. Handler said with great courage and conviction. People just didn't talk to the President that way. But it was time for some straight talk, and she knew that he was a gutsy politician that did not shy away from a controversy and did not ignore the elephant in the room or politically inconvenient topics.

She was right. The President laughed and said, "Bravo Dr. Handler. I applaud your courage and candor."

President Parry said, "OK, I would like to hear from Dr. Pirot on ideas to reform the educational system. I am sick of having whole generations of nitwits with no skills running around my country."

DR. PIROT ON REFORM OF THE EDUCATION SYSTEM

Dr. Paul Pirot, Director of the Department of Education got up and walked to the podium.

"Thank you Mr. President for giving me the opportunity to make a contribution here. Yes, I agree with you that we are facing the end of this country as we know it. Something drastic must be done, and I will support you no matter what you want to do. The United States is currently ranked 23rd in the world in reading comprehension, 26th in the world in general education and 31st in the world in math and science competence. Those are truly frightening numbers. We have kids graduating from high school who cannot balance a checkbook or point out where Brazil is on a globe. We have good jobs in numerically controlled machine operation going begging because kids do not understand decimals. We cannot have a productive, competitive economy where our workforce is made up of a bunch of nitwits as you so eloquently put it.

I would recommend following the Finnish example. They recruit their teaches from the top 10% of their classes and pay them like lawyers and doctors. They get smart, hard working students out of their school systems, and that is what we need. Accordingly, I would recommend firing all the teachers who did not graduate in the top 10% of their classes and giving competence tests to the ones who are not fired and giving competence tests to the recruits who are hired from the top 10% to replace the ones who did not make the cut. I would set a national pay standard for teachers at the levels at which first year associates in major law firms are paid, and implement heavy taxes on cigarettes, alcohol, soft drinks and unhealthy fast foods to pay for it.

I would implement grade level minimum competency tests each student has to pass to move on to the next grade, and fire any teacher caught teaching the tests. I would then establish a system of federally subsidized trade schools to teaching welding, CNC machines, plumbing, construction, drywall, carpentry, auto mechanics, waitressing, cashiering, assembly line skills, aircraft manufacturing skills and other very practical skills to the students who cannot pass their grade level competency tests after three tries or any other student who chooses to work in blue collar jobs regardless of their level of competency. That is what I would do. The teacher unions will go ballistic, but we have to do something drastic. Thank you sir."

President Parry, who did not have union support anyway, erupted.

"Screw the unions. Those guys drove wages and benefits up so high they decimated entire industries as the jobs all moved to China. I have no soft spot for unions. I think globalization was the biggest policy mistake in the long history of policy mistakes. The benefit of lower cost goods to American consumers is far outweighed by the decimation of entire industries and towns and the creation of a class of 47 million Americans who cannot even afford basic health care. It is time to get America going in the right direction again. I don't care what the talking heads say about me or what the people think about me or how they vote. I took this job to try to help America regain its strength, and I could not care less if I get re-elected. I don't need the money or this job. We are going to do what is right and people are just going to have to make some sacrifices. It is just not right that the only ones making sacrifices are our brave men and women in uniform."

PRESIDENTS ORDERS AFTER RANTS

And with that brave speech having been spoken, President Parry concluded the meeting with:

"OK. Lets get busy. Thank you all for coming. I would like the Joint Chiefs to draft orders for my signature along the lines recommended here this morning by Mr. Steadman, Mr. Rogers, Mr. Headman, Mr. Wilmont and Mr. Picket. I would like you Dr. Handler to draft a bill I can introduce into Congress cutting off all foreign aid, stopping interest payments to the Chinese and reforming the Social Security system along the lines you recommended. I would like you to supervise the

Office of Management and Budget to draft another bill to implement a flat tax system which is not voluntary which imposes a flat 10% income tax on all citizens and corporations and other entities, a 10% value added tax and a 10% national sales tax and drops the capital gains tax to zero and eliminates the death tax forever. Depreciation deductions are to be allowed as they encourage people to buy capital equipment and that creates jobs. Deductions for contributions to private retirement plans are to be retained since the social security system and military retirement plans might not make it out of this paradigm shift alive. I would like you to also draft a bill for temporary emergency food aid to U.S. citizens only Dr. Handler, and citizenship will have to be proven to receive the aid. That bill should implement a national ID card and bar state and federal agencies from giving aid or benefits to illegal aliens. That bill should also heavily fine any employer caught using illegal aliens and implement surprise INS raids on employers to check citizenship status of their employees. Mr. Pirot, I want you to supervise the Department of Education in drafting a bill which mandates competency testing in our high schools at every grade level, fires all existing teachers and re-hires only the ones who are from the top 10% of their classes and top 10% in performance of their students and sets national pay scales for teachers at the pay of beginning law school grads in the large law firms. Any teacher whose students do not pass consistently pass competency tests at their grade levels is to be fired in an on-going quality control effort. Any students who consistently fail to pass competency tests is to be kicked out of their high schools and shunted to vocational schools to learn manufacturing and construction and other blue collar skills. I also want a special task force set up by the FBI and Justice to investigate fraud in the collection of medicare and social security benefits by U.S. citizens and by illegal aliens who scam their way onto the system, and I want that task force to also investigate fraud in the social security disability system. I want the task force to also investigate all complaints of age discrimination. I also want the law amended to set up a presumption of guilt of age discrimination against all companies who do not have in their workforce a percentage of workers over 50 which is equal to the percentage of workers over 50 in the population. And I would like the full retirement age raised to 70 and no income restrictions for people over 65 that would adversely affect their social security benefits. And I want it made illegal for all lobbyists to assist in or write legislation. I also want taxes raised on the oil companies and pharmaceutical companies, and off shore tax havens closed. I also want drugs legalized and taxed so as to put the cartels out of business. I would like those bills on my desk three weeks from today to initiate the legislative process. Thank you and the meeting is adjourned."

REACTIONS TO PRESIDENT'S ORDERS

And with that, the President set America on an economically sustainable course into the future. The move by the president was politically suicidal and cataclysmic in its effect on established institutions in America. The Democrats and liberals went ballistic as did the American Association of Retired People, all the liberals and most of the other social security beneficiaries. All the foreign countries whose foreign aid was cut off cried foul, especially Pakistan. Ironically, Pakistan screamed and yelled just as yet another Al Quaida leader was found hiding in Pakistan and was killed by a missile strike from a Predator drone. That event followed the discovery during the previous week that Pakistan had for years been selling nuclear technology to Iran's nuclear weapons program.

The Chinese were apoplectic when they found out that America was going to stop paying interest to them on the U.S. government bonds and T-bills held by China. That was the biggest default by a government on its obligations ever in the history of the world, and it set the U.S. on a collision course with mighty China. China had been a third world backwater when Nixon opened the country to foreign trade. Now, because its extremely low labor rates and the massive outflow of manufacturing jobs from the U.S. and other countries to China, and massive investment by the Chinese government in development of weapons systems, China had become a legitimate superpower with a blue water, super carrier navy and a fearsome missile force and fighter forces. While that had been happening, the U.S. had been on a steady decline with falling average income, declining performances by its school children on standardized tests, continued exportation of jobs to China and India and rising national debt.

And so it started. President Parry had kicked the beehive, but he did not back down from any of it. He had several idiosyncratic characteristics. For one, he was willing to do what was right for the country regardless of the personal cost to him. He was also willing to call a spade a spade, and had no regard for political correctness. In short, he was willing to do what needed to be done and say what needed to be said regardless of the effect it had on his personal well-being or the damage it did to his political career. He was, in short, not your normal politician. The country badly needed more men like him.

The media and the people in the country whose oxen had been gored did not see it the President's way. Most people in the country believed that the only people who needed to sacrifice to preserve our way of life were the brave men and women in uniform. They were just plain wrong about that, but nobody could convince them thereof. Self-centered personalities had become the social norm. The can-do "lets all pull together" attitude, willingness to sacrifice for the war effort and volunteerism of the days following Pearl Harbor were gone. People all over the country started rioting.

The media started a feeding-frenzy smelling political blood in the water. Three days after President Parry's new bills were introduced into Congress, the Wall Street Journal ran a headline on the front page in huge type: "PRESIDENT PARRY HOSES EVERYBODY—STARTS

WAR WITH CHINA". The Senators and Congressmen all started trying to distance themselves from him, even the ones from his own party.

NEWS CONFERENCE AFTER PARRY HOSES EVERYBODY FOR THE GOOD OF THE COUNTRY

Not surprised by the chaos in the streets and in the media and the halls of Congress, President Parry called a news conference in prime time with representatives from all the media outlets present.

"Yes, Ms. Riviera?" President Parry said responding to the upraised hand of Kimberly Riviera, CNN anchorwoman for one of their most popular prime time news programs.

"Mr. President, are you not afraid that defaulting on the interest payment obligations to China will lead us into war with China?" Ms. Riviera asked.

"Yes of course I am concerned about this and its impact on our relationship with China. I fully expect that an armed conflict with China will result from this move. We know from overhead imagery from our spy satellites that China has greatly increased their military training activities and may be preparing an invasion fleet as we speak. Do not panic. We do not think that they intend to invade the U.S. because, frankly, we no longer have much in the way of resources they need except perhaps our farmland. We think though that the U.S. will be drawn into an armed conflict with China in aid of some other country which is the target of their aggression. To that end, I have issued orders to our military forces to begin preparations for war with China. We do not know, when, if or where such a conflict will arise, but we are going to be ready for all contingencies."

"Yes, Mr. Canon?" President Parry said looking at Stuart Canon, anchorman for the NBC Evening News.

"Mr. President, why did you elect to introduce a bill implementing a flat income tax, a value added tax and a national sales tax?" Stuart Canon inquired.

"Mr. Canon, we are facing a dire economic situation. The unfunded liability of the federal government for the various entitlement programs enacted by Congress over the years is massive. In order to pay those obligations, the U.S. has had to borrow heavily in the form of selling T-Bills and U.S. government bonds to whoever will buy them. The national debt is in the trillions of dollars now. The interest payments that the U.S. government has to pay on the money it has borrowed will soon total 95% of the total income the federal government takes in every year. That means that soon, there will be no money to pay our troops, fuel our ships and planes, buy and maintain weapons systems or do anything else without borrowing more money. Many civilizations in history have disappeared because their national debt became so great they could no longer afford to defend themselves. It is imperative to save this country that we cut expenses drastically and raise the level of income the federal government takes in. The tax structure I have proposed will address one half of the problem. The cuts in government payouts I have proposed will address the other half of the problem. "

"Yes, Ms. Kandora?" the President said looking at Katy Kandora, anchorwoman of ABC's Evening News Program.

"Mr. President, the teacher's unions are up in arms about your proposal to fire all the existing teachers which are not from the top ten percent of their classes, implement competency testing for teachers and students and about the blue collar track that students who cannot pass the competency tests will be forced into. What do you have to say to the teachers?" Katy Kandora said.

"The teachers have done us no favors. The U.S. now ranks 31st among the world's nations in math and science test score averages nationwide. The U.S. has been on a long, slow slide toward massive mediocrity in the quality of our graduates. Silicon Valley is loaded with engineers from India and China. Many high school graduates cannot balance a checkbook or point to where Brazil in on a globe. This is unacceptable, and I will no longer tolerate it. It is time for a massive paradigm change, and that is what I have proposed. The U.S. cannot survive in a competitive world economy with a bunch of stupid people running around not able to support themselves. With regard to the blue collar track, the vast majority of jobs in America do not require more than a high school education. How many times have you gone into a store and asked a question about something and found out that the person working with you did not know there job or did not know enough about their products to answer your question?"

"Yes, Mr. Gonzalez?" President Parry said pointing at Hector Gonzalez, anchorman for Univision's evening news program.

"Mr. President, the Hispanic community is incensed by your proposal to implement a national ID card and to carry out surprise INS raids on employers to verify the immigration status of their employees and fine them heavily if they are found to be employing illegals. Why did you make such proposals and aren't you afraid that this will cost you your job when you are up for re-election next year?" Gonzalez asked.

"Mr. Gonzalez, I know for a fact that this position and the other positions I have taken will cost me my job next year. I don't care about that. I care about saving this great country of ours and I am willing to sacrifice my own political ambitions and my job security to try to do what needs to be done. There are twenty million illegals in this country doing jobs that I think Americans would do if given the chance. I would certainly do them if I had been unemployed for two years and was out of options like many of our good citizens. I have heard all the arguments by employers, and I simply do not believe that Americans who are desparate and who have been long term unemployed would not do the jobs the illegals are doing. I want the illegals out of the country for good regardless of how long they have been here illegally, and I want employers to hire Americans. It is as simple as that. Any employer caught knowingly hiring illegal aliens will be heavily fined and supervised. We are turning the magnet off."

"Thank you all for coming. That is all the time I have for questions right now. The nation is in crisis, and I must attend to my duties." President Parry said closing the press conference.

There was a major buzz after the press conference. No president save perhaps for Abraham Lincoln, had acted so boldly with so little regard for his own political career to do what he believed in to save the country. The reporters were stunned. They rushed to file their stories for the next news cycle. The headlines screamed the next day. The Los Angeles Times page 1 headline was two inches high and read PRESIDENT STOMPS ON MEXICANS, OLD PEOPLE AND TEACHERS. That really pissed off the illegal aliens and all the Mexicans in general. It also got the AARP in a tizzy and sent the teacher's unions to the barricades.

The special interest groups all immediately called their lobbyists and promised millions to fight the new laws to prevent them from being passed. A horde of lobbyists, who had been supplying tickets and campaign contributions over the years to the various members of the Senate and House of Representatives, all descended on Washington, D.C. in a horde. They started calling in favors to fight the new proposed laws that upset so many of the carefully laid plans of their well-heeled clients. The Congressmen geared up for a protracted battle with the White House to try to preserve the rights of their "constituents" that were paying so much money into the PACs and the coffers of the Congressmen's re-election committees. A verbal fist fight broke out in the press between the White House and the Senators and Representatives in the Senate and House of Representatives.

But the worst of it was in East Los Angeles where the illegals, Chicano gangs and even the legalized Mexicans went wild and started rioting. Homes and cars were burned. Cops were attacked and they responded LAPD style with massive police brutality which made the evening news. This was like pouring gasoline onto a fire. Soon the Mexican gangs were spreading out into the rich suburbs and invading homes and committing horrendous crimes against the occupants of the homes.

Rich people in fancy cars were nothing but rolling targets. Often they were dragged out of their cars and beaten or raped, and sometimes murdered, often in front of news cameras. News crews were attacked at random if the gangs did not want the public to see what they were doing. LA became a war zone with the middle class, rich people and white and yellow people defending their property and lives with guns. Firefights erupted every night in neighborhoods the Mexican gangs visited. The hospitals were overwhelmed with casualties.

PRESIDENT DECLARES MARTIAL LAW

The next week, after watching numerous horrendous assaults on TV, President Parry was disgusted. He addressed the nation in a prime time address. In his address, he first apologized to the youth of the United States for the condition of the country they were to inherit in general and the huge national debt in particular. He said the entitlement programs were a grand idea and generous and compassionate in their concept, but hugely flawed in their implementation and riddled with fraud. He said the debt service or interest payments on the money the U.S. had to borrow to fund all the deficit spending the Congresses over the year had approved had now risen to the level that the continuation of the very existence of the United States as we know it was now in doubt. The President concluded his apology with a declaration that because of the widespread rioting, rampant lawlessness and general chaos throughout the country, he was declaring martial law. In doing so, he bypassed the financially compromised legislative branch of government and implemented all his proposals without further delay or filibuster.

Under martial law, the Marine Corp and Army reserves were called up and given shoot to kill orders to take out the Mexican gangs and stop the looting, vandalism, home invasions and all other violent crimes. It was a bloodbath for awhile, and then things settled down as there became fewer and fewer gangs with enough non KIA members to still function. The ones that did have members still standing, got the picture and decided it was not worth the cost of their lives. The looting and murders and rapes stopped and the food riots were quelled in the United States with handouts of emergency rations.

CHINESE GO BALLISTIC OVER DEFAULT

As anger in China rose over the President's proposed default, they began rattling their sabers and threatened to invade Taiwan and to attack the U.S. if the U.S. came to its aid. They never mentioned their plans to invade Brazil and take over the Tupi Oil and Gas field off the coast of Brazil. They also demanded payment of the interest they were owed. The U.S. tried to calm them with promises to pay and said that this was only a temporary situation, but the truth was that the U.S. had a choice between spending its federal income on defense and other essential services or pay interest to the Chinese. The U.S. secretly chose to pay for essential services like defense and let the chips fall where they may regarding China. The die was cast. War with China was inevitable.

None of the legislation proposed by President Parry passed the House of Representatives or Senate.

CHAPTER 3

THE DRUMS OF WAR

CHINESE ARMADA STARTS SAILING FOR BRAZIL

President Parry's phone rang at 2AM on April 1.

"Sir, you better come down here and see this." It was William Headman, director of the National Reconnaissance Office calling from the situation room with his National Security Advisor, Mike Maloney calling from the situation room.

"This is an April Fool's joke right? What could possibly be so urgent to wake me up at 2 AM?" the slightly irritated President said.

"Just get down here sir. This is no joke." Headman said.

"OK, I will be down there in ten." the President said.

Now fully awake and somewhat alarmed, the President got up and got dressed. His lovely blonde wife Monique sat up in bed and said, "What's wrong dear?"

"I am not sure yet, but I think the shit is finally hitting the fan." President Parry said.

"Oh dear God. Be strong my love. The free world depends upon you for leadership." Monique said.

"Yeah I know. Love you. See you whenever. If we need to have you moved to the bunker, I will send the staff to get you." the President said.

"OK. I love you too." Monique replied, now thoroughly alarmed.

President Parry walked down to the situation room thinking about what he might find when he got there and thinking about what he might have to do about it. As he walked in, he saw that many of the major players in his administration had gathered. Roger Picket, Chairman of the Joint Chiefs was there along with Richard Rogers, Head of the CIA. Tom Wilmont, Head of the National Security Agency was also there as was General Tim Steadman, Director of the Defense Intelligence Agency.

"You better sit down sir." Headman said. "We have some images from our KH-13 spy satellites to show you."

As President Parry took his seat, the first of the images was displayed on the huge flat screen at the end of the conference table. The satellite photos showed a huge armada of ships leaving the secret underground naval base at the southern end of Hainan Island in China.

"Tell me what is going on." President Parry said.

CHINESE DESTROYERS TOWING SUBMERGED KILOS

"Well it looks like Chinese have launched an armada big enough to invade and take over many countries of the world. It is not big enough to invade the United States and win, but it is pretty big. They have launched six super carriers with attendant Aegis-type cruisers and Aegis-type destroyers as well as enough tenders and support ships to make up six carrier strike groups. We think they have launched two boomers too, and they are towing nine surfaced Kilo submarines behind the destroyers in the carrier strike groups. They may also be towing some sonar arrays.

They also have launched enough Landing Ship Transports to carry about six divisions of Chinese marines, special forces and supporting troops and two amphibious mechanized divisions. They also have launched some LSTs that seem to be loaded with mobile missile launchers. We are not sure what kind of missiles those are, because their Long March strategic intercontinental ballistic missiles look just like their truck mounted ASBMs." Headman said.

KILOS AND ASBMS OBSERVED IN ARMADA:
President briefed on apparent purpose of armada

"Holy shit. Possible truck mounted ICBMs? Any idea where they are going or what they are up to yet? President Parry exclaimed.

"Well sir, we are not sure yet. They do not appear to be heading for either Taiwan or Hawaii or Canada. They seem to on a course that would take them to the tip of South America. From there they could proceed to attack our East Coast, South America, Europe, Africa or Saudi Arabia. We are not exactly sure where they are going or why yet." Headman replied.

"Why would they be towing submarines?" Parry asked.

"That would indicate they are expecting a submarine battle, because that is why they would need a towed sonar array and Kilos. Kilos are best suited for hunting other submarines although they can also be used to attack surface ships with submarine-launched anti-ship missiles. Because we know they are towing Kilo-class submarines, we would expect that whatever battle they are expecting to fight is more than 6000 kilometers away from China because that is the range of the Kilo-class submarine. Since they have no Chinese Navy bases anywhere other than China, they may be choosing to tow their diesel-electric submarines to conserve bunker oil in their tenders to re-fuel the LSTs and other non-nuclear ships. They seem to have launched enough tenders to carry large amounts of jet fuel above and beyond what the carriers can carry themselves indicating they may be expecting to have to wage a big air battle wherever they are going." Headman continued.

"Mr. Wilmont, what has the NSA learned about the intentions of the Chinese from decryption of their encrypted message traffic? President Parry said turning his attention to the director of the National Security Agency. The NSA intercepts all forms of message traffic, emails, military transmissions, phone calls, etc. and has acres of super computers and armies of code breakers to decrypt the encrypted traffic.

"We have not learned anything yet about their destination or their intentions. Just as they launched the armada, they changed all their military message traffic encryption codes to codes we have never seen before. We are working hard at cracking them, but they are excellent codes, and we have not cracked them yet. We have not picked up any information from the phone calls, emails and diplomatic message traffic we have intercepted over the past few months or over the past few days. They must have planned this operation using strictly face-to-face meetings with no electronic message traffic at all. That is very odd and very ominous. They REALLY wanted to keep this thing secret which means it is extremely important." Wilmont replied.

"Hmm, I see. How long before they get to the tip of South America? Once they get there we should be able to know a little more about where they are headed from the course they set after they round the tip of the horn right?" Parry said.

"Correct. It should take them about three weeks to get to the tip of South America at the speed they are making as a group now." Headman replied.

"OK, keep me informed of developments on this situation. In the meantime, I am going to contact the Chinese Ambassador and ask for an explanation of what is going on and contact the allies and bring them up to speed and see if they know anything more than we know. Thank you for bringing this situation to my attention gentlemen, and good night." Parry said.

The President made his way back up to his bedroom, and tried to sneak back into bed, but his wife woke up and asked him what was going on. He said, "I was right. The shit has hit the fan. The Chinese just launched a huge armada and we don't know what they are up to or who they plan to attack, if anybody."

"Do you think they are going to attack us?" Monique asked.

"No. They do not appear to be heading for Hawaii, Alaska or our West Coast. But they have launched a huge force. If they attack anybody, it is going to be a big fight."

"Are you going to ask them what is going on?"

"Yes. First thing in the morning."

And with that, they tried to go back to sleep, but sleep would not come to the President.

CHAPTER 4

LIES AND FRIENDS

FOUR WEEKS BEFORE THE WAR OVER THE TUPI FIELD STARTS

President Parry called the Secretary of State Dr. Suzanne Saddler first thing in the morning and read her in.

"Good morning Dr. Saddler. The Chinese have launched a huge armada with six carrier strike groups and enough troop ships to carry a six divisions of marines and a couple of divisions of mechanized amphibious landing forces. It is going to be an interesting day. What is on your agenda for today?" President Parry said.

"Holy shit! I am preparing for some trade talks with China. That is about it. Are they going to attack us?" Dr. Saddler asked incredulously.

"We don't think so. I need you to contact the Chinese Ambassador Hu Chang and get him over to the White House for a conversation ASAP. Will you do that for me and plan on attending yourself." Parry said.

"Oh certainly sir, I will get on that right away. Do you want me to cancel the trade talks that start next week?

"Yes. Thank you. See you later today hopefully." President Parry said.

CHINESE AMBASSADOR LIES
ABOUT INTENT OF ARMADA

"Ambassador Chang, Suzanne Saddler. How are you today?" Dr. Saddler said into the phone.

"I am fine thank you. To what do I owe the pleasure of your call?" Ambassador Chang said into the phone.

"Mr. Ambassador, President Parry has asked me to invite you to the White House for a conversation as soon as possible. Can you make it this afternoon possibly? Dr. Saddler said.

"Yes, I can do that. What does he want to talk about?" Ambassador Chang said.

"I think he wants to talk about what China's intentions are with regard to the buildup of China's forces and the launching of the armada earlier this week." Saddler said.

"I see. What time would you like me to come over?"

"Two O'Clock at the White House please." Dr. Saddler said.

"Alright, I will be there." Ambassador Chang said.

"Mr. President, Suzanne Saddler. Ambassador Chang said he would be over at two this afternoon."

"Thank you Suzanne. See you then." President Parry said.

"General of the Army Lo Binxiao, this is Hu Chang, Chinese Ambassador to the United States. May I speak with you for a few minutes?" Chang said into the encrypted phone. The Chinese had anticipated this inquiry from the White House and had changed their encryption codes used on their embassy's secure phone system. Thus, although the NSA was intercepting the conversation, they were not able to decrypt it.

"Certainly Ambassador Chang. What is on your mind?" General Binxiao replied.

"I have been summoned to the White House to explain our actions in launching the invasion armada. What do you want me to say?" Ambassador Chang said.

"We want to keep the site of the invasion and our plans to take over Brazil and the Tupi Oil and Gas Field secret. So lie to them. Say we are sailing to Africa to secure our investments there from the rioting and to prevent governments there from nationalizing our natural resource recovery plants and equipment." General Binxiao said.

"You want me to lie to the President of the United States, the most powerful military superpower in the world?" Chang said.

"Yes, precisely. They are not the superpower they once were and we have been building our military strength for two decades to prepare for this day. We are not afraid of the United States." General Binxiao said with confidence in his voice.

"Alright I understand. I will do what you say, but don't blame me if this blows up in our faces. Thank you for your time." Ambassador Chang said.

"Don't be such a pussy. It is time to man up." General Binxiao said.

Two o'clock rolled around and the President's phone rang in the Oval Office. "Mr. President, Ambassador Hu Chang and Dr. Suzanne Saddler are here to see you." the President's secretary announced.

"Excellent. Send them in please and have the kitchen send up a coffee and tea service please."

"Certainly sir."

"Ambassador Chang, good afternoon. Nice to see you. Good afternoon Dr. Saddler. Tea Ambassador? Coffee Dr. Saddler?" President Parry said.

"Good afternoon Mr. President, and yes that would be lovely." Ambassador Chang said.

"Yes please." Dr. Saddler said.

The coffee and tea service arrived and the President's guests were served.

"Ambassador Chang, our spy satellites have taken overhead photographs of a massive fleet with six carrier strike groups and enough LSTs to hold six divisions of Chinese marines and two divisions of mechanized landing forces that have set sail out into the Pacific from your navy bases at Hainan Island and Zhanjiang. We have overheads of some LSTs that have been loaded with mobile missile launcher trucks too. Some of the ships appear to be towing something which we think are submarines. There appear to be ballistic missile submarines with the armada also. What are China's intentions?" President Parry inquired with a stern face.

Ambassador Chang took a moment to compose his thoughts. He then began to speak quietly.

"Do not be alarmed Mr. President. China does not intend to attack the United States. Our intent is to stabilize Africa and protect our substantial investments there from being nationalized by the various governments of Africa during this current climate of worldwide strife. We have invested billions of dollars in development of natural resources recovery plants in various countries in Africa, and we feel with the current economic situation worldwide, that the governments there may be even more unstable than they have been in the past. We fear they may seize our plants and refineries and divert the streams of natural resources we have been extracting for their own use and sale. That is all we are thinking about." Ambassador Chang lied as he looked calmly and sincerely into the President's eyes.

Ambassador Chang lied, and everybody in the room suspected it, but yet the story was plausible.

Hmm, that's almost believable the President thought to himself. "I see. But why are you sending six super carriers and two ballistic missile submarines with the armada? And why are some of the ships towing Kilo class submarines?" President Parry pressed.

CHINESE AMBASSADOR EXPLAINS WHY THE KILOS

"Oh, we fear that the European powers such as England and France may attempt to interfere with our operations with their carrier and submarine forces, and we want to be prepared to deter them and defend if they attack with their carriers. The ships are also towing sonar arrays to defend against submarine attacks." Chang lied again.

President Parry was quiet and thought for a moment. Finally, after what seemed an eternity, the President spoke.

"Alright Ambassador, but please advise your government that the United States will not tolerate with any interference with or attack by China on any U.S. operations or assets anywhere in the world and will come to the aid of any country under attack by China where that attack adversely affects U.S. strategic interests." the President said.

Ambassador Chang shifted slightly in his chair, but did not break his composure.

"Oh we are quite aware of that and understand your concern." Ambassador Chang replied.

"Very well Ambassador, that is all I had to discuss with you for the moment. Thank you for coming over."

"You are welcome and don't hesitate to contact me if you have any further questions." Chang said.

After Ambassador Chang left, President Parry turned to Dr. Saddler and asked her what she thought about what the Chinese Ambassador had said.

"I think the Ambassador has a black belt in bullshit and that is exactly what his superiors told him to say." Dr. Saddler opined.

"Me too." the President replied.

CHAPTER 5

CALL TO ARMS

The commander of the Peoples Liberation Army Navy invasion fleet Shang Jiang (Admiral) Chian Wing Liu, stood on the bridge of the former Russian super carrier RFS *Varyag*, renamed the PLAN *Jiangnan*. She had been renamed *Jiangnan* after the shipyard in China where she was finished after being towed from the Russian shipyard where her construction was begun. She had been purchased by the Chinese from Russia when 70% complete by a tourist venture out of Macau with the idea that she would be converted into a floating hotel and casino. However, the Peoples Liberation Army Navy (PLAN) had hijacked the development several years earlier, and had her completed as a super carrier for carrying several squadrons of Su-27MK2 naval Flanker-Gs and Chinese autonomous navalized drones similar to the U.S. X-47B. The *Jiangnan* was now a fearsome super carrier class ship on a par with the super carriers of the U.S., the United Kingdom and France.

It was a varsity night, with a howling gale blowing 60 knots across the bows of the Chinese ships, and all the ships of the invasion fleet crashing through 50 foot waves of icy water. Everybody was sick including Admiral Liu. But they pressed on in dogged determination, because the survival of China hung in the balance, at least in their view. China had grown so large and energy hungry that the world's energy markets could no longer supply her voracious demands for oil, liquefied natural gas and coal without sending prices sky high although they were already very high. China had decided to take matters into its own hands and just take what it needed regardless of what the rest of the world thought.

Admiral Liu had forgone the narrow Strait of Magellan passage. The invasion fleet was huge, and the Strait of Magellan was only two kilometers wide at its narrowest point. He needed more room than that to spread his ships out so as to not trap them into a narrow killing zone in case they were attacked. More space would give them room to maneuver also should the need for evasive action arise. So the Drake Passage, one of the world's most dreaded sea passages with the wildest weather and the roughest seas, was his only choice. Now all the Chinese sailors were paying the price of Chinese aggression, many below decks panicked and went up to the top decks. Some were vomiting over the side while hanging on for dear life, and some were being swept into the ocean by huge waves crashing across the deck. The fleet did not bother to stop and look for them. To turn around in 50 foot waves was to risk capsizing. To launch rescue helicopters in 60 knot winds was suicidal. So the men swept over the side were just left to drown. War is hell.

"Navigator, what is the direct course to the Tupi Field from our current position? And what is the distance?" Liu inquired.

"Admiral of the Fleet, the initial direct course to the Tupi Field from our current position is 036 degrees, distance 4189 kilometers sir." the young Chinese officer serving as principal navigator for the fleet said.

CHINESE LAUNCH ANTI-SATELLITE
WEAPONS AND START CYBER WAR

"Radio room, Admiral Liu. Change codes to the Yellow Dragon code set, and make signal to the State Central Military Commission of the Peoples Liberation Army as follows: 'Invasion fleet is exiting Drake Passage. Launch the anti-satellite weapons. Order Wicked Rose and the hacker network to open the trap doors and wreak havoc on the directories of the military and government computers of the U.S., the power grid and other utilities. We are turning the corner.'" Admiral Liu spoke into the interphone to the radio room. "After you have finished the message to the State Central Military Commission, make signal to the rest of the ships in the invasion fleet on the invasion fleet frequency to change their code set to Yellow Dragon and set their course to 036 degrees, all ahead flank and stay in combat spread formation."

"Captain Wang, set your course to 036 degrees, all ahead flank." Liu said with grim determination in his voice speaking to Captain Choo Wang, captain of the *Jiangnan*.

"Helmsman, set your course to 036 degrees magnetic. Engine room, make turns for flank speed." Captain Wang said to the sailor at the helm of the ship and to the engine room over the interphone.

At the Xichang Satellite Launch Center, 64 km northwest of Xichang City, Liangshan Yi Autonomous Prefecture in Sichuan Province, 54 anti-satellite missiles lifted off their launch pads in the middle of the night, each aimed at a different one of the spy satellites and communication satellites of the United States, Britain and France. The war for control of the Tupi Oil and Gas field off the eastern coast of Brazil had officially started.

About 20 minutes later, the kinetic kill vehicles of all 54 anti-satellite missiles impacted their targets thereby substantially blinding the United States, U.K. and French spy satellite constellations and taking the U.S., British and French satellite-based voice and data communications networks offline.

Simultaneously, notorious hacker Wicked Rose, now in the employ of the Peoples Liberation Army started his work to disrupt the computers of the United States. Wicked Rose had been such a successful Chinese hacker working for his own account before he was forced to work for the Peoples Liberation Army. Wicked Rose had been forced into service for the PLA on pain of arrest and imprisonment after he had hacked into PLA networks and other networks of computers operated by the Chinese government. The PLA had put Wicked Rose in charge of the Evil Security Team, the Honker Union of hackers and the hacker force of the Sichuan Military Command Communication department.

GINWUI ROOTKIT

While working for the PLA, Wicked Rose had developed the GinWui rootkit and installed it surreptitiously on many if not all the Department of Defense Computers, as well as the computers of many utilities in the power grid, water utilities etc. The GinWui Rootkit spread virally by the exchange of word processor documents between computers, and, by now, had been widely distributed among DoD computers and the computers of many other critical infrastructure functions in the United States. The GinWui Rootkit installed a trap door in the infected computer through which the Chinese hackers could access the directory structure of the infected computer and wreak all kinds of havoc.

Upon receiving the command from the State Central Military Commission to launch the attack, Wicked Rose ordered his hacker network to contact all the computers upon which his GinWui Rootkit was installed and start conducting cyber-warfare. The hackers were directed to attempt to disrupt and disable the American DOD communication and fire control networks and snarl the operations of the utility and traffic systems of the U.S.. Attacks were carried out by opening the trap doors on the infected American computers, and taking control of them. Once inside and in control, the hackers sought to find and destroy files, create their own files, manipulate services, and start new processes and kill processes then underway. The hackers were also able to get information about the computer and its user, access and alter the computer's registry, as well as lock, restart or shut down the operating systems.

These attacks put the DOD computers and the computers of various critical utilities into a state of chaos, forcing their users to be innovative and work around the problems created. IT people all over the United States started working around the clock to find the source of the problem.

When they found the GinWui Rootkit, they were impressed and dismayed at the same time. Americans had always been patsies when it came to security, and now they were paying the price. The IT guys did the best they could, but things were very disrupted and backup and obsolete communication systems, control systems and data networks had to be called back into service out of retirement. Slowly, but surely, some semblance of communications and control were re-established albeit without the full functionality afforded by the newer systems which had been trashed.

White House Situation Room, 0300 Local Time, April 23

The phone rang in President Parry's bedroom in the White House at 3 AM startling the President and his wife out of their slumber.

"Sir, its Roger Picket. Bill Headman at the National Reconnissnce Office just advised me that the Chinese government just shot down all of our KH-11 spy satellites and our military communications satellites along with those of the British and the French."

"Holy shit, that is essentially a declaration of war." President Parry said. "How do we know it was them? Also, where is their invasion fleet now?"

"Our missile defense early warning satellites detected contrails and infrared blooms and hot tracks rising from the Xichange Satellite Launch Center As far as the location of their fleet goes, we know they had reached the tip of South America, but then they killed our spy satellites. The last time we had a fix on them, they were just rounding the tip of South America." Picket said.

"Any word yet on their destination? Do you think they are going to attack the East Coast of the U.S.?"

"No sir. And I don't really know. But I do not really think they are going to attack the United States. They are not quite strong enough yet, but they are getting close. Furthermore, they want the type of natural resources that we don't have much of anymore after the environmentalists succeeded in getting fracking banned. Specifically, what they need the most of is oil. They get plenty of coal to fire their electricity generation plants from Austrailia, so there is no need to attack us for our coal." Picket said.

"We better find them then and get some intelligence on their location, course and speed don't you agree?"

"Yes sir."

"Launch the Auroras to go find them and keep tabs on their course and speed." President Parry said.

"Aye, Aye sir." Picket said as he hung up.

AURORAS FLY TO FIND FLEET

Forty-five minutes later, three hypersonic Aurora spy planes lifted off their launch pads at Area 51 at Groom Lake in the desert outside of Las Vegas. The Auroras sped straight up for several miles to the very edge of space on their solid fuel boosters until they attained sufficient speed to light off their main engines. As they arced down to horizontal flight parallel to the surface of the earth, they lit their liquid-methane-powered ramjet engines and accelerated to mach 6 or a little over one mile per second. Each had been assigned a search grid in the ocean north and east of the tip of South America to cover so they set their on-course headings to cruise directly to block 1 of search grid 1. Tankers had been arranged periodically along their route of flight to refuel them. Even counting the intervals during which they had to descend and slow down to the tanker speed and then climb back up to their assigned cruise altitudes, they were at the tip of South America in 2.1 hours. After meeting their last tanker, they each set courses for block 1 of their assigned search grids.

Fifteen minutes later after the first Aurora had reached block 1 of its search grid and started its search, "Falcon 1", the first of the Auroras, found the Chinese invasion fleet about 500 miles northeast of Drake . "Eagle 6 this is Falcon 1. Bogey is located my grid, course 036, speed 35 knots. Current position is South 51 decimal 23 decimal 16 by West 62 decimal 02 decimal 33." Falcon 1 was reporting that the Chinese Fleet had been found at his location just West of the Falkland Islands, about 630 kilometers Northest of Drake Passage heading northeast at 35 knots.

This encrypted radio transmission was received and decrypted and digitized and encrypted again by an Argentina Navy ground station at the tip of South America that had hastily been recruited by NSA and DOD because of the loss of our military communication satellites. The CIA station in Buenos Aires was too far away from the action to receive a VHF transmission, so recruiting the Argentinians and reading them in was DOD's only choice. The Argentinians were given the Aurora's tactical mission frequency and advised the time they would be in their airspace and requested to listen for transmissions and to send them to a specific email address at the NSA via encrypted packets. The Argentinians were also given a public key to use for PGP encryption and requested to exchange public keys with the analyst at the given email address. Having been the recipient of American foreign aid for many years, the Argentinians, even though they openly harbored many of our former Nazi enemies, were glad to help in any way they could despite the fact that further foreign aid had just been cut off. They were afraid of the Chinese and worried that if the Chinese target was Brazil, they would be next.

After the radio transmission from Falcon 1 had been processed, it was sent to the NSA over the internet in a series of encrypted TCP/IP packets. A message was sent back to the Argentinians via the internet and encrypted packets for decryption and transmission by an Argentinian radio operator to the Auroras.

It read, "Roger that Falcon 1. Return to the barn via assigned route and rendezvous with Falcons 2 and 3 at first tanker position. First tanker position is South 48 decimal 47 decimal 16 decimal 04 by West 68 decimal 56 decimal 33 decimal 98."

They were taking a chance by giving the actual coordinates of the tanker, but since the mode of communication was new and the Chinese would not have the private keys, the risk was warranted.

The message continued, "Stay on frequency for further transmissions from agents at predetermined locations regarding positions of the remaining tankers."

The National Command Authority, i.e., the President was ordering the Auroras to return to Area 51 after rendezvous with their first tanker over Santa Cruz, Argentina.

Falcon 1 relayed the order to Falcon's 2 and 3, and by routes calculated by their on-board GPS navigation systems, each turned to a heading calculated to take each of them, respectively to the position of the first tanker. After refueling there, each turned to a heading to take them over the CIA station in Lima, Peru. That CIA station transmitted to them by encrypted radio transmissions the position of their second tanker, and they all flew to that tanker and filled up their tanks again.

From there, they flew to positions over the CIA stations in Guatemala City, Guatemala and Cabo San Lucas, Baja, Mexico and repeated the process until they got back to Area 51 and made conventional airplane landings on the long runway at Groom Lake.

Several other search sorties of the same nature were flown by the Auroras over the next week or so to re-locate the Chinese fleet and report their course and speed. It was concluded, that, unless the Chinese were taking a very bizarre route that was not fuel efficient at all, their destination was most assuredly not Africa.

Alarm started to rise as the possibility of an attack on the East Coast of the United States appeared to be more and more likely.

Ultimately, the DOD and CIA determined that the commercial weather satellites had sufficient resolution to find the Chinese fleet so long as there was no cloud cover. The infrared capabilities of the commercial weather satellites were designed to sense the temperatures of the clouds, but were no good for sensing hot spots such as ship stacks on the surface if cloud cover was in the way.

CHINESE LAND ASBM MISSILES AT PORT ALEGRE

It was noticed by this awkward and less than optimal intelligence gathering mechanism, that several LSTs dropped off the Chinese formation off the coast of Brazil at approximately the latitude position of Porto Alegre and stayed there. Nobody could figure out why this had happened, and eventually, in the excitement that followed, this fact was lost in the confusion. It was not noted by U.S. commanders that a battalion of Chinese special forces had snuck ashore at night over the beaches at Porto Alegre and had seized control of a warehouse complex outside the city.

All communications with the Brazilians at Porto Alegre was lost when these Chinese special forces took out the local Brazilian army contingent and silenced all internet and phone traffic. The Chinese commandos silenced all the ISPs and central switches of the telephone network and destroyed all satellite uplink dishes. All long distance communication and internet traffic was thereby squelched. However, since the U.S. including the CIA had no assets in Porto Alegre, the fact that they could not communicate with anybody in Porto Alegre was not noticed.

The CIA, having lost their military communication satellites and having also lost their civilian communication channels, was unable to contact their assets on the ground elsewhere in Brazil to find out much of anything. Without spy satellites, the CIA and National Reconnaissance Office were unable to see the Chinese special forces moving their truck mounted ASBMs into the warehouses in Porto Alegre.

Likewise, the CIA and NRO were unable to see a Chinese amphibious landing force setting up setting up a network of anti-aircraft SAM sites linked to Russian stealth defeating radar systems.

CHINESE ANTI STEALTH RADAR NETWORK AND HOW STEALTH WORKS

The Russians had actually invented stealth, but they did not know it. Stealth was discovered one day in the 60's when a brilliant engineer at the Lockheed skunk works was reading a scientific paper written by a Russian author. This engineer realized from one of the formulas in the paper that a stealthy aircraft could be built by using the teachings of that formula. That was the beginnings of stealthy aircraft design.

This engineer noted that by making the surfaces angled in just the right way to reflect radar waves of the X-band wavelength commonly used in anti-aircraft and airborne search radars away from the plane and not back toward the radar and coating the airframe with radar absorbing coatings, the radar cross-section of a plane could be greatly reduced. But that all hinged upon the assumption that the inbound radar waves were X-band or K-band, both of which were very high radar frequencies.

Once stealthy aircraft designs like the F-117 and the B-2 became public, and their effectiveness was proven over Baghdad, the race was on to find anti-stealth technologies. The post-Soviet Russians, ever mindful of business opportunity, figured out that if they used older VHF band radars with longer wavelengths than the X band radars, they might be able to detect stealth aircraft.

The Russians imported a system devised by the Czechs. The Czechs devised a clever passive radar which uses emitters of opportunity such as commercial transmissions instead of emitting its own radar pulses. Because it does not emit its own pulses, it is passive and undetectable by radar warning receivers of incoming warplanes. This system is called "bistatic passive coherent location system" and it is a system which the Russians use as a first layer of defense to detect stealth planes.

This bistatic passive radar uses emissions from civilian transmitters such as cell towers or TV transmitters which get reflected away from a stealth aircraft. The system measures the time delay between the time a signal is received on a direct path from the TV or radio tower and the time the same signal is reflected off a stealth plane and received. This time delay gives the bistatic range since the radio and TV signals propagation speed, i.e., the speed of light, is a constant. The Doppler shift of the echo and its direction of arrival gives the speed of the object and the direction to the object from the receiver. A rough estimate of the position, speed and bearing can be derived from several such readings. The stealth plane does not know any of this is happening as it happens since the system is passive.

Another passive system called Vera-E invented by the Czechs uses time delays at multiple physically separated receivers for receipt of electronic emissions emitted by a stealth plane.

KEYS TO DEFEATING PASSIVE RADARS

The keys to defeating bistatic passive radars is in not emitting any signals from the stealth aircraft and destroying all commercial transmitters used by the system or destroying all the receivers in the system or flooding the band with false signals. The Czechs and Russians tried to export these system to China, but the U.S. blocked the sales. Or thought they did. In reality, they did not, and the Chinese obtained this technology through the back door.

But the bistatic passive radar was only the first line of the Chinese anti-stealth defense. The second line was Very High Frequency (VHF) target acquisition radars mounted on trucks. These radars received an initial fix on where the target probably was from the bistatic passive radars and then were focused on that area. The Chinese bought these Russian VHF radars specifically for defense against stealth jets. They looked like huge box springs mounted on trucks. VHF radar was World War II technology which had be upgraded with digital technology to turn them into Active Electronically Steered Phased Arrays (AESA).

The VHF radar operated at a much lower frequency than the X-band and K-band radars the stealth planes were designed to be stealthy against. The radar system was comprised of transmit-receive channel modules integrated into each antenna element, analog-to-digital conversion of each channel and fully digital signal processing of the radar return signals to improve resolution and decrease noise.

The VHF radar system had been designed by the Russians to automatically adapt to electronic countermeasures and digitally process out interference from bad weather and intensive chaff bombing.

The Russian upgrades were like putting a supercharger on an old GTO. The system could detect smaller stealth fighters like the F-35 and the F-22 Raptor, but the Batwing B-2 bomber was still large enough to defeat the longer wavelengths. Fortunately, for the U.S. pilots, the system was huge, easy the see, hard to hide and hard to deploy rapidly, and it was active so it could be detected and homed in upon by anti-radiation missiles.

THIRD LINE OF STEALTH DEFENSE

The third line of the Chinese anti-stealth defense was a series of truck-mounted phased-array target engagement radars. These target engagement radars received data on where the target was from the VHF radars. These large trucks had flip-lid target engagement-fire control radars that were to be used to obtain a better fix on where the target was, and guide mach 6 surface-to-air missiles toward the stealth fighter target. The idea was to guide the missile toward the target by transmitting steering commands to the missile until it was close enough that the missile's own radar in the missile nose cone takes over for the kill.

Even a stealth fighter will show up on an X-band radar if the plane is close enough to the radar. That was the whole point of the first three lines of defense – to find the stealth planes and get the missile close enough to the stealth jet that the missile's own radar could see it.

ANTI-STEALTH SAM BATTERIES

The final line of the Chinese anti-stealth defense was the truck-launched Russian S-300PMU-2 anti-aircraft missile batteries. These missile launching trucks were networked to the radars of the first three lines of defense.

The missiles were single-stage, solid-fuel, 25-foot long, mach-6 missiles. Each received mid course guidance from the phased-array target engagement radars until it got close enough to the stealth jet that the missile's own seeker radar could take over. This allowed the missile to home in on the target without the help of the radars on the launch vehicle or the ground radars on the second and third lines of defense which were all vulnerable to HARM anti-radiation missile attack as long as they were transmitting.

AMERICANS MISSED THE FACT THAT AN ANTI-STEALTH RADAR SYSTEM HAD BEEN SET UP

The fact that this anti-stealth defense network had been set up surrounding the Chinese ASBMs at Porto Alegre had escaped the notice of the Americans. The blinding of American, British and French intelligence by the loss of their spy satellites at the commencement of the Chinese attack was a crippling blow.

ONE MISTY STEALTH SATELLITE SURVIVED

The single Misty stealth spy satellite that survived the attack did not have an orbit that allowed it to cover Brazil as far south as Porto Alegre.

The President was starting to get worried. "I am pissed General. And I am really starting to worry that they are going to attack somewhere on our East Coast. What can we do to these Chinese pricks?" Parry said to the Chairman of the Joint Chiefs of Staff, General Roger Picket.

PRESIDENT ORDERS A RAID ON
MISSILE LAUNCH COMPLEX

"Well sir, I recommend first taking out their missile launch complex. That would be the Xichang Satellite Launch Center 64 km northwest of Xichang City, Liangshan Yi Autonomous Prefecture in Sichuan Province. The Chinese are known to have nuclear tipped ICBMs capable of reaching the United States, and they could launch them from there. Then I would take out their spy satellites and targeting satellites for their Anti Ship Ballistic Missiles." General Picket replied.

"Perfect. Set up a raid." President Parry replied.

General Picket strode to the secure phone in the Oval Office, and asked the White House operator to connect him to the Secretary of the Air Force. "Jerry, Picket here. I am with the President. He wants us to plan a raid to take out Xichang to prevent the Chinese from launching nuclear tipped Intercontinental Ballistic Missiles at the U.S. mainland. Set up a strike package. I am on my way over. Picket out." And with that, he strode briskly out of the Oval Office with a professional "I'm on it sir."

PICKET SETS UP SHOOT DOWN OF CHINESE SPY AND ASBM TARGETING SATELLITES

When General Picket reached his office, he set up a secure landline conference call between the Commander of US Navy's Navspasur satellite detection and surveillance system, Rear Admiral Ron Adams and CINCLANT Admiral Chester Jones.

"Gentlemen, General Picket here. The President wants to shoot down the Chinese spy and ASBM targeting satellite constellations and it is going to be up to you to do it. He wants it done ASAP. I am sure you are aware by now that they shot down all our spy and communications satellites early this morning. Admiral Adams, I want Navspasur to give the locations of the Chinese satellites and their orbits to CINCLANT Admiral Jones to help the AEGIS cruisers point their AS/SPY-1 radars in the right direction to find each satellite. Admiral Jones, I want you to set up an AEGIS cruiser to make the shots using SM-3 Missiles. Get it done. Any questions?" There were none. "OK then, Picket out."

SPRINT IRIDIUM SAT PHONES USED
for attack on Chinese satellites

The team swung into action with Admiral Jones ordering the Ticonderoga class AEGIS cruiser USS U.S.S. *Lake Champlain* to sea out of Norfolk. The Captain of the U.S.S. *Lake Champlain* was given an encrypted Sprint Iridium satellite phone as was the Commander of Navspasur. The sat phones allowed them to communicate with each other over the commercial Iridium satellite network which the Chinese had unwisely not shot down.

Once the U.S.S. *Lake Champlain* had received the position of each satellite in turn, it turned its AEGIS system radar to point at the target satellite, and its Aegis Weapon System MK-99 Fire Control System calculated a solution to the target. A launch command was given, and an Aerojet MK 72 solid fuel rocket booster propelled the RIM-161 Standard Missile 3 out of the Mark 41 Vertical Launching System. The RIM-161 missile had had its software modified for satellite intercept as opposed to its usual mission of intercepting ballistic missiles mid-course before their re-entry.

In flight, the SM-3 missile established communication with the U.S.S. *Lake Champlain* for mid course guidance corrections. When the booster burned out, the Aeroject MK 104 solid fuel dual thrust rocket motor took over to propel the missile through the atmosphere. The missile continued to receive mid course guidance corrections from the U.S.S. *Lake Champlain* and was aided by the GPS data received by the on-board GPS receiver.

After the second stage burned out, the ATK MK 136 solid fuel third stage rocket motor provided propulsion in space until 30 seconds before intercept.

At 30 seconds to impact, the third stage separated, and a Lightweight Exo-Atmospheric Projectile kinetic warhead began to search for the target satellite using pointing data from the U.S.S. *Lake Champlain*. An ATK solid fuel divert and attitude control system maneuvered the kinetic warhead in the final stages of the intercept.

In terminal phase of the intercept, the kinetic warhead sensors identified the satellite and tried to find the most lethal point of impact. Once identified, the kinetic warhead was steered to the impact point until actual impact occurred and the satellite was destroyed.

This process was wildly successful in killing all 16 satellites of the Chinese spy and ASBM targeting satellite constellations.

PLANNING FOR RAID ON SATELLITE LAUNCH FACILITY

Meanwhile, the planning stages for the raid on the satellite launching complex started. The Secretary of the Air Force, Adam Smith, after he hung up with Picket, immediately called the Commander of the U.S.

Air Force base at Kadena, Okinawa by secure land line with an outline of the plan and asked for help refining it.

When General Picket walked into his office 40 minutes later, Smith was ready with a preliminary plan.

"Here's what we've got so far General Picket. I can launch a strike package of twelve Marine F/A-18s and six Air Force F-22 Raptors out of Kadena this afternoon armed with laser guided bombs, AMRAAMs and Sidewinders."

"Good. What are their defenses around Xichang?"

"They have an air base nearby. We know they have two squadrons of Flankers there. We believe, but cannot confirm that they are Su-30MK2 thrust vectoring Flankers with the AF-41 engines." Pattison replied.

"Hmmm, that will be trouble for the Hornets. Can't you send more F-22s?" Picket asked.

"No sir. We just don't have enough of them, and a couple of them are down for maintenance, so if you want to launch this afternoon, six is all we have available." Smith replied.

"OK do it. I will be crossing my fingers. Those thrust vectoring Flankers are going to be a handful for the Hornets, but the Raptors should be able to handle them if they don't run out of missiles before shooting them all down."

"The Hornet pilots are not completely helpless against the Flankers. If they know how to do it, they can beat a Flanker."

"Lets hope they know how to do it."

That afternoon, the twelve F/A-18's and six F-22s launched from Kadena Air Force Base on Okinawa and headed for Xichang. The Chinese radar picked up the F/A-18s as they crossed the coastline, but the Chinese early warning radar did not see the F-22s because of their superior stealth.

Twelve Su-30MK2s were scrambled to intercept the F/A-18s and a fierce dogfight ensued. The Flankers flew straight up out of the ground clutter to attack the F/A-18 formation. Not a good tactic since it bleeds so much energy from the attacker before the battle even begins, but the Flankers with the AF-41 engine had power to spare. The Flankers had flown their intercept course on the deck in the ground clutter to evade the search radars of the F/A-18s. They did not know about the presence of the F-22s, but by flying on the deck, they also avoided the search radars of the F-22s. The F/A-18s and the F-22s were caught by surprise, and this resulted in the F-22s being late arriving at the dogfight. The Hornets fought valiantly and ferociously.

Unfortunately for the brave Navy and Marine pilots in the Hornets, the thrust vectoring and superior thrust-to-weight ratio and wing loading factors of the Flankers were too much for the F/A-18s. The Hornets took devastating losses. Eleven of the F/A-18s were shot down in the first 60 seconds. Realistically speaking, the F/A-18s had very little chance of all getting through once the Chinese radars discovered them and the Flankers were scrambled for the intercept.

The F-22s, flying high cover, did not see the Flankers on their search radars till they zoom climbed out of the ground clutter. The Raptors swooped down into the furball, but were just seconds too late to save the first eleven Navy and Marine pilots.

The twelfth F/A-18 flown by a Marine escaped and re-engaged the Flankers along with the F-22s. The Air Force F-22s furiously engaged the Chinese pilots, and fought brilliantly and with a ferocity that intimidated the Chinese pilots. They wiped out all twelve Flankers in the next minute and a half.

The Chinese pilots had trouble locking their fire control radars onto the stealthy F-22s in order to launch their radar guided missiles.

The Chinese infrared guided missiles equivalent to our Sidewinders proved unreliable also because of the stealthy design of the heat signature of the F-22s and the brilliant evasive maneuvers flown by the Raptors. The Raptor missiles had no problems locking onto the Flankers, because the Flanker radar and infrared signatures were huge.

The Russians, never having been accused of subtlety, designed the Su-30 MKK Flanker for power, speed and maneuverability and not for stealth. In fairness to the Russians, the Flanker was designed before stealth became a factor in aerial combat.

The lead F-22 pilot locked his fire control radar on six of the Flankers simultaneously and took them out with AMRAAM missiles at 3 miles in fire-and-forget mode. The Flankers, detecting the incoming AMRAAMs on their IRST systems, scattered and launched countermeasures, but the missiles were on them in the blink of an eye, and the countermeasures did not work. Three huge fireballs erupted in the Chinese sky as the first three Flankers disintegrated.

The remaining six Flankers then turned into the formation of six F-22s and a straggler F/A-18 to engage them. The first Flankers took on the lead F-22, and, his wingman, the second Flanker engaged the wingman of the first F-22. The remaining Flankers each engaged one of the remaining F-22s and a roiling furball ensued.

The sole surviving F/A-18 got an all-aspect Sidewinder lock and launched the heat-seeker when the third Flanker flew past the merge. The missile made a sharp turn in pursuit. The Flanker's Infrared Search and Track system picked up the inbound Sidewinder, and the Chinese pilot made a hard break and launched flare countermeasures just in time to evade the Sidewinder. But in so doing, he turned across the flight path of an F-22 who got a lead pursuit angle guns solution on the Flanker and took him out with a fusillade of 20 mm cannon shells. All seven American jets then turned their attention to the five remaining Flankers. The lead F-22 took out another one of the Flankers with a Sidewinder shot and a third Flankers was splashed when the second F-22 launched a Sidewinder at him and the Chinese pilot made a break to evade the missile that took him directly into a 20 mm cannon shell fusillade fired by the last F/A-18. The fourth and fifth Flankers were taken out by an F-22 that had locked them both up on his radar and launched AMRAAMs in terminal guidance mode on them. The missiles were on them so fast, they had no time to react and were destroyed The remaining Flanker then bugged out.

Unfortunately, the raid on the Satellite Launch Center had to be aborted, because the F-22s were armed for dogfighting and not ground attack. Thus there was not enough laser guided ordinance left on the single surviving F/A-18 to take out the missile launch complex. The planes were forced to return to Kadena Air Force base.

President Parry was furious and felt the continued existence of the Chinese missile launch complex was a grave threat to the U.S. mainland. President Parry grilled General Picket about why the mission failed for an hour. Picket explained that there were not enough F-22 Raptors available to fly cover for the attack bombers and that the F/A-18s were simply no match for the thrust vectoring AF-41 powered Flankers with their IRST systems.

"Goddamnit. I knew canceling that F-22 program was a mistake. We have spent so much money on other programs to keep the old and infirm afloat and being the policeman of the world that now we cannot afford the weapons we need to save the entire country. Of all the people we have helped in the world with our foreign aid and disaster relief efforts, I am betting nobody comes to our aid if the Chinese attack us or hijack the Brazil's oil supply."

"I agree with you sir. But we have to focus on what we can do now with what we have and leave the rest up to Congress." Picket said in a low tone trying to calm a clearly agitated President Parry down.

"OK, OK, of course you are right. What do you think?"

PICKET'S PLAN AFTER FIRST RAID ON SAT LAUNCH COMPLEX FAILS

"If I were Commander-in-Chief, I would mount a submarine-based cruise missile attack on the PLAAF air base at Yuanmou 150 miles northeast of Xichang to crater their runways and blow up their fuel depots. I would sneak a boomer into the South China Sea with several cruise missiles aboard in the Trident tubes and launch them from just off the coast of Dongyu. I would arm them with runway cratering bomblets so as to keep the Flankers down. Then I would send in a strong force F-22 Raptors to protect a squadron of B-52s and some tankers out of Kadena Air Force Base on Okinawa to carpet bomb Xicheng. Even if they send some Flankers up or even some J-20 Stealth fighters, the F-22s will take them out and the B-52s will get through and accomplish the mission. That is what I would do sir." General Picket said.

"OK Roger. That sounds like a better plan. Make it happen." President Parry said.

General Picket was on his secure phone before he even left the Oval Office. The USS *Florida*, SSGN-728, which was patrolling the western pacific was ordered to the South China Sea to infiltrate to a position near the coast of China in the Taiwan Strait. She was ordered to fire a salvo of six Tomahawk Cruise Missiles at each of the PLAAF Airbases at Yuanmou and Xining and then hastily retreat for the waters off the Japanese coast. Six B-52 Buffs and two squadrons of F-22 Raptors and six tankers were ordered to fly to the Xichang Satellite Launch Center out of Kadena Air Force Base and level it after the cruise missile attack had disabled the runways at Yuanmou Airbase.

The attack went off without a hitch. A squadron of Su-30 MKK Flankers out of Xiangyun Midu Airbase tried to intercept the B-52s, but the F-22 Raptors quickly dispatched them.

CHINESE GO NUCLEAR ON ASBMS AFTER SAT LAUNCH FACILITY DESTROYED

Now the Chinese were really pissed. After the U.S. stiffed them on their U.S. bond and T-bill interest payments and leveled their prized missile launch complex, they decided to take off the gloves and fight bare knuckles.

Orders were sent to the invasion fleet to arm their ASBMs with nuclear weapons when attacking U.S., British and French carriers. It was on as far as the Chinese were concerned.

RICKY AND COMPANY IN HAWAII WHEN THEY GET THE CALL TO ARMS

Ricky, Carmen, Amber, J.J., Alexandra and Neil and Tommie "Taco" Thomas were at a luau at the Oahu Hilton when Ricky's cell phone rang. The aviators had been in the islands for a few days of R and R after Top Gun training and before they resumed their duties at their squadrons.

Ricky's lawyer friend Amber Wong had taken a few days of vacation to be able to make the trip. Ricky and Amber had been seeing each other on and off whenever she could get away from her practice and Ricky was available.

Ricky and J.J.'s Black Knight squadron of F/A-18s had been embarked on the super carrier USS *Carl Vinson* which had been sent to Pearl Harbor for war games training missions after Top Gun, so Ricky and J.J. met the boat at Pearl. Carmen's squadron of F-35s was also to be embarked on the USS *Carl Vinson*, but was currently still at Eglin AFB in Florida for further training. Carmen had taken some leave to join the boys in Hawaii.

Ricky and Amber had been getting along well, and their relationship had grown close even though Amber could be self-centered and demanding at times. Ricky liked Carmen just as well although he could not see her often as he saw Amber since Carmen was still stationed on the East Coast and was there most of the time.

Ricky recognized Veronica's ring tone and answered the call. "Hello?"

"Ricky, its Veronica. Where are you?" Captain Veronica Chase, the Marine Corps representative at the National Reconnaissance Office said with a slight tone of urgency in her voice.

"Veronica baby, how are you? We are in Hawaii. What's up? You sound a little uptight." Ricky said through the slight haze of a mai tai or two. It had been happy hour in Hawaii before the group went to the luau.

VERONICA REPORTS WHAT THE CHINESE HAVE DONE

"Saddle up cowboy, we are going to war. The Chinese just shot down all but one of our spy satellites and all our communication satellites. We are blind and our communications networks are all down. The Chinese also hacked most of DOD's computer and scrambled the power grid and traffic control grids. It is chaos back here on the mainland. President Parry is pissed. He carpet bombed their satellite launch complex at Xichang and shot down their spy satellites and their ASBM targeting satellites. Who is with you?" Veronica said.

"Holy shit! Really? Wait a minute isn't shooting down our satellites against the International Treaty Barring the Militarism of Space?" Ricky said.

"Yeah. Remind me to sue them when the war is over." Veronica said sarcastically. "But for now, seriously dude, who is with you. Your squadrons are looking for you, and, if I know you, you are with J.J., maybe Neil, probably Carmen etc. You silly bastards need to get back to your squadrons ASAP. The President is going to deploy several carrier strike groups, and yours is one of them. Did you watch the President's prime time address the other night and his recent press conference where he said it looks like war with China is inevitable after we hosed them on the interest we owe them on the T-bills and bonds they bought from us."

"Yeah we watched it and could not believe it. The shit is really hitting the fan. We watched the Chinese Ambassador get up in front of all the news cameras and try to tell the world the big fleet they launched is only for stabilizing the Africa region to protect their investments. We all thought the guy was lying. Our S2 officer did not know anything though when we checked with him. All he knew was that it was a big fleet, and that nobody knew where it was headed. Where do you think the battle is going to be?" Ricky asked.

"Don't know, but I am betting on Brazil. The last place we have overheads of the fleet from our satellites is down in the Drake's Passage regions south of the Cape of Good Hope. Right as they were about to exit Drake's passage, the lights went out on our spy satellites and all hell broke out with our computers. The President sent some Auroras down to find them and they found them close to the Falklands and heading north on a course which indicates Africa is not the target despite their protestations to the contrary.

Nothing works right and we are having trouble not only with seeing what is happening on the earth's surface, but also in voice communications with the Pentagon and data transmission. We know the Chinese have hacked our computers, because our IT guys tell us they did, and our directory structures keep changing and files we know were there are now missing. Some of the computers just freeze and others spontaneously shut down without a command to do so. It's a mess.

The CIA tells us that they have been finding something called the GinWui Rootkit on our computers that a Chinese hacker named Wicked Rose installed. It allows him or one of his hacker drones to open a back door to our file structures and do whatever they want. We have not figured out how to stop it yet. For now, we are just making do with backup systems. I have to report to the Commandant of the Marine Corps this afternoon to keep him apprised of what is happening out here so I better sign off for now." Veronica closed the conversation.

"OK Veronica, thanks for the heads up. We are on it. My carrier is out here in Hawaii right now on training exercises. I invited Carmen and Neil to come join J.J. and I for some liberty after the Red Flag battle at the end of Strike Fighter Tactics Instruction in Fallon. We have been chilling out for a couple of days."

CARRIER ASSIGNMENTS

"Tell Carmen the Commandant thinks the Chinese are going to attack Brazil, and that the Navy is going to have to bring the West Coast carriers around to support the East Coast carriers in countering the Chinese fleet. He has decided to provide F-35 support to the West Coast carriers. He has ordered her squadron to Miramar to deploy on a carrier out of San Diego in support of F/A-18 operations off the other carriers stationed at North Island. Carmen's squadron is to be moved to the USS *Carl Vinson* when the carriers meet near the tip of South America. So Carmen needs to call her squadron immediately for orders. The President is going to order your carrier USS *Carl Vinson* and its strike group to make for Drake Passage off Cape Horn ASAP to shadow the Chinese invasion fleet from behind, and will be sending two other carrier strike groups from NAS North Island with you." Veronica continued.

"OK I will tell her that and tell J.J. and Neil what is happening. Keep in touch Veronica. We all miss you." Ricky said re-assuring Veronica.

"I miss you guys too. Be safe and fly smart. Let's kick these little yellow bastards in the teeth. Chase out." and with that, she hung up the phone and was off to get ready to brief the Commandant.

"Hey guys listen up. That was Veronica Chase. Veronica says we all need to call our squadrons for orders. The shit has hit the fan, and we are going to war with the Chinese."

Ricky then filled everybody in on what Veronica had told him. "Everybody call your squadron right away and get on the phones and start making plane reservations back to your squadrons. J.J. and I will contact our operations officer to find out how soon we move out."

"I'm on it." Carmen said. She immediately got on her cell phone and called the operations officer of the VMAQ-3 Moon Dogs at MCAS Cherry Point, North Carolina to find out what was happening.

"Ditto." Neil said. He got on the phone to his operations officer at the Navy's Black Knights squadron, VFA-154, at NAS Lemoore. He and Taco were told to fly back to San Diego immediately and that the Black Knights were being deployed on the CVN-76, USS *Ronald Reagan* and that they would sail in three days time as Carrier Strike Group Seven. The operations officer told Neil that somebody else would fly his plane down to NAS North Island and to meet Tommie and Neil's Weapons System Officer Tom "Squishy" Moore at North Island.

"Hey Carmen, did you hear the news?" Carmen's operations officer said from his office at Cherry Point.

"Yes, I was just calling in for details. What's up?" Carmen replied.

SOUTHERN STRIKE GROUP COMPOSITION

"Get your butt on a plane and fly to San Diego and report to MCAS Miramar, ASAP." Carmen's operations officer said into the phone. "They are dividing the Moon Dogs up and distributing our F-35 capabilities to strengthen the Marine F/A-18 squadrons deployed on the various carriers to give them vertical take-off and landing capability, stealth and DAS infrared capability. You and Tequilla are moving to MCAS Miramar tomorrow. I will have somebody else fly your plane out to Miramar and you can meet up with Tequila and the rest of the squadron there. Ultimately, we are going to be deployed on CVN-70, the USS *Carl Vinson* as part of Carrier Strike Group 1." Carmen's heart skipped a beat. She knew Ricky and J.J.'s Black Knights squadron was deployed on the USS *Carl Vinson*. "We are getting the band back together." she thought to herself.

She snapped back to reality when her operations officer said, " We sail in three days time out of NAS North Island. We have orders to join up with U.S.S. *Nimitz* which is steaming toward the southern tip of South America from Hawaii as we speak. The *Nimitz* will join the USS *Ronald Reagan* and the USS *Carl Vinson* and form a Southern

Expeditionary Force trailing the Chinese invasion fleet. Three more Carrier Strike Groups are sailing out of Norfolk in three days to act as the Northern Expeditionary Force and head south to intercept the Chinese invasion fleet. A new squadron of F-35's has been hastily formed from RAG pilots, and will deploy on one of the Northern Force carriers. Can you get to San Diego tomorrow?"

"Yup, I am on my way." Carmen replied. "Tell whoever is going to fly my plane, not to ding it up or he will have to deal with me." The operations officer just laughed, said "Roger that" and hung up.

That night in her hotel room, Amber had a hissy fit.

"Ricky, how can you just leave me her in Hawaii high and dry? I came all the way out here to spend some time with you, and this is how you treat me? Can't you get a waiver or take some leave or something and catch up with the ship later? I cannot believe this shit! You could be killed out there. Then where would I be?"

Ricky just looked at her in amazement.

"Amber this is my job. There are no waivers or leave when something like this happens. My squadron needs me, J.J. needs me and the Marine Corps needs me. I need to be there for my buddies. We are going to war with China, and that just trumps all other concerns of any nature. It is not all about you. My life and those of my fellow pilots will be at risk and we know that. We signed up for it and have accepted the risk. There is no crying about it now. So there it is. You need to get on a plane and go home. If you have a bomb shelter at your house, stock it up and get in it. If you don't, build one. The Chinese have nuclear-tipped ICBMs that can reach the United States, and, if they have the audacity to shoot down our satellites, they might just nuke the mainland. That is unlikely though since we just leveled their Satellite Launch Center at Xichang. But they have boomers, so it is not out of the realm of possibility since we don't even know what their target is yet."

"You are scaring me Ricky."

"Sorry, that is just the way it is. We have driven ourselves right up to the edge of a possible extinction event for the U.S. By not conserving energy and developing alternative energy fuel sources to fuel our cars and trucks fast enough. They need oil to keep their economy running and so do we. Conflict over the remaining oil was inevitable, and now it is starting. To make matter worse, we stiffed the Chinese on the interest on their US bonds and T-bills, so they are really pissed. They have three trillion of US debt instruments they are holding. What would you do if you were them?" Ricky said with a very serious look on his face.

"I guess you are right Ricky." Amber said calming down. "It is our own damn fault. But there is no way in hell I am going to live in a bomb shelter. If I die, I die. At least I will be comfortable right up until the end." Amber gave Ricky a kiss and said, "See you stud. Fly safely to the extent that is possible in a war zone."

CONVERSATION WITH PRIME MINISTER OF ENGLAND

Picking up the secure phone in the Oval Office, President Parry called the Prime Minister of the United Kingdom, Paul Putter. "Prime Minister Putter, it is President Parry. Good evening sir. Sorry to be calling so late your time. I hope I did not wake you."

"Good evening President Parry. No you did not wake me. I am in our situation room right now looking at our options, and was actually just about to call you. Your timing is impeccable." Prime Minister Potter said.

"I spoke with the Chinese Ambassador a couple of weeks ago and inquired of him what the Chinese intentions were with regard to the huge fleet of ships they recently launched out of their Navy base at Hainan Island." President Parry said. Parry continued:

"The Chinese Ambassador told me that their intention with regard to the big fleet is to stabilize the African region where they have so many investments in natural resources. When I asked him why they launched such a big fleet with six super carriers, ballistic missile submarines, probably kilo class submarines and enough LSTs to land two divisions of Chinese Marines, he just said the Chinese were afraid that the U.K. and France would interfere with their operations and attack them with aircraft carrier-based forces as they were conducting their operations in Africa. I don't believe a word of it since I just got word that the Chinese have just shot down all our spy satellites and our military communications satellites. Further, there is no reason to bring ballistic missile submarines on such a force unless they are planning to nuke Britain and France. What do you think?"

Prime Minister Potter was shocked. "They shot down your spy satellites and communications satellites too?. Buggers! Yes, we concur, their "stabilize Africa" story is hogwash. Our TopSat spy satellites showed the same things as yours in terms of the composition of the fleet although not with quite the same photographic resolution. We too think it is too big and too well armed to contemplate only a stabilization of the African regions, and we are quite alarmed. None of those countries down there have much in the way of military power. We think they are going to attack Washington D.C. or somewhere on the East Coast of the U.S or possibly Europe or one or more of the oil producing countries. So I have ordered a carrier force centered on the HMS Prince of Wales super carrier to prepare for sailing in three days time to intercept the Chinese fleet and engage them if necessary. I was going to call you for help. We have already assumed you will be doing the same thing and that our forces can coordinate with yours to share intelligence and provide additional firepower. We will also send our other super carrier the HMS Queen Elisabeth as soon as we can get her ready to sail. That should be in about a week. We will have cruisers, destroyers and frigates accompanying both carriers and two fast attack submarines. We don't know where the Chinese fleet is right now, because they shot down our TopSat spy satellites this morning, and the President of France confirmed that the Chinese shot down the French spy satellites as well. Do you know where they are and are heading yet?"

President Parry paused a moment. He had not known the Chinese had shot down the British and French spy satellites till this conversation. "Thank you for your report. It looks like this is a very serious situation. I did not know they had shot down your spy satellites till just now. I am afraid we don't know where they currently are either. The last time we saw them with our satellites, they were just exiting the Drake Passage at Cape Horn. Then they shot down our spy satellites this morning, so we are looking at alternatives right now to find them. I have already launched our spy planes to overfly the southern Atlantic and find them, and we should be hearing from them soon. We will keep sending our spy planes to monitor their position and course until we figure out where they are going and what we think they are going to do. In the meantime, we are checking with private operators of Earth Observation satellites and operators of our weather satellites to see if those birds have enough resolution to find these ships. We plan to check with the Russians too to see if their spy satellites have sent down overheads of the fleet's position if the Russians still have any spy satellites in orbit. Keep me informed if your people find the Chinese fleet and determine where they appear to be going. I am going to sign off now, as there is much work to be done, and I need to call the President of France. Goodbye for now and we will talk soon."

"Right then. Cheerio. I will keep you posted." Prime Minister Potter said cheerily.

You gotta love the British. They are big game players. Even the Nazi juggernaut could not intimidate them. Their RAF pilots flying Spitfires had taken out 1000 Nazi planes in the Battle of Britain while only losing only 500 of their own and saved the country from invasion. As Winston Churchill famously said, "Never in the annals of history has so much been owed by so many to so few."

CHAPTER 6

BATTLE TUPI

APRIL 15: THE TUPI OIL AND GAS FIELD 125
MILES OFF THE COAST OF RIO DE JANEIRO

Miguel Perez had been working as a drill pipe rigger on the Riga Cluster Deepwater Drilling Platform for five years. He was married with five children and a devout Catholic who went to mass every Sunday in the makeshift chapel on the ship. He only got to see his family once every other month when the Petrobras chopper landed on the ship and ferried some of the crew home for some R & R. The crew took turns going ashore and his turn was coming up the following weekend.

PIPE FITTER IN TUPI ON PLATFORM
SPOTS CHINESE FLEET

"This is Captain Silva of the Riga Cluster Deepwater Drilling Platform out in the Tupi Field. We have a massive naval formation closing on our position and are not sure what is going on. We request clarification and instructions." said Captain Silva.

"I see. Hold the line please.""Captain Silva, this is Ricardo Rega, CEO of Petrobras. Have any of the ships approached your platform yet and done any hostile act?"

"No sir. They are still pretty far away, maybe twenty miles to the closest one so far." Silva replied.

"Alright, keep me apprised of the situation. I am going to call the government in Brazilia and see if they know anything, and I will call you back." Rega promised.

"President Emmanuel, this is Ricardo Rega, good afternoon sir."

"Hello my good friend, how are you?" President Manny Emmanuel greeted his good friend and top campaign contributor. "What can I do for you?"

"Sir, one of my Platform Captains out in the Tupi Field just called me and reported that there are Navy ships in the Tupi Field and they spread out for as far as the eye can see along the horizon. He is worried and wants to know what is going on. I was hoping you knew." Rega said.

"I am sorry my friend, I do not know. Let me call the President of the United States and see if he knows anything, and I will call you back in a few minutes."

"Alright, thank you." Rega said and hung up. So far the Chinese plan was working brilliantly. Nobody knew what was going one. Surprise is one of the major principles of war that all great generals strive mightily to use.

President Emmanuel asked his secretary to dial the White House immediately with priority flash traffic. She was able to get through to the President's office immediately as the White House had been monitoring the situation closely and was very curious.

"President Emmanuel, good to hear from you. This is President Parry. What is going on down there?"

"Well sir, I was just about to ask you that. The President of Petrobras just called me and told me that a massive naval formation has just showed up in the Tupi Oil and Gas field off the coast of

Rio de Janeiro. They have not done anything hostile yet, but he was wondering what they are doing there. He asked me what they want and what they intend to do. He asked me what I know about the situation. I told him I did not know the answers to any of his questions and that I would call you to see if you knew anything more. Do you know what is going on?

Actually we do not know what is going on exactly. We have been watching this formation of Chinese ships with concern since they left China awhile ago. It is a big formation loaded for bear with six carrier battle groups, troop carriers, amphibious LSTs, ballistic missile submarines, and we think they have kilo class submarines with them. They have been saying publicly that they are headed for Africa to stabilize the region to protect their investments there, but we do not believe them...."

Just then the line went dead as a Chinese cruise missile streaked in from a Chinese Aegis cruiser and blew up the switch that was carrying the telephone conversation. President Emmanuel heard a deafening roar and raced to the window of his office and saw a formation of Chinese Su-30 MK2 Flankers streak overhead heading for the airbase at Brasilia to attack the Saab Gripen fighters of the Grupo de Aviação de Caça (GAvCa). Most of the Gripens were caught by surprise on the ground and destroyed. The few that made it into the air did not stand a chance against the superbly trained Chinese pilots and their thrust vectoring Flankers. It was a bloodbath.

Simultaneous raids took out the Brazilian fighter groups at their air bases at Santa Cruz and Anapolis. Helicopter, support and close air support squadrons at the air bases at Natal, Salvador, Florianopolis, Belem, Porto Velho, Manaus and Campo Grande, Canoas, Belem, Recife and Boa Vista were wiped out in other raids by carrier-based Chinese fighters and cruise missiles lauched from Chinese cruisers in the carrier task forces. The Brazilian Air Force was nothing but a pile of smoking rubble in less than three days. Things were looking very grim for the defense of the motherland.

Without the benefit of air cover, the Brazilian Army's effort's to repel the assaults of the Chinese Marine Divisions and Special Forces units on their air fields, oil refineries and oil export terminals were doomed to failure. Likewise, the Brazilian Navy was pretty much behind the eight ball in attempting to defend the oil drilling platforms out in the Tupi Oil and Gas field. With quiet and small Kilo class submarines lurking in the depths that they could not see on their sonar and outgunned on the surface and with no air cover, the Brazilian Navy could pretty much see the handwriting on the wall.

The fighting on the ground raged for a month. The Chinese, fighting far away from home, had no men to spare to man prisoner of war camps took no prisoners. When Brazilian soldiers surrendered, they were executed. When word of this spread through the ranks, the Brazilians got seriously motivated, but, in the end, they were simply unprepared, outgunned, and overwhelmed by the superior firepower and technology of the Chinese. Nevertheless, both the Brazilian Army and Navy fought valiantly. The Brazilians fought to the death—the battle was not over until the last man and woman in the Brazilian Army was dead or so seriously wounded they could not fight anymore.

Suffering fearsome casualties, the Brazilians did manage to inflict some damage on the Chinese, sinking a Chinese Cruiser and downing two Flankers. Several platoons of Chinese Marines were caught in ambushes and wiped out to the last man. In the end however, the Chinese controlled all the major airfields in Brazil and the oil refineries at Canoas, Maua, Paulinia, Sao Jose dos Campos, Cubatao, Duque, de Caxias, Mauaus, Fortaleza, Betim, Araucaria, Sao Francisco do Conde, Pelotas, Grupo Peixoto de Castro and Repsoi YPF.

The Chinese also controlled the town of Mecae, the center of Petrobras operations to the offshore platforms and home to many of its facilities and the ports of Pecem and Fortaleza.

The Chinese quietly set up their truck launched Anti Ship Ballistic Missiles in the middle of the night at a secret location inside a warehouse facility in the far south of the country. These ground-based ASBMs were to augment the ASBMs deployed on two Chinese boomers under the waters of the Tupi Field. Together, they lay in wait for the unsuspecting American carriers to stumble into their trap.

The Chinese had achieved what they wanted to achieve defensively with the ASBMs. The ground-based launchers were completely invisible to aerial reconnaissance since they were hidden inside a giant warehouse in a small town far to the south of Rio. They could roll their truck launchers and satellite dishes out from the warehouses when the skies were clear of planes or satellites to download initial target fixes from their ocean surveillance satellites. They could then load the initial target fix into their missile guidance systems just prior to launch, and roll the ASBM missiles out on their truck launchers and launch them.

Now all they had to do was wait for the unsuspecting American carriers to cruise into range, and then nuke them.

CHAPTER 7

DISASTER STRIKES

"Well there is our answer." President Parry said to Admiral Roger Picket, Chairman of the Joint Chiefs. "Its Brazil. Must be their oil and gas they are after." They were sitting in the Situation Room where there were assembled the Joint Chiefs, the Director of the CIA, Richard Rogers, the director of the National Security Agency, Tom Wilmont, Director of the National Reconnaissance Office William Headman, Mike Malone, National Security Advisor and General Tim Steadman, Director of the Defense Intelligence Agency.

"What else could it be? Its not their women. The Chinese would not know what to do with a hot Brazilian in a thong." Mike Maloney National Security Advisor wisecracked with a grin.

PRESIDENT'S SPEECH ON THE CHINESE AND FRUSTRATION WITH OUR LACK OF MONEY

"Shut up you wise ass and stop insulting the Chinese. They are way smarter than us." President Parry snapped stunning the room.

"The Chinese have for years been quietly making deals all over the world for natural resources like oil, coal, aluminum, timber, copper, water, rare earths ore, rubber and other stuff they will need in the future. They have been way smarter than us. Back in 2009, they bought the mineral rights to an entire mountain full of copper in Peru. They have been making friends all over the world. Until now, they have done it peacefully. Now they have taken it to a whole new level, and we have our tit in a ringer. In contrast, we have been sitting around not planning for this day. We need that oil from Brazil, and an interruption in that supply will have grave consequences to our economy and will put us into a severe recession or worse.

To make matters worse, the Chinese have put together a first class military with super carriers, stealth fighters, navalized thrust vectoring Flankers, anti-satellite weapons, nuclear-tipped anti-ship ballistic missiles, intercontinental ballistic missiles, many divisions of Chinese Marines and Army, a first class Navy including ballistic missile and attack submarines.

For our part, we are broke and we do not have the kinds of weapons systems we should have at this point in the numbers we need to meet this threat. All this buildup by the Chinese has been happening right under our noses. So now we have to do what we usually do – close the barn door after the horse has already escaped.

I get very frustrated with the way things go with this country as you can tell. We let things get so out of control in Germany back in the 1930s by dithering, that 6 million people died before we were able to whack that Nazi scumbag lunatic.

But here we are, and we are stuck with what they call in Jamaica a 'situation', so now the question is what the hell are we going to do about it."

The room was stunned again by the President's uncharacteristically salty language. President Parry was spitting mad.

"Alright calm down Mr. President, I think we can still get this thing under control." Admiral Picket finally said after a long silence trying desparately to defuse the situation. The President was still fuming, but he finally sat down and turned to Admiral Picket attentively.

"What is the status of our carriers and where are they now?" the President asked. "What are the allies sending if anything. Where are our subs?" "Talk to me. Give me a plan. How are the Brazilians doing, and are we completely blinded? Do we have any good intel at all? What is the situation in Brazil right now?"

"Mr. Headman, why don't you and Mr. Roger's start us off with the situation in Brazil right now." Admiral Picket said.

Headman got up and gave an orderly a command to project several overhead satellite shots in sequence slowly taken by the one spy satellite that survived. He let the sequence of overheads roll in silence for effect. Some shots showed Brazillian airfields covered with Chinese transport planes, helicopters and fighters. Other shots showed a massive Chinese fleet of aircraft carriers and accompanying missile cruisers, destroyers and tenders of six carrier battle groups cruising off the coast of Brazil ready to repel invaders. Still other shots showed Chinese oil tankers and Liquified Natural Gas tankers queued up at the oil terminal ports and LNG compression plant ports of Brazil loading oil and Liquefied Natural Gas into their tanks for transport back to China. Still other shots showed Chinese troop emplacements, anti-aircraft gun positions, anti-aircraft missile batteries, communications facilities and artillery positions around ports, refineries, LNG processing plants, airfields, military bases and likely invasion beaches. Still other shots showed Chinese troops aboard the oil drilling rigs, drilling ships, and exploration ships standing guard over the Brazilian workers.

Finally Headman broke his silence.

"As you can see, the Chinese have completely taken over the Brazilian oil and gas drilling, exploration, production, refining, pumping and LNG compression facilities. They have also defeated the Brazilian Army, Navy and Air Force and are in full command of the Brazilian military infrastructure including all their military bases, airfields and communication facilities, radar stations and satellite uplink and downlink facilities. We have human intelligence reports that they have enslaved the Brazilian oil rig and refinery workers and are forcing them to work and are executing them if they refuse to work."

"How did you get these shots?" the President asked.

MISTY AND TACSAT AND CUBESATS DISCUSSED

"The Chinese missed one of our Misty stealth recon satellites that they did not see on their radar prior to their attack on our spy satellites. It was in an East-West orbit that we were able to alter enough to get partial coverage of Brazil. In addition, we had a TacSat-6 next generation mini spy satellite sitting on the shelf, so we launched it out of Vandenburg last week into a polar orbit over Brazil. It is returning great shots in both visual, infrared and radar spectrum as we speak.

The TacSat-6 is a smaller, cheaper version of the TacSat-3 we developed back in 2012. It is about as big as a refrigerator and only costs about 25 million to build, and can be built in about 6 months. We have already started building two more. The TacSat-6 uses hyperspectral imaging using visual, infrared and radar and has resolution down to 2 meters.

In addition, the French space agency CNES working with Dassault Aviation launched a cubesat spy satellite into orbit over Brazil yesterday using their Aldebaran launch system. They launched it from the underbelly of a Rafale fighter off the French nuclear super carrier *Charles de Gaulle* which is enroute to the Tupi field right now. The *Charles de Gaulle* is about 900 miles away from the Tupi Field as we speak. The French cubesat is in orbit now and returning good visual spectrum pictures and providing data and communications links. They say we can use their Aldebaran launch system to launch communication cubesats of our own to support our drones and tactical operations if we need to, but I don't think we will need to. We have the Pegasus system from Orbital Sciences that can launch satellites via a rocket attached to the underbelly of a modified jumbo jet. We can put cubesats and TacSat-6 satellites into orbit that way also, so the loss of our communication satellites and spy satellites will only temporarily hinder our operations."

"Good. Get a replacement spy and communication satellite constellation in orbit as soon as you can using TacSat-6s and Cubesats so we can use our the data links of our weapon systems and our military communications systems." President Parry said.

"Yes sir."

GINWUI ROOTKIT DAMAGE DISCUSSED

"Tell me about the damage to our military communication and fire control systems Wicked Rose and the hacker force of the Sichuan Military Command Communication Department have done." the President said.

"Well sir, they have caused quite a bit of initial disruption using a diabolical mechanism they have infected most of our computers with called the GinWui root kit. The GinWui root kit allows hackers in China to open back doors into almost all of our DOD computers and remove files and entire directories and shut down critical processes. We do not know what information they were able to steal yet, but they would not have been able to steal any critical tactical war planning, because we have not done any yet since this was a surprise attack.

DOD HAS DETECTED ROOT KIT FOOTPRINT AND CAN REMOVE IT

Our cyber security forces have been able to detect the fingerprint of the GinWui rootkit and detect it on all DOD computers and remove it. So, as of today, the Chinese hackers can no longer access our computers through a back door and take control of our operating systems. The threat of further disruptions is over now, but we are watching for further attempts at intrusion. All DOD computers have timed backup systems, so all systems are being backed up to a state they were in just before the attack so only files generated since the attack which a hacker noticed and deleted will be lost. We should be back online and fully functional shortly sir."

"Very good. So tell me more about what these satellite shots mean." the President said.

CHINESE HAVE TWO BOOMERS AND FOUR FAST ATTACKS IN AREA

"These shots are bad news. They show the Chinese fully control all the seaports of Brazil as well as all her airfields, the airspace above Brazil and the sea lanes off her coast. In short, the Chinese have Brazil locked down tight. We think the Chinese have two nuclear-powered, ballistic-missile submarines and four nuclear-powered, fast-attack submarines in the area from information from our undersea hydrophone network. We have detected six distinct sonar signatures that we have never heard before. We think these are subs they built in secret at their underground naval base at Hainan Island out of view of our spy satellites, so we have never seen or heard them before. Their boomers may have anti-ship ballistic missiles aboard, and their fast attack subs will probably have cruise missiles to attack land targets and possibly missiles that can be launched from submerged positions to attack aircraft.

"Regardless, we have four *Virginia*-class and two *Seawolf*-class, nuclear-powered, fast-attack submarines enroute to the area to gather intelligence and start taking out whatever submarines they have in the area, but they are not there yet. All are equipped with an acoustic cloaking shell that directs sound around the submarine. It relies upon density and bulk modulus of the shield material to make the sub completely disappear by bending sound waves around the sub and avoids absorbing the sound waves so as to also avoid a shadow. That technique came out of Duke University. We love those people.

"Go Blue Devils!" the President interjected laughing.

"With regard to the Boomers, we don't know what weapons the Chinese have loaded on them, but since the Chinese clearly should have anticipated a naval battle, it is a safe bet they loaded them with DF-21D anti-ship ballistic missiles.

We are pretty sure they have some Kilo-class diesel subs down there too, but those little things are so quiet and small they are hard to hear and hard to see and we are still listening and looking for them."

If they do have Kilos, they will have torpedoes and Sizzler anti-ship missiles on-board. China is known to have acquired the Sizzler from Russia. It is a particularly nasty, supersonic sea-skimming missile which can deliver a 450 kilogram warhead at a range of 300 kilometers and perform defensive maneuvers enroute including curving around islands. The warhead has a rocket motor of its own, and that rocket then ignites and accelerates the warhead from mach 1 to mach 3 in the terminal phase for the kill. That makes it much more difficult for our radar-guided Phalanx guns to shoot it down.

We have a new trick in our bag though. We have fitted our ships with the French Sofradir multi-channel missile detection system to integrate radar, infra-red and visible light sensors into a single tracking unit which compares data from all three channels for a better chance at lock on to the incoming warhead and shoot it down.

We have also retrofitted all our carrier battle groups with the Raytheon Laser Area Defense System (LADS) which can blow incoming shells and small rockets apart with laser beams. This system should back up the Phalanx system and will never run out of ammo like the Phalanx system could under heavy assault."

"Mr. President, if I could interrupt here for a minute?" Mr. Rogers, Director of the Central Intelligence Agency interjected.

"Yes, Mr. Rogers, what do you have?" the President inquired.

CIA DESCRIBES KILL SWITCHES THAT HAVE BEEN SNUCK ONTO SIZZLERS

"Thank you sir. The CIA has had a black program going on for some time to penetrate the foundry and design facility where the Russians get their microprocessors for their guidance modules for the Sizzlers. We have succeeded in placing a mole engineer on the design team for the Sizzler guidance system. This mole has, in a surreptitious manner, placed a 'kill switch' in the design of the Sizzler active radar homing terminal guidance module so that we can kill an inbound Sizzler at will by transmitting a kill signal from our ships.

"Fantastic. How does that work?" President Parry asked.

"Basically, the Sizzler guides initially after a sub launch using an inertial guidance system to an initial point set into its guidance system which is close to the target. The warhead then separates from the main rocket motor, an lights off its own rocket motor and accelerates to mach 3 and enters an active radar homing mode where it transmits radar pulses and listens for echoes and homes in on the echoes. It is during this terminal stage that we lock onto the incoming pulses, mimic them and send them back along with a spread spectrum abort signal. The spread spectrum abort signal is invisible to all receivers not having the same spread spectrum pseudorandom code sequence key which the kill switch receiver has. The mimic echo signals we send back also has changed timing, and since it is the strongest echo signal the inbound missile receives, the missile locks onto our echo instead of the legitimate echo. Because we changed the timing, that alone will cause the missile to miss even if the kill switch has been discovered or does not work.

The 'kill switch' demodulator we snuck into the missile warhead radar receiver design works like this. It receives the spread spectrum abort command and unencodes it with the same pseudorandom code sequence we used to create it. When it decodes the abort command signal, it understands it is homing on a U.S. ship. It then feeds further false guidance data into the guidance system of the missile. The false guidance data causes the missile to go nuts and harmlessly crash into the sea." Rogers stated matter of factly.

"Are you kidding me? That is outstanding!" the President exclaimed. What is spread spectrum? Do the allies know about this, and have the capability to send the signal?"

"No, we were afraid of leaks, and have not told them about it yet, so their ships are in danger from the Kilos and any Chinese fast attack boats that are armed with Sizzlers. Spread spectrum is a way of spreading the energy of a signal out over a wide range of frequencies by either chirping the signal, that is rapidly changing its frequency during each each radar pulse, or by encoding each radar pulse with a pseudorandom code sequence. The way that works, is a pseudorandom string of ones and zeroes running at a bit rate which is much higher than the radar pulse rate is encoded into the radar signal by exclusive-ORing the data that defines when the radar RF pulses are transmitted with the pseudorandom string of ones and zeroes that we call the key. The result is a transmitted signal with its energy density spread out over a bandwidth of frequencies that is about 100 times more broad than the original radar signal. That makes it undetectable, and it does not interfere with the narrowband radar pulse echo signals in the same frequency range occupied by the spread spectrum signal." Rogers said.

CHINESE ALSO HAVE YJ-91 ANTI SHIP MISSILES AND ASBMS IN AREA

"Don't get too excited just yet Mr. President." Admiral Picket interjected. "First, the Chinese have developed their own sea-skimming, anti-ship missile from the Russian Kh-31P anti-radiation missile. It is called the Ying Ji YJ-91, and they have adapted it for submerged launch as well as for air launch. It is a mach 4.5 missile with a range of 50 kilometers. It has active radar homing which turns on in terminal phase when the missile drops down from 20 meters above the sea surface to only 7 meters. It can also be programmed to pop up and dive like our Harpoon. If we get lucky, the Kilos will only be armed with Sizzlers, but if they have the YJ-91 Ying Ji anti-ship missiles, we are going to have to shoot those down the old fashioned way.

PRESIDENT TOLD MUST TAKE OUT ASBMS ON LAND

Second, in addition to attacking our ships with Ying Ji missiles, if the Chinese have Anti-Ship Ballistic Missiles down there, our carriers and other ships should not be sent into the Tupi field area until we eliminated the ASBM launching platforms. That means we have to take out the boomers, and if they have mobile truck mounted launchers, we have to find them all and destroy them. The DF-21D is capable of carrying a 500 kiloton nuclear warhead, so one of them can wipe out a carrier and perhaps an entire carrier battle group if the ships of the battle group are not spread out far enough. We are not sure yet whether or not we can stop one of those missiles once it takes off. We have weapons that can destroy one in the boost phase, and our Aegis cruisers can fire SM-3 missiles to shoot down incoming missiles, but we have never tested the SM-3 against an ASBM in a vertical death dive from the edge of space since nobody has ever had one before. It is a major gamble sending carriers in there now sir."

"Where are our carriers and can we send them in to start an invasion? And what forces are the allies sending?" President Parry asked.

"An invasion would be a bad idea right now until we have control of the airspace above Brazil. We will not have control of the airspace until we can send in our carriers and win the air battle. We cannot send in the carriers until we eliminate all their ASBMs, and sink or disable their carriers or win the air battle with their carrier based aircraft and control or knock out their airfields."

PRESIDENT TOLD FLANKERS ARE
BETTER THAN F/A 18S

"Winning the air battle with their carrier based aircraft is going to be a dicey proposition. Their navalized Flanker MIGs are better jets than our F/A-18s and our F-35s. Their Su-27MK2 Flankers are fearsome weapons systems, and our Navy and Marine F-35s and F/A-18s are not going to be able to go toe-to-toe with them one-on-one and win every time. Our pilots are going to be at a severe disadvantage."

NORTHERN AND SOUTHERN EXPEDITIONARY FORCES:
WHICH CARRIERS ARE BEING SENT

"As far as what forces the allies are sending in, right now the British are sending *HMS Queen Elisabeth* carrier battle group, and the French are sending the *Charles de Gaulle* carrier battle group .

We have three carriers headed down from the East Coast, and three carriers headed toward the southern tip of South America from the West Coast and Hawaii.

The East Coast Contingent, comprising the Northern Expeditionary Force, are the *U.S.S. Enterprise*, the *U.S.S. George W. Bush* and the *U.S.S. Harry S. Truman.*

The West Coast contingent, comprising the Southern Expeditionary Force, are our carriers *U.S.S. Carl Vinson*, the *U.S.S. Ronald Regan* and the *U.S.S.* Nimitz.

Three of our Carrier Strike Groups from the Norfolk, Virginia Navy base, based around the *U.S.S. Enterprise* the *U.S.S. Harry S. Truman* and the *U.S.S. George W. Bush* are about 1700 miles away from the Tupi Field right now and proceeding southward at flank speed.

Two of our Carrier Strike Groups from NAS North Island, based around the *U.S.S. Carl Vinson* and the *U.S.S. Ronald Reagan* are rounding the tip of South America with the *Carl Vinson* being about 1500 miles south of the Tupi Field and the *Reagan* Carrier Strike Group is about

1700 miles south of the Tupi Field. The third Carrier Strike Group based around the *U.S.S. Nimitz* is behind them having been diverted from excercises in Hawaii. They are just now reaching the southern tip of South America.

The French and British supercarriers *Charles de Gaulle* and *HMS Queen Elisabeth* and their carrier battle groups are within 900 miles of the Tupi field right now."

"Alright, cut orders as you have recommended, and contact the Commander of the Southern Expeditionary Force to get out of ASBM range until we take out those boomers and find any land based launchers. Send in some Force Recon MARSOC teams from the Marines to find any ASBMs on land. Pass word to the commanders of the *de Gaulle* and *Queen Elisabeth* that we recommend that they do the same thing. The meeting is adjourned." And with that, President Parry turned on his heel and walked briskly out of the room.

CHINESE NUKE THE BRITISH CARRIERS

Atlantic Ocean, 124 Miles Northeast of Rio de Janeiro
Aboard the Type 094 Jin-Class Peoples Liberation Army Navy
Ballistic Missile Submarine *Huludao -1*
April 16, 0320 Hours

(Translated from the Mandarin)

"Attention on deck! Captain on the conn" the Chief of the Boat screamed as Captain Ka Cheng strode into the conning tower of the *Huludao – 1.*

"Bow planes to 15 degrees up angle. Take us to periscope depth. All ahead one third. Trail the floating communication wire and raise the satellite communication antenna on the main periscope when we get to periscope depth. I want to download the satellite optical and radar pictures of surface contacts in the area and get their positions and get any orders from the fleet command." the Captain ordered.

"Aye sir, roger that." the Executive Officer Kin Sheng confirmed the order.

"Periscope depth sir." the bow planesman reported.

"Raise the SigInt periscope and confirm the floating communication wire is deployed." Captain Cheng ordered.

"Aye sir. SigInt periscope is raised, and satellite communication antenna is deployed."

"Very well, communications room, establish communication with the Yaogan-IX Ocean-Surveillance-System satellite constellation and download a satellite picture of surface ship contacts within 1200 miles of the Tupi Oil and Gas Field. I want exact current positions of each ship, identification of each ship as ours or belonging to somebody else. Also establish contact with the Yaogan-VIII Synthenthic Aperture Radar satellite. I want you to download an SAR radar image of each enemy ship within range and store the radar images in memory for upload into the anti-ship ballistic missile guidance systems if we get launch orders." Captain Ka Cheng ordered. "I also need any orders for us from Fleet Command that come in over the floating wire."

"Aye, sir. Right away." the communication technician reported.

"Sonar, situation report. Any hostile contacts yet?"

USS VIRGINIA IN RANGE OF CHINESE BOOMER WHICH LAUNCHES ASBM

"We have a large number of surface contacts, all ours and one very weak submerged contact at 50,000 yards. From it sonar signature, to the extent our computers can tell, it appears to be a U.S. *Virginia*-class hunter-killer submarine. But it appears and then just disappears sir and reappears in a different place. Each time it reappears, it is a little closer. We do not know what it is sir, or whether there is something wrong with our gear. We have checked our gear, but we cannot find anything wrong." the Sonar Officer Lt. Jiang Wang reported.

"Alright Lt. Wang. Just keep and eye on it and keep me posted. It is probably nothing." Captain Ka Cheng ordered.

"Captain, Communications Room. We have received the ocean surveillance system satellite picture of the western Atlantic off the coast of Brazil. There is a British supercarrier *HMS Queen Elisabeth* and a French super carrier, the *Charles de Gaulle*, within range of our missiles sir! There is a U.S. carrier to the south, the *U.S.S. Nimitz*, but she is out of range of our missiles, and there are three more U.S. carriers to the north of our position, but they too are out of our range. Also sir, we have received orders from Admiral Chian Wing Liu, Commander of the Invasion Fleet to sink the British and French super carriers."

"Get me the Admiral on the secure channel." Cheng ordered.

"Captain Cheng, what can I do for you?" Admiral Chian Wing Liu inquired.

"I received your orders to sink the British and French carriers. I just wanted to make sure it was not a mistake and you want China to start a war with Britain and France?" Captain Cheng inquired hoping Liu was not serious in wanting to start a multi-front war.

"How dare you question my orders you impudent little prick. I will have you executed for this. You sink those carriers immediately am I clear?" Liu bellowed.

"Yes sir. Cheng out." Captain Cheng trembled. "Fucking douche bag. He wants to start a war with the Americans and now he wants to add the British and the French. What a grandstander. I guess he did not learn anything from Hitler's failures." Cheng said to himself under his breath as he left the communications room.

0330 Hours

"XO, take us to missile launch depth. Spin up missiles 1 and 2 and load our present position into their guidance systems. Load the SAR radar picture of the *HMS Queen Elisabeth* in the terminal guidance system of missile 1, and load the *Queen Elisabeth's* present position as the inertial guidance systems initial guidance point into the first stage guidance system. Load the SAR radar picture of the *Charles de Gaulle* in the terminal guidance system of missile 2, and load the de Gaulle's present position as the inertial guidance systems initial guidance point into the first stage guidance system. Report missile ready." Captain Cheng ordered.

"Aye sir." Executive Officer Kin Sheng reported.

After about ten minutes passed, Sheng reported the solid fuel DF-21D anti-ship-ballistic missiles ready to fire.

"XO confirm nuclear weapons release order Sierra Tango Five Echo Niner Xray Quebec Seven Baker Four" Captain Cheng said.

"I concur." the XO said.

Both officers removed launch keys from around their necks and inserted them in the key slots.

"On my mark. Three, Two, One, Mark." Captain Cheng said, and both officers turned their keys. The submarine lurched as both missiles leaped out of their launch tubes in blasts of compressed air and broached the surface. Their solid fuel boosters lit and they took off with a tremendous roar straight up, each headed toward their initial guidance points in the vicinity of their victim ships.

GORY EFFECTS OF NUCLEAR BLASTS

Ten minutes later, British supercarrier *HMS Queen Elisabeth* and French supercarrier *Charles de Gaulle* were each vaporized in 500 kiloton atomic fireballs. The inky black of the Atlantic night lit up as if a magnesium flare went off. Sailors on the Strike Group support ships within a mile of the fireballs who were above deck at the time of the explosions had their flesh flash barbequed and then torn off their bones by the 400 mile per hour winds of the blast waves. The flashes burned holes in the retinas of sailors on the cruisers and destroyers of the British and French Carrier Strike Groups who looked at the fireballs for more than a second and who were within five miles of the carriers. Tsunamis towering 120 feet rocketed out from the respective ground zeroes traveling at 600 miles per hour and capsized all the ships of the Carrier Strike Groups the waves caught broadside throwing thousands of screaming sailors into the salty Atlantic which was once again inky black. The capsized ships trapped thousands more men and women below decks dooming them to watery graves terrified, possibly alone, screaming and in the dark. Mercifully, the 12,130 men and women enlisted and officers on the carriers felt nothing. Altogether, the death toll was 13,858 KIA and 432 wounded and sick from radiation poisoning with four cruisers and four destroyers lost to the tsunami waves created by the nuclear detonations in addition to the two carriers. Chinese fighters were dispatched from carriers nearby to interfere with rescue attempts that commenced the next morning. They shot down rescue helicopters as they were trying to make rescues, and shot down rescue helicopters after they had taken wounded aboard and were returning to their ships. Chinese fighters also strafed and bombed ships trying to pick up survivors in the water.

The British and French governments immediately declared war on China, but ordered the remnants of the Carrier Strike Groups that were still afloat to withdraw until the anti-ship ballistic missile threat was neutralized. The British and French planned to wait for air-superiority to be gained by the Americans, if ever, before they moved any ships back into the area.

Several divisions of British and French troop regulars were ordered to prepare for an invasion. French Foreign Legion detachments and British SAS commandos also were mobilized and given specialized missions in coordination with the American plan for the assault.

AMERICAN VIRGINIA-CLASS FAST ATTACK
SUBS TAKE OUT CHINESE BOOMERS

Atlantic Ocean, 124 Miles Northeast of Rio de Janeiro
Aboard U.S. Block III Virginia-Class Fast Attack Submarine
USS South Dakota SSN-790
April 16, 0300 Hours

"Conn, Sonar. There is no indication that Chinese boomer knows we are here yet sir. She is at periscope depth with her scope up making noise like its New Years Eve. WhisperShield seems to be working like a four leaf clover sir."

The USS South Dakota was a block 2 *Virginia*-class fast attack submarine that had been fitted with stealth technology to provide a zero wake and no Bernoulli hump. The technology, invented in the metamaterials lab at Duke University, was comprised of a fluid cloak that had thousands of small water jets housed in a water permeable sheath. The jets accelerated water as it entered the sheath and decelerated it as it left the sheath leaving no net change in the water speed such that the water closed around the submarine seamlessly with no disturbance as if it had never been there. The sheath-provided fluid cloaking eliminated wake noise as well as the Bernoulli hump on the surface of the ocean and the resulting V-shaped trail known as the Kelvin wake. A submarine travelling through the water as deep as 1000 feet creates a bulge in the water on the ocean's surface called the Bernoulli hump which can be detected by aircraft. The Bernoulli hump causes a V-shaped Kelvin wake. By fluid cloaking to cause the water to close around the submarine with no net disturbance, both were eliminated. The fluid sheath is made of metamaterials with different densities that cause sonar waves to speed up when they hit the cloaking fluid sheath and slow down when they depart it thereby causing no net distortion. The effect is to effectively bend sonar waves around the submarine without causing any reflections which can be detected by an enemy.

"Good. Report upon any significant change in status of the boomer. Any idea what she is doing?" Captain Tom Weingartner asked. "Bearing and range to target?"

"No sir. Not exactly. Probably communicating or downloading satellite data since there are no U.S. ships in the area to be looking for visually. 179 degrees, 40,000 yards sir."

"Keep me apprised on bearing and range."

"Aye, Aye sir."

"Conn, steer 179 degrees, propulsor to all ahead 2/3s for 10 seconds then glide for 30 seconds, then all ahead 2/3 for 10 seconds then glide for 30 seconds in intervals till we close to 5000 yards. Keep WhisperShield deployed." Captain Weingartner ordered. "When we get to 5000 yards, we will creep up till we are right on top of her, then smoke her."

WisperShield is a new acoustic cloaking technology developed at Duke University. Its effect is to bend sound waves around a submarines so that it is invisible to sonar. It surrounds the sub in a shell of material which has a density and bulk modulus which is such that sound waves are bent around the sub instead being reflected from it thereby rendering the sub invisible to sonar operators. It was deployed on all U.S. *Virginia*-class fast attack submarines in 2025.

0320 Hours

"Captain, sonar. 176 degrees now, 5,000 yards. Still no indication she knows we are here. Still don't know what she is doing."

"Conn, steer 176 degrees, all ahead 1/3 for 10 seconds, then glide for 10 seconds, then all ahead 1/3 for 10 seconds, then glide for 10 seconds in intervals till we get to 1000 yards then shut down and rig for silent running and glide to our firing point.

0330 'Hours
US FAST ATTACK SUB SINKS CHINESE BOOMER

"Captain, Sonar! She just launched two missiles! She's at bearing 178, range 600 yards now."

"Fire Control Coordinator, Conn, set the Chinese boomer as Master 1 and calculate a firing solution."

When the Fire Control Coordinator was satisfied with his firing solution, he so informed Captain Weingartner.

"Torpedo Room, Conn. Make all tubes ready. Open outer doors on tubes one and two. Firing point procedures. Make tubes one and two ready in all respects. Fire tubes one and two."

Two MK-48 Mod 10 torpedoes lept from their tubes, and, traveling at 74 kilometers per hour, closed the gap to the Chinese submarine in 31 seconds.

0330 Hours

"Captain, Sonar! Two torpedoes in the water. They are American MK-48s! I don't know where they came from, but they are right on top of us, range 200 meters, coming from port and closing!"

"Shit! Launch countermeasures. Hard to port. All ahead flank. Where did those guys come from?" Those were Captain Cheng's last words.

0331 Hours

"Conn, Sonar. Two explosions sir. We got the boomer. She's toast."

"Good work Lt. Wright. Keep your ears open now for escorts coming looking for us." Captain Weingartner ordered.

"Aye, aye sir. Good shooting."

"Rest in peace you Commie bastards." Captain Weingartner snarled to himself. "You can't just randomly invade a country and commandeer their resources for your own purposes. The world is going to have something to say about that."

"Conn, make your depth 800 feet, steer 015, all ahead flank. Lets get out of here before they find us. We just kicked the beehive." Weingartner barked.

A swarm of Chinese destroyers and ASW helicopters with dipping sonars converged on the scene, but by the time they got there, the South Dakota was well out of the area and had gone quiet and had deployed her WhisperShield acoustic cloaking device. She had found a big metal drilling rig to settle in deep and hide next to and that would fool any magnetic anomaly detectors if the Chinese used ASW planes equipped with MAD (Magnetic Anomaly Detector) booms. For now, she was safe. She was, for all intents and purposes, invisible to the Chinese anti-submarine warfare equipment known to the western world. But with Chinese ASW ships and planes everywhere and helicopters dipping sonar listening devices, and Chinese ships towing Continuous Active Sonar arrays, there was no telling how long the *South Dakota* would be safe from detection since she was vastly outnumbered by Chinese submarines, surface ships and planes, all now knowing she was there and looking for her.

SECOND CHINESE BOOMER SANK BY USS CALIFORNIA

About 600 miles to the south, the second and last Chinese nuclear ballistic missile submarine *Huludao −2* suffered a similar fate. The Chinese died at the hands of the *U.S.S. California*, SSN-781, another U.S. *Virginia*-class fast-attack submarine. The *Huludao −2* never got off a shot — she never heard the *California* nor had any idea the American hunter-killer sub was there. The first thing *Huludao −2* heard was two torpedoes in the water from directly abeam and three hundred yards away. She never had a chance.

ASBMS AT WAREHOUSE MADE READY TO LAUNCH ON NIMITZ

Alto Comercio Warehouse Complex, Porto Alegre in the southern extreme of Brazil
April 16, 2026, 0320 Hours Local Time
(Translated from Mandarin)

"Zhong Wei (First Lt.) Xiu, move the launcher for missile #1 out of the warehouse and into the parking lot, spin up missile #1 and connect your launcher to the LAN and make ready missile #1 for upload of the missile's current position, the initial target point into the first stage guidance system and upload of the Synthetic Aperture Radar scan of the target into the missile's terminal guidance system." shouted Shaio Zaio (Major) Fo-hai Zheng, commanding officer of Kilo Company, First Missile Brigade, Chinese Second Artillery Corps which was the truck mounted ASBM detachment at Porto Alegre. The target was the USS *Nimitz* approximately 1200 miles to the southeast out in the inky-black, pre-dawn Atlantic.

First Lt. Gao Xiu gave Zheng a quizzical look, and said, "We have launch orders sir?"

"Yes. Shang Jiang (Admiral) Chian Wing Liu has located an American carrier within range of our missiles, the USS *Nimitz,* and wants us to sink it. Report when you are coupled to the LAN and are ready to upload data into the missile. I have downloaded our current position, the current position of the *Nimitz* and an SAR radar picture of the *Nimitz* from our satellites. Standby for upload." Zheng said sternly.

Xiu was shocked that the war with the Americans was starting so soon, but did as he was told and got into the cab of the truck launcher, and ordered the enlisted driver to drive it out of the warehouse and into the parking lot. Xiu hooked up the missile's guidance system network interface to the 100BaseT Ethernet LAN cables.

"Major Zheng, the missile is ready for upload of targeting data." First Lt. Xiu reported.

"Very well. Standby for upload. Report successful data capture."

"Major Zheng, the missile reports successful data capture and all systems ready."

"Very well, erect the launcher, disconnect the LAN cables, release the locks, clear the area and report ready for launch."

"Aye sir.

Five minutes later, the missile was ready for launch, and First Lt. Xiu reported, "Missile Long Spear 1, ready for launch sir."

"Very well, report to me with your missile launch key."

Xiu reported to Zheng in the makeshift control room set up inside the warehouse. He could see the satellite image of the Atlantic Ocean taken the previous afternoon off the southeastern coast of South America with its azure seas, puffy white clouds and the majestic, Navy gray USS *Nimitz*. "What a pity." he thought to himself to destroy such a powerful and storied ship and kill all those brave sailors and marines."

"Confirm nuclear weapons release order Tango Echo Four Bravo Eight Kilo Quebec Six Xray Three."

Xiu snapped out of his reflection, "I concur." and inserted his key into the launch console as Zheng simultaneously inserted his key.

"Launch on my mark. Mark"

ASBM LAUNCHED AT NIMITZ

Both officers turned their keys, and a tremendous roar erupted from the parking lot as a huge plume of red-orange flame erupted from the solid fuel booster of the DF-21 as she lifted off from her launcher. The parking lot shook and the night lit up as if it were broad daylight. A huge column of white, acrid smoke enveloped the parking lot and warehouse as the missile rose slowly at first and then, steadily gaining speed, accelerated out of sight into the inky black of the night sky. Death was on its way to the *Nimitz*.

US DETECTS ASBM MISSILE LAUNCHES AT
SEA AND PORTO ALEGRE

U.S. Space Command
Space Tracking and Surveillance Mission Control Station
460ᵗʰ Operations Group
Buckley Air Force Base, Aurora, Colorado
April 16, 0335 Hours

"Multiple missile launch detections!" the watch officer monitoring the Space Based Infrared System (SBIRS) satellite monitoring system screamed. The SBIRS satellite system was a constellation of infrared monitoring satellites in high elliptical orbits and geostationary orbits which could detect the hot plumes of missile boosters. The SBIRS satellites could also detect the red-hot warhead and decoy re-entry vehicles as they plunged back into the atmosphere and were heated to a cherry red color by the friction of the air as they dove back into the thicker air from space at mach 10.

"What are the origins of the launches?" Captain Rick Salazar, USAF, senior controller inquired of the watch officer. Captain Salazar was the duty officer in charge that night of the Air Force SBIRS missile launch detection system.

"I have two sea launches of ballistic missiles 124 miles northeast of Rio deJaniero, and one ballistic missile launch from the Porto Alegre area in the south of Brazil, 696 miles southwest of Rio de Janeiro. It's the Chinese sir." the watch officer replied.

"Do you have headings and projected targets on them from the computer yet?"

"Yes sir. You don't want to know. The two sea launches are headed for the British supercarrier *HMS Queen Elisabeth* and a French super carrier, the *Charles de Gaulle*, respectively. The land launched missile is headed for the U.S.S. Nimitz sir." the watch officer said.

"Holy Mother of God. Try to raise the Captain of the *Nimitz* right away, and see if you can get through to the British and French carriers ASAP. Second Lieutenant Smith, get on the secure line and raise the Joint Chiefs and try to get the White House on the line. We have a situation here." Captain Salazar barked.

Both junior officers snapped to and started working on trying to get through to the carriers and the Joint Chiefs, but the communications system had been severely crippled by the loss of the primary communication satellites. Watch officer Lieutenant Stacy Chang was able to get through to the *Nimitz* using a kluge communication system patched together using a constellation of cubesats that had hastily been put into orbit, but she was not able to get through to the British and French carriers in time to give them any warning.

Aboard the U.S.S. Princeton Ticonderoga-class Aegis cruiser screening the U.S.S. Nimitz 1190 miles southeast of Porto Alegre April 16, 0345 hours

SILVERTON SHOOTS AT AN ASBM FROM USS PRINCETON

"Inbound ballistic missile, range 620 miles, bearing 343 degrees, altitude 73 miles, speed mach 10!" Petty Officer First Class Henry Schmidt screamed to nobody in particular looking up from the Air and Missile Defense radar console at which he sat in the Combat Information Center of the U.S.S. *Princeton*, CG-59.

The U.S.S. *Princeton*, an AEGIS guided missile cruiser in the escort formation for the U.S.S. *Nimitz* supercarrier, had been newly re-fitted, and carried the latest Standard Missile –3 or SM-3 for mid-course intercepts of inbound missiles, and the Standard Missile-2 Block IV for terminal phase intercepts. The *Princeton* had also been fitted with the Megawatt Laser Area Defense (LADS) system which had just come online in the Navy weapons inventory. The *Nimitz* was the first U.S.

carrier to reach the southern Atlantic off the coast of Brazil. The *Nimitz* was still about 1200 nautical miles south of Porto Alegre.

The boyish, slight, blonde-haired, blue-eyed Schmidt said "It looks like it may be a Chinese Anti-Ship Ballistic Missile in hunting mode sir." this time directing his clearly alarmed tone towards CIC watch officer Lieutenant Brenda Silverton.

"Very well Schmidt. Call weapons and tell them to start spinning up an SM-3 for a mid-course intercept, and report ready to fire to me. I will call the Captain." Silverton said matter-of-factly. She was a cool customer. Tall, slim, attractive all-business, brunette, Annapolis lifer who had been through hell and back at Canoe U and come out the other side tough and smart.

"Captain, Lt. Silverton. Schmidt reports an ASBM inbound 620 miles out arriving at mach 10. We think it is Chinese and they are shooting at the *Nimitz* sir. We are spinning up an SM-3 for a mid-course intercept."

"Good work Lieutenant Silverton. I concur." the handsome, 6'2" ex-Annapolis wide receiver Commander Brad Cutbarth intoned. "I just got a heads up from the Captain of the *Nimitz* that U.S. Space Command at Buckley AFB just informed him that they observed three Chinese ASBM missile launches via the SBIRS infrared satellites."

"Three sir? We only see one"

"Yes, three. They think the other two are headed for British and French carriers up north of us off the coast of Rio closer to the Tupi Field. There is no proven defense against these things Lieutenant so lets pull out all the stops. Fire two SM-3s at it for mid-course intercepts to increase the probability of kill ratio. Then fire a terminal phase interceptor Standard Missile-2 Block IV at it when it starts its death dive in terminal phase. Once it enters the death dive, we have less than a minute to kill it before it kills the carrier. Also, it will maneuver to avoid attack by our missiles, so the probability of a kill during the terminal phase using the terminal phase interceptor missile is not high.

We have a better chance of killing it with the laser in terminal phase, because it cannot dodge a light beam. Unfortunately we have never successfully tested that system against an actual ASBM. At any rate, get the high power Megawatt Laser Area Defense System ready to fire at the warhead re-entry vehicle as soon as it is in range."

"Aye, aye sir." Silverton said as she sprang into action.

"Weapons officer, CIC Silverton here." she barked. "Spin up another SM-3 for mid-course intercept of the inbound ASBM. Then spin up an SM-2 Block IV for a terminal phase intercept and launch it as soon as the warhead is in range if the warhead makes it past the SM-3s. Light up the Megawatt LADS, and fire it at the warhead as soon as the warhead is in its death dive and in range. Don't miss you douche bag, or I will come down there and kick your ass assuming you are still alive. Silverton out."

"Aye Maam!" her lover and Harry Potter look-alike, Lieutenant Junior Grade Brad Keenan, said.

CHINESE ASBM HUNTING USS NIMITZ

As they were speaking, the Chinese Anti-Ship Ballistic Missile was screaming along at the edge of space at mach 10 looking down at the ocean below with its synthetic aperture radar looking for its target. It had stored in its memory a synthetic aperture radar image of the U.S.S. *Nimitz* which the Chinese ocean scanning satellites had taken the day before. As it passed over each ship on its flight path, it compared the synthetic aperture radar image of the ship to the stored image of the *Nimitz.*

"Firing solution achieved. Missile 1 away M'aam!" Lt. Junior Grade Keenan reported as the first SM-3 blasted out of it launch tube. The *Princeton's* fire control computers had computed an intercept on the inbound ASBM and were ready to transmit guidance information to the SM-3. The Chinese ASBM was now within the 270 mile range of the *Princeton,* with an SM-3 exo-atmospheric interceptor missile with a kinetic warhead streaking up toward it and communicating at breakneck speed with the *Princeton's* fire control computers to receive guidance information. This was not going to be easy. The problem was literally how to hit a mach 10 bullet 270 miles away and 79 miles up at the edge of space with a mach 8 bullet launched from the surface of the sea.

Two minutes later, "Missile 2 away M'aam" Keenan reported as the second $24,000,000 Raytheon RIM-161 Standard Missile-3 missile rocketed out of its Vertical Launching System tube and lept into the sky literally streaking out of the huge orange and red fireball created by its massive, finless, thrust-vectoring Mark 72 solid fuel booster with an ear-splitting roar.

Both missiles semi-active radar homing guidance systems listened to the radar signals reflected off the Chinese ASBM that were transmitted from the *Princeton's* radar system and listened rearward to guidance signals transmitted from the *Princeton* to avoid electronic countermeasures transmitted from the ASBMs. Both missiles calculated their closing velocities and set the angles of their seeker head antennas. They then used their long wavelength infrared sensors and their monopulse radars to calculate angle error measurements, and started sending flight path corrections to their guidance systems. Both missiles missed.

"Miss! Both missiles M'aam." Petty Officer Schmidt reported. "Chinese ASBM has found its target and is starting its death dive. Mach 12 now, 68 miles."

"Shit, that 4.5 billion dollar carrier is toast. That is 6000 guys." Silverton thought to herself. "And we may go down with it." "Weapons, Silverton. Both SM-3s missed. Say status on SM-2 Block IV. Once that re-entry warhead starts to maneuver in the death dive, the chances of hitting it are not good. What is the status of the laser."

Just then, a tremendous roar erupted as the SM-2 Block IV terminal phase interceptor missile blasted out of its launch tube belching smoke and fire and lighting up the night in orange and red hues.

"SM-2 is away, LADS is ready to fire M'aam."

"Fire the LADS right fucking now. We have less than a minute to impact."

No sooner had she finished her sentence than all the lights on the cruiser dimmed as the megawatt Laser Area Defense laser drained almost all the juice available from the cruiser's massive electrical powerplant to start is lasing reaction. A brilliant yellow-white beam instantly lit up the sky like God's blowtorch and found the white hot re-entering warhead and laid the wrath of Hades on the warhead's structure.

BALLISTIC NON NUCLEAR HIT ON THE NIMITZ

Fifteen seconds later, the Chinese ASBM crashed into the arresting gear system on the landing portion of the flightdeck of the *Nimitz* at mach 12. It did not explode. The 500 kiloton nuclear warhead, had been rendered inert by melting of its arming and ignition circuits by the laser. But the re-entry vehicle of the ASBM was so heavy, that it crashed though the flight deck, penetrated the hanger deck beneath the flighdeck and kept right on going. The warhead crashed through the second, third and fourth decks and finally came to rest in the engineering spaces below fourth deck, destroying one of the screw driveshafts and the mechanism that controlled the two ships rudders. The *Nimitz* would not sink, but it was out of the fight for good. She could not be steered into the wind. Since that ability was essential for aircraft launch and recovery, her fighting days were over until she could be repaired.

DAMAGE TO THE NIMITZ REPORTED TO THE PRESIDENT

White House Situation Room
April 16, 0510 Hours

Assembled in the White House Situation Room in the basement of the West Wing were Joint Chiefs of Staff, Secretary of Defense, Director of the CIA, Director of the National Reconnaissance Office, the National Security Advisor, and President Parry.

"I am afraid I have some bad news to report Mr. President." Admiral Picket, Chairman of the Joint Chiefs of Staff said. "The U.S.S. *Nimitz* has been hit by a Chinese Anti-ship Ballistic Missile and has been disabled. She is not able to steer and her arresting gear has been destroyed so she cannot recover planes. In addition, the British supercarrier *HMS Queen Elisabeth* and a French super carrier, the *Charles de Gaulle* have been sunken by sub-launched, nuclear-tipped, Chinese Anti-Ship Ballistic missiles with great loss of life. Further, several of the strike group cruisers and destroyers have capsized and been sunk by the huge tsunami wave the nuclear detonations created. Both the French and the British are pulling what is left of their carrier strike groups back to home port. We are completely on our own sir."

"Holy mother of God, the Chinese nuked the British and the French? Why didn't they nuke the *Nimitz?*" President Parry asked.

"That is the one of the two items of good news I have for you. We know the Chinese ASBM that was launched at the *Nimitz* was nuclear-tipped, but that our megawatt Laser Area Defense weapon disabled the nuclear weapon's arming and firing circuitry during its terminal phase. When it hit the *Nimitiz*, it did not explode but acted like a large kinetic weapon crashing through the flight deck in the recovery area and destroying the arresting gear equipment in addition to putting a massive hole in the landing area of the flight deck. It essentially destroyed much of the aft area of the ship, crashing through all four decks and into the engineering spaces below the fourth deck where it destroyed the rudder control machinery and disabled the drive shaft for one screw. She is not dead in the water, but she cannot steer with her rudders or recover aircraft, so she is out of the fight."

"I see. Loss of life aboard the *Nimitz?*"

"Sixty-five sailors and marines killed, ninety-eight wounded sir."

"What about the French and British casualties?"

"12,130 men and women enlisted and officer KIA on the British and French carriers alone." Mr. President. "The resulting tsunamis from the nuclear detonations capsized and sunk four cruisers and four destroyers altogether with further loss of life. Altogether, the death toll was 13,858 KIA and 2432 wounded and sick from radiation poisoning. Chinese fighters dispatched from carriers nearby shot down rescue helicopters during rescue attempts. Then, after surface ships picked up wounded but alive men from the water and brought them aboard, the Chinese fighters strafed the surface ships."

"Those Godless little yellow bastards. Isn't there any good news Admiral?"

"Yes sir. Two of our *Virginia*-class fast attack submarines torpedoed and sunk two Chinese boomers, one of which was the boat which launched the two ASBMs that sank the British and French carriers. They report that their acoustic cloaking technology is working beautifully, and the Chinese boats never heard anything until the torpedoes were in the water that killed them. Our boats snuck up on them until they were right on top of them and then fired Mark 48 torpedoes. The Chinese only had seconds to figure out what was about to hit them.

OUR VIRGINIA CLASS SUBS PINNED DOWN AFTER SINKING BOOMERS

But our subs report they are pinned down now and cannot move because every ASW capable destroyer and helicopter in entire Chinese armada is out looking for them all day and night. To make matters worse, there are still stealthy Kilo-class boats down there that will be looking for them also as well as posing a danger to any ship that enters the area.

In short, the situation is too hot right now to risk losing two three billion dollar boats by sending them after the Chinese carriers. We are afraid that the Chinese will be able to find them and sink them regardless of the acoustic cloaking technology."

Can we shoot at their carriers? How may carriers do the Chinese have down there?" President Parry inquired.

"Six sir, and no, we cannot shoot at their carriers yet because our subs are pinned down, and cannot move into position to launch anti-ship missiles nor launch from where they are for fear of giving away their positions. We cannot attack them by air for two reasons. First, we cannot get our carriers within 1500 miles of the Tupi Field, because we have not destroyed their truck launched ASBMs yet. Because we do not have air superiority yet, we cannot get any Air Force bombers or F-22s close enough to launch an air-to-surface anti-ship missile. It would take tankers and AWACS and fighter High Value Combat Air Patrol detachments flying in Chinese controlled airspace to carry out an Air Force mission from the bases in the U.S. Those high value AWACs and tanker assets would be easy pickings for the Chinese fighters who could overwhelm the HavCAP fighters."

SEAL DELIVERY VEHICLE TEAMS DISCUSSED FOR ANTI KILO OPS

"OK, it sounds like we have to get some help to those *Virgina* class subs. Do we know whether the ASBM that hit the *Nimitz* came from another boomer or from somewhere else? President Parry asked.

"U.S. Space Command reports two of the missile tracks originated from points at sea, and the third track originated from somewhere in the Porto Alegre area on the coast of Brazil." Admiral Picket said.

"Where is Porto Alegre?" the President asked.

"It is 696 miles southwest of Rio de Janeiro on the Atlantic coastline."

"So they have mobile land launchers for these things? Do we know exactly where they are?"

"No sir, not yet. We have some visual and infrared imaging nanosats that we put into orbit last week to cover Brazil, but so far they have seen nothing. It looks like Chinese spies in the U.S. have informed the Brazilian forces that the U.S. has put up some new surveillance satellites and the Chinese have detected them somehow and figured out their orbital cycle and are moving the mobile launchers into hides whenever the satellites are overhead."

"How do you plan to find those ASBMs then?"

"We have dispatched several MARSOC special operations teams from the Marine Corps and a couple of Navy SEAL teams to infiltrate the area and find the ASBMs. I will get back to you as soon as they find them." Admiral Picket

"OK keep me posted. I presume our Carrier Strike Groups cannot get within striking distance of the Tupi field until we find those ASBMs and take them out."

"Correct." Admiral Picket replied

"We also need to get another Carrier Strike Group down there right away to replace the *Nimitz*. Make it so." the President ordered

"Aye, aye sir." Admiral Picket responded. "Another thing sir. The Kilo class subs are the biggest danger to our *Virginia*-class hunter killer subs right now, and they are a big danger to our carriers also. They are armed with the Sunburn class of anti-ship missiles and rocket-propelled torpedoes. We have to eliminate the Kilos. The problem is they are so quiet, our conventional ASW forces cannot find them until they shoot. We think we can find them using Seal Teams towing CAS passive sonar arrays though. We can deploy four SEAL Delivery Vehicle Teams into the area from Norfolk and Coronado. They can use their very quiet submerged SEAL Delivery Subs towing Passive Sonar Arrays and deploying Continuously Active Sonar (CAS) sonobuoys to find the Kilos. There is so much active sonar being emitted by the Chinese ships and surface ships looking for our subs, that the Passive Sonar Arrays may pick up returns from Chinese pings bouncing off the Kilos. The towed passive arrays will also pick up sounds from the Kilo crews and machinery.

The CAS sonobuoys emit a continuous, low power sonar signal and collect signals reflected off targets for signal processing. The processed signals create a very detailed and accurate picture of what is in the ocean within range of the system. The sonobuoys transmit their raw data to satellites which relay them down to our surface ships for signal processing. The surface ships are stationed safely out of range of the ASBMs. Position information on any Kilo found by the sonobuoys can be relayed to our *Virginia*-class attack subs via their floating wire communications link and to the SEAL submarines via their satellite communications gear.

Once a SEAL Team finds what they think is a Kilo sub using a broadband search, they can focus down to the specific bearing and do a narrowband search. That will positively identify it as a Kilo. Then they can take take multiple readings over time to get its position, heading and speed and report that data by their satellite uplinks. We can communicate that data to one of the *Virginia* class subs and silently launch an armed drone to swim over to the Kilo's position and torpedo it. The drones swim out of the sub's torpedo tubes so quietly, they cannot be detected. The drones can be programmed to swim very far away from the sub before starting their programmed strike mission. These drones swim very quietly using electric motors and hydrogen fuel cells to generate the electricity. They are armed with miniature versions of the wired guided Mark 48 ADCAP torpedo which also has an active/passve sonar seeker head to guide the torpedo during the terminal phase. The warhead is large enough to easily sink a Kilo."

"How would you insert the SEAL teams?" the President asked.

"That is the hard part. Without air superiority, we are taking a risk dropping them in with a High Altitude Low Opening (HALO) jump, because their transport plane would probably be shot down. We would not be able to give them Combat Air Patrol protection from fighters since the carriers are being held too far away from the Tupi Field by the ASBMs. Any tankers in Chinese controlled airspace would be shot down, so we would lose all the fighters. We could air drop their SEAL Delivery Vehicle submarine from a C-130 Hercules, but again, we would be risking the C-130. We could attempt to sneak the SEALs in by a HALO jump from a regularly scheduled airliner flying over the area, say from Brazil to Paris, but we would have to infiltrate the SEALS and buy all the seats on the flight so that when the door was opened at 35,000 feet for the jump, there would be no passengers to suffer an explosive decompression. A flight going out basically empty except for six SEAL teams of six men apiece would be a dead giveaway.

We think it is best to neutralize the ASBM threat on land first and then send in our carriers and start an air battle to keep their AEGIS-type destroyers and cruisers busy with air and anti-ship missile defense to take the heat off the two submarines currently pinned down. We should send four more *Virginia*-class fast attack submarines down there equipped with the acoustic cloaking technology to deliver the SEALS and their SEAL Delivery Vehicle submarines and towed passive sonar arrays. The SEAL submarines are driven by Lithium-Ion batteries driving electric motors, so they are extremely quiet, quieter even than the Kilos. The SEALs can find the Kilos, and the fast attack submarines can kill them, and then start attacking the Chinese carriers and their escorts with anti-ship missiles." Admiral Picket said.

Admiral Picket's expression was filled with great pride for the success of the very expensive *Virginia*-class boats and their acoustic cloaking technology.

"OK I agree. Make it so." President Parry ordered.

USS California, Virginia-class Fast Attack Nuclear Submarine 163 miles off the coast of Rio de Janeiro, Brazil in the Tupi Oil and Gas Field

Navy SEAL Lt. Jerry "Ninja" Pattison marshaled his team of three Special Warfare Combatant Crew SEALS in the air lock of the *California* for a final re-cap of their briefing.

"OK frogmen, one last time, here is how it is going to go. After we exit the submarine, marshall at the SEAL Delivery Vehicle mounted on the stern of the submarine. Gator, you double check the coupling between the towed passive array and the SEAL delivery sub and check the passive array for operation. Thumbs up if it is working. I will check the SEAL Delivery Vehicle for operation and thumbs up if good. Twenty-three, you open the stealth web when you see thumbs up from me and Gator. Payton, you release the sub hold downs when you see a thumbs up from me and Gator and see that the stealth web is open, then take your station in the sub. I will drive the sub out the opening and stop. Twenty-three, you close the stealth web after the SEAL delivery vehicle clears it and take your station in the sub. Gator, you fire up the passive array as soon as we clear the web. I will drive the sub in a search pattern and Twenty-three and Payton will release CAS sonobuoys on my command to establish a pattern. The sonobuoys are programmed to start emitting at 0030 Zulu time. That will give us time to get far enough away from the pattern that the Chinese won't find us when they come looking for the source of the Continuously Active Sonar signals. Gator, be heads up on the passive array as soon as the sonobuoys fire off, because that is going to surprise the Chinese sonarmen and Captains in the Kilos, and they may have a Chinese fire drill and start scrambling around and making noise. Got it?"

"Roger that LT." Gator said.

"What if the Chinese do come looking for us LT and they find us." asked Twenty-three.

"They won't find us. I will shut the sub down and we will commence silent operation when the sonobuoys start emitting. The re-breathers don't emit any bubbles that would make noise. Even when it is running, the sub is so quiet, that it cannot be detected. So the only way they will find us is if active sonar pings get sufficient return from the sub to detect us. If the Chinese do find the SEAL Delivery Vehicle using active sonar and fire a torpedo at us, bend over and kiss your ass goodbye. Remember what they told us at BUDS. Hardly any of us will live to see our 30th birthday."

"Thanks for that inspiring locker room speech LT. I am super motivated now." Twenty-three said with a grin.

"Kiss my ass Twenty-three. Do you want me to tell your Dad you are a pussy?" Lt. Pattison said with a smile.

"No sir."

"Alright then. Lets do this." Lt. Pattison said as he sealed the air lock door. "Con, Dagger-1, we are ready to go. Flood the air lock. Give us 5 mikes for the egress." The SEALS of Dagger fire team donned their re-breather apparatus and prepared to face the cold water of the southern Atlantic.

"Dagger-1, roger 5 mikes. Standby for egress in two. We will be right here waiting for you unless things get too hot and we have to maneuver." Captain Stanley Baldwin said over the intercom indicating his understanding that it would take the SEALs five minutes to check for proper operation of the towed array and sub, release the sub and drive it through the opening in the stealth fabric surrounding the California. "All stop. Flood the air lock and standby for SEAL egress."

The egress went smoothly. Lt. Pattison drove the sub in a search pattern and ordered sonobuoys deployed at regular intervals. The sonobuoys rose to the surface and waited for the programmed time before they started emitting.

At the appointed time, the sonobuoys started emitting their continuous wave low frequency sonar signals. Simultaneously, they sent digitized echo return signals to a geosynchronous U.S. satellite overhead for relay down to a signal processing center on the U.S.S. *Truman* of the Northern Expeditionary Strike Force. It was there that a fairly high resolution picture of the ocean floor and two Chinese Kilo submarines hiding in the area covered by the sonobuoys emerged.

Aboard Chinese Kilo Submarine Yuan Zhend 64 Hao

DEPTH 800 FEET, 124 MILES OFF THE COAST OF RIO DE JANEIRO IN THE TUPI FIELD, HIDING UNDER THE RIGA-3 DRILLING PLATFORM

"(From the Mandarin) Con, Sonar, we have multiple Continuous Active Sonar sources at the surface painting us! They appear to be U.S. sonobuoys. Range 5 kilometers, bearing 020 to the closest one."

"What the fuck! How did they get there? Communications, Con. Find out if any U.S. anti-submarine warfare planes have flown over." Shang Xiao (Captain) Ching-Wai yelled into the intercom.

"Con, Communications. Surface ships report no U.S. planes have flown over."

"All ahead 1/3. Make your depth 1200 feet. I want to get below the thermocline." Captain Ching-Wai ordered.

"LT, I picked up a Chinese voice and now I am getting faint screw noises, bearing 043, range 6 miles." Gator reported aboard the Dagger fire team SEAL Delivery sub.

"Take another bearing in two minutes Gator after we have moved. I am taking us toward the Riga-3 drilling platform. We are going to have to get out of the water."

"Roger that LT."

Gator waited two minutes and then took another range and bearing reading on the screw noise. "Bearing 045 now, range 5.5 miles."

"Triangulate that and report that subs position." Lt. Pattison ordered.

Gator triangulated the position and reported to Garcia. "I have that sub at bullseye for 2, at 020 degrees." Bullseye was the position of the Riga-3 drilling platform.

Lt. Pattison got on the satellite communications rig. "Papa Bear, Dagger-1, we have a submerged contact at Bullseye for 2, at 020. Probable Kilo."

"Dagger-1, Papa Bear, we concur. Get out of the water and let us know when you are out." the mission controller on the *Truman* ordered.

"Hammerhead, Papa Bear. Probable Kilo at Bullseye for 2 at 020 degrees. Launch the drone." the *Truman* mission controller ordered the U.S.S. *California*, SSN-781.

"Sonar, Con. SEALS report probable Kilo at Bullseye for 2 at 020 degrees. Do you have him now?" the captain of the *California* inquired.

"Con, Sonar. Yes sir we have him now. We hear Chinese voices. Chinese submarine for sure. Probably a Kilo from the screw noises."

"Torpedo room, Con. Program drone-1 to cruise to Bullseye for 2 at 020 degrees and commence a search pattern. Launch of the drone torpedo to be on my mark. Program the drone to swim silently out for one mile from the sub before starting her cruise mode. Launch the drone as soon as you have her programmed."

"Aye, aye sir."

Lt. Pattison steered the SEAL delivery vehicle submarine to one of the hulls of the semi-submersible Riga-3 drilling platform and ordered his SEALs to board and be ready to take out the Chinese Marines guarding it. It was 0230 local time. The SEALS tethered the sub to the platform hull, locked and loaded and silently climbed the boarding rungs welded to the side of the hull. They had to climb about 80 feet up to the platform's operations deck. Lt. Pattison led the way. When they got to the top, Lt. Pattison held up his fist in a hand signal for all the SEALs to stop where they were. He stuck his head above the platform and did a quick recon for sentries. He saw four men on the rails of the operations platform at spaced out locations leaning on the rails and looking out to sea. Three of them were smoking and one appeared to be asleep.

Lt. Pattison moved silently back below the level of the platform and gave hand signals telling the other three SEALS where the sentries were and their status and assigning each a target. With a thumb dragged across his throat, he ordered the SEALs to dispatch the sentries using their combat knives for silence. Lt. Pattison decided to take the one that was sleeping. The dumb ass would never know what hit him.

Silently the SEALS made their way up onto the deck and into the shadows of the various pieces of machinery and other structures on the deck. They each got as close as they could to their targets, and upon a brief command from Lt. Pattison in their wearable communication sets, they sprang into action like Pumas. They each closed the gap between their concealed positions and the unsuspecting sentries in the blink of an eye. On contact, they each clasped their left hands over the sentry's mouths and drove their combat knives into the sentry's liver and rotated their knives. Each quickly withdrew his blade and brought it up to the sentry's throat and, with a lightning fast stroke, slit the sentry's throat and severed his carotid artery.

Slowly each SEAL lowered his victim to the deck as the man bled out, and withdrew to the shadows, dragging the man behind him.

Lt. Pattison did a quick recon of the structures on the platform and determined that a platoon of Chinese marines were sleeping in the crew quarters with a handful of Brazilian oil workers tied up outside.

Ninja gave hand signals for flash bang grenades followed by frag grenades and then a mop up with their Heckler and Koch MP5 close quarters submachine guns.

Lt. Pattison silently crept up to the door of the sleeping quarters giving the shssh sign to the Brazilians who were awake and watching him. He motioned for the other SEALS to join him and they did. Each SEAL pulled his night visions goggles down over one eye, pulled out a flash bang grenade and a frag grenade and pulled the pins. Ninja then opened the metal door suddenly, and they all rolled their grenades into the sleeping quarters. Pattison closed the door quickly and each SEAL ducked behind it to shield their night vision and their night vision light amplification tubes from what was about to happen. A few seconds later four blinding flashes of light and deafening explosions turned the enclosed room into a trip into the interior of the sun. A second or two later, WHAM, WHAM, WHAM, WHAM followed as the frag grenades went off and shredded the room and its occupants. Lt. Pattison opened the door quickly after the fourth blast, and the four SEALS charged into the chaos inside. Each SEAL picked targets of opportunity that appeared to have survived the blasts and dispatching them with double taps, one to the heart and one to the forehead. It was all over in a matter of seconds. 16 Chinese Marines KIA.

Quickly, the SEALS untied the Brazilians and sprinted to their submarine. Lt. Pattison radioed that the team was safely out of the water. The drone had reached the last known position of the Kilo a minute earlier, and had commenced its search pattern and had found its target with passive sonar and signaled the acquisition of a target and its position back to the U.S.S. *California*.

The skipper of the *California*, having received notice that the SEALS were out of the water, ordered launch of the drone's torpedo. The mini-Mark 48 left the drone and streaked to its target at 65 knots closing the distance to the target in 20 seconds.

"Con, Sonar. Torpedo in the water sir! 590 meters, 049 degrees, constant bearing, homing!" the sonarman of the Yuan Zhen 64 Hao reported.

"Shit! Launch countermeasures. All ahead full, hard right rudder!" the Captain ordered, but it was too late.

No sooner had he uttered the words than he heard the sound of every submariner's worst nightmare.

BOOOM. Direct hit amidships. Then he heard the sounds of the hull cracking and them collapsing and the sea water rushing in and the sounds of screaming sailors. The darkness and salty seawater took him to his second life in hell seconds later.

Dagger fire team heard the explosion about 3 miles away from the drilling rig, and knew it was the Kilo they had found buying the farm. The quickly mounted up in their submarine and hustled back to the U.S.S. *California* for recovery.

This process was repeated three more times from the *Virginia*-class fast attack submarine U.S.S. Washington, in the waters of the Tupi field 92 miles off the coast of Rio de Janeiro and by the fast attack submarines U.S.S. *Indiana* and the U.S.S. *Colorado* in the waters off Porto Alegre before the night was over. Four of the six Chinese Kilos had been summarily dispatched to their watery graves. Two more were still in hiding in the vast waters of the Tupi field.

MARSOC TEAMS AND SEAL TEAMS INFILTRATE PORTO ALEGRE

Captain Cruz "Drive-by" Wilmont, 1st Platoon, G Company, 2nd Marine Special Operations Battalion, MARSOC looked at his team. "Final equipment check. Two mikes to drop. Helmets on, unbuckle, switch to your bailout bottles, stand up." Wilmont said over the interteam radio. "Team two ready?"

"Two is ready." Captain Adam "Slick" Sims reported. Team 2 was to freefall to a drop zone outside the West side of the city. Wilmont's team was to freefall to a drop zone on outskirts of the East side of the city.

Drive-by extended his arms straight out at shoulder level, palms up, and bent it to touch his helmet. That was the signal for the team to move to the rear of the cargo bay where the ramp was about to come down.

It was 0200 hours. They were in an MC-130 Combat Talon at 35,000 feet over Porto Alegre flying 50 feet below a commercial jetliner that was on a regularly scheduled flight from Rio de Janeiro to Maldonado, Uruguay. To Chinese radars below, they looked like one target – a harmless commercial airliner on a regularly scheduled flight. Team 1's mission was to find the ASBMs and paint them with laser designators for an airstrike scheduled for three days hence. Team 2's mission was to find and identify Chinese air defense positions.

Both teams switched their masks from ship's oxygen to their portable oxygen bottles and stood up as the ramp lowered at the back of the cargo bay. As it opened, the frigid night air at −35 degrees F roared in and swirled around them. "Piece of cake boys. Cowboy up. Light your IR strobes and turn on your NVGs."

The teams powered up the infrared strobes on their helmets. They would be invisible to Chinese radar in freefall, but they would be able to see each other's IR strobes with their night vision goggles while they screamed earthward in head-first free fall at terminal velocity − 200 miles per hour. Air surfing by GPS to spots above their drop zones, when their altimeters read 1000 feet MSL, they opened their ram air parachute systems. From there, they would glide silently down in formation for the last 1000 feet to silent landings at their respective drop zones.

The jump light turned green, and the teams sprinted down the ramp and dove into the pitch blackness. The roar of the engines and turbulent air was replaced with dead silence and blackness except for the sound of the air whistling past their ears at 200 mph. Each man looked for the IR strobe lights of their teammates and steered with his arms and legs toward the remaining members of his team. Each team had different strobe frequency, Team 1 fast and Team 2 slower.

A stealth HALO jump like this one was the only safe way to get recon marines on the ground this far behind enemy lines when no air superiority existed.

Once on the ground, Wilmont's team extinguished their chem lights by burying them, moved into the woods and established a star defensive perimeter.

Captain Wilmont pulled out his scrambled Sprint satellite phone, and dialed a number. "Goldilocks, Drive By, grid 020 for 10, 0530 zulu." Wilmont was setting up a time and location for a meeting with their local CIA contact who had been secretly gathering information from locals about the whereabouts of the ASBMs. The meeting was to be 10 statute miles from bullseye at a heading of 20 degrees, and was to occur at 0530 Greenwich Mean Time, about an hour from the present local time.

Goldilocks was a stunningly beautiful Brazilian bombshell named Theresa Diaz. She was dressed in a T-shirt and cargo pants that accentuated her ample bosom and pert little buns. Captain Wilmont struggled to concentrate on his mission.

"I talked to some locals who were outside the night of the launch on the *Nimitz*. They reported that they saw a flash of light and a streaking column of red and yellow fire rising up from the Northern outskirts of the city." Theresa reported. "They told me that they drove to where they thought they saw the column of fire rise from, but they found nothing but a bunch of warehouses. That is all I have for you, but at least it will give you a place to start."

"Good work Ms. Diaz. That helps."

"Oh call me Theresa please. It was very nice meet you Captain Wilmont. Be very careful Captain. There are Chinese patrols and soldier garrisons everywhere. You have my number if I can be of further assistance." She obviously was well educated, probably in the United States and had flawless English.

Drive-by was thinking of a few things he would like her to assist him with, but thanked her and sent her on her way. "I will call her later." he promised himself. It was a long hump, and they only had a few hours of darkness left. "Saddle up boys, we have some ground to cover. The team buried their chutes and jump equipment and set off at a jog toward the general area Ms. Diaz had indicated on the map.

They reached the area indicated by the locals at dawn and set up in hidden reconnaissance positions to watch activities. They watched for hours during the daylight, but did not see any ASBMs, mobile launchers, antiaircraft gun or missile emplacements. They did not even see any Chinese soldiers. As the gathering dusk enveloped them, Drive-by called the team together.

"OK guys, we are going to have to go to plan B to find these ASBMs. I have contacted SOCOM command and asked them to get the Misty stealth satellite re-tasked to take optical and synthetic aperture radar pictures of this general area tonight. I have also asked for a cubesat to take infrared images of the area tonight."

Looking at Lance Corporals Jake Skidmore and Don Rivera, Drive-by whispered,

"Skeeter, at 0200 you are going to set up a flight plan for the Swarm on ECCHO on your iPad™ and launch the insect drones to fly a box search pattern which overflies each of these warehouses right here. I want you to gather thermal and acoustic fly-by data on each warehouse. There should not be anybody in them working that late at night. Riverboat, you launch the Puffer at 0210 and set it up to fly round trips all night over these warehouses to intercept cell phone calls and radio transmissions and stream audio and video packets back to your laptop so we can listen in on any cell or radio communications coming out of these warehouses. Set the scanners to the local cell phone frequencies and the tactical frequency band for the Chinese Marines. Team 2 reports they have not found any SAM or anti-aircraft gun sites yet. I am going to call SOCOM command and have them send a Phantom Eye drone off one of the carriers to fly overhead at 0400 at 65,000 feet. That will be too high for the Flankers, but not too high for the SA-2 surface to air missiles. If they have any of those around, they may pull one out of hiding and fire it, and we will lose a drone, but know where they are hiding the SAMs. Go get ready. Dismissed."

By 0200, Lance Corporal Skidmore had programmed the predefined flight path for a group of electrically powered, virtually-silent insect sized drones called the Swarm. They would assemble in the air into a formation that covered a large area, establish their own local area network and divy up the territory below. Each drone would take thermal images and listen for sounds coming from its area, and transmit the data back to a receiver to which Skeeter's iPad was interfaced. The data would be assembled into a composite thermal image and sound map of the entire area covered by the Swarm at any particular time and displayed on the iPad. The Swarm would fly on autopilot along the predefined flight path and send back data. The team could listen in on any noises coming from inside the warehouses and see any heat signatures within them. The iPad would show the team on the iPad in real time where the Swarm was when it took the thermal images and heard the sounds of the sound map displayed on the iPad. By touching an icon signifying an intercepted sound, the team could listen to what was intercepted.

The Puffer was a pneumatic-cannon based drone system which shot an Italian-designed drone with folding wings out by air pressure. Launch was virtually silent. The Puffer drone's wings unfurl when the drone leaves the cannon. It takes off using a silent electric motor driven propeller, and flies its preprogrammed route on autopilot. As it flies, it reports back intercepted cell calls and radio transmissions in a stream of audio packets.

The drone launches went off without a hitch. The team divided into two sections, one recon marine watching the returns from the Swarm drones and another standing lookout, another recon marine watching the returns from the puffer with a fourth standing lookout.

The drones were good spies. By 0330, the drones had overflown all the warehouses in a five square mile area, and a pattern had emerged. Man-sized heat signatures and various sounds of men laughing, drinking, watching a movie, snoring and playing cards were found in three warehouses.

At 0400, the Phantom Eye drone launched from the carrier was approaching the area, and Puffer reported a brief burst of radio communications. Shortly thereafter, the team observed trucks rolling out of two of the warehouses. Misty and Cubesat SAR radar and infrared imagery was relayed to their iPads by SOCOM on a scrambled satcom channel. The spy satellite data showed one truck bearing a radar array and two other trucks coming out of a different warehouse bearing a second radar array and an SA-2 surface-to-air missile. At 0410, when the Phantom Eye was overhead, a huge plume of orange and yellow flame erupted from the SA-2, and 30 seconds later, the Phantom Eye disappeared in a ball of flame high overhead. They had their answer. The Chinese were hiding their missiles and radar in the warehouses to keep them from being discovered by spy satellites. Now they had to find the ASBMs.

The Captain Wilmont dispatched Skeeter and Riverboat to the location of the third warehouse with fiber optic spy equipment. They snuck up on a rear loading dock door and snaked their fiber optic camera in through a crack. They observed six mobile truck launchers loaded with DF-21 anti-ship ballistic missiles. They had their answer.

PRESIDENT INFORMED MARSOC HAD FOUND THE LAND BASED ASBMS

"Mr. President, Force Recon MARSOC special operators have found the ASBMs in Porto Alegre. We are ready to launch an airstrike on your command." reported General Ron Majors, Commandant of the Marine Corps and member of the Joints Chiefs.

"How did they find them?" the President asked.

"They used an insect swarm of small drones. The individual drones look like small insects, and fly very quietly using electric motors. The team on the grounds sets up a flight path for the drones by touching points on a map displayed on the iPad. The swarm then flies the route automatically. The drones organize themselves in a swarm formation, each drone taking video of part of the area that drone covers. They set up a local area network among themselves to share video and communicate among themselves to coordinate their flight paths. The team downloads the video where it gets pieced together into a larger images using an app on an iPad™. The drones are too small to detect and shoot down since they are invisible to radar, and the swarm flies high enough that they are not seen by the human eye." General Majors said with a smile.

"Very clever General." President Parry said.

"Is not like the Old Corps." General Majors said with a laugh despite the gravity of the situation. Everybody in the room laughed.

"What's next General?" the President said instantly killing the buzz.

"Well we have to take out those missiles. As long as those truck launchers are intact, we cannot send any carriers into the theatre close enough to establish air superiority preceding an invasion. History has proven that an invasion over the beaches without air superiority is suicidal."

"How do you propose to take them out? What have your MARSOC teams reported on air and ground defenses?" President Parry asked.

"We have two teams on the ground. They have reported seeing Su-MK2 Flankers flying over the area, usually in sections of four. They have also heard jets flying at night, but could not get a visual on them even with their night vision gear. They have not reported seeing any antiaircraft missile batteries or antiaircraft guns other than the mobile radar trucks and mobile SAM launchers Team 1 reported hiding in warehouses. As far as troop strength, they think the area is being guarded on the ground by two battalions of Chinese Marines."

"Hmmm, sounds like the area is fairly heavily defended. What do you think is the best thing to do to take them out?"

"We cannot hit them with stealth fighters or stealth bombers from the states because we don't have air superiority. That means the tankers needed on stations over Brazil to get the stealth aircraft to the target and back would be shot down. It would require a fairly large number of tankers to get the planes on target from their bases in the U.S. The air bases of our allies in Peru or Chile might be a possibility. Those bases are not well defended, and the Chinese could take our stealth bombers out on the ground before they ever took off. The Peruvian and Chilean air forces are no match for the Chinese. Further, they probably would not be willing to risk their pilots and planes to go up against the Chinese to help us save the Brazilians and their gas and oil from domination by the Chinese. I think we will have to launch a long range airstrike from one of our carriers that rounded Cape Horn. Those carriers are still pretty far offshore, so we have tanking issues, but that seems to be the only option right now. Without air superiority, we cannot send in the Airborne Rangers. Their transport aircraft would be shot down before they could even jump. We are going to have to figure out something using our carriers." General Majors said grim faced.

"Ok figure it out, and launch an airstrike as soon as possible."

TACO RAID WIPED OUT

Admiral Wallace "Cornwall" Courtney, Commander of Expeditionary Strike Force 2, the southern force of U.S. carriers, pondered the situation. He had a massive force of three Carrier Strike Groups and three Expeditionary Strike Groups with three Marine Expeditionary Units embarked under his command in the southern Atlantic. He had orders from OpNav, and the Joint Chiefs and Commander in Chief, Atlantic Fleet (CINCLANT) via POTUS to invade Brazil from the south. The general plan of attack was to establish air superiority, incapacitate the Chinese command and control structure and then carry out a pincer movement with the Expeditionary Strike Force 1. Strike Force 1 would be launching their three embarked Marine Expeditionary Units from the northern part of Brazil. Admiral Courtney's Expeditionary Strike Force 2 would be invading from the southern part of Brazil and the three embarked Marine Expeditionary Units would establish a two-front war for the Chinese who would have major force components north of them and south of them.

But the Admiral was totally handcuffed by the presence of the Chinese Anti-Ship Ballistic Missiles Force Recon had found at Porto

Alegre. One strike from the nuclear tipped ASBMs could sink a carrier and many if not all of its support ships depending upon how spread out they were. But they could not be too spread out, because the Chinese were known to have silent, tiny, almost un-detectible kilo class submarines operating in the theatre of operations. A Chinese kilo-class submarine could sneak inside the defensive shield of the escorts and loose a salvo of nuclear-tipped torpedoes and anti-ship missiles and sink one or more of his carriers, cruisers, destroyers or troop ships before it could be found and sunk.

Admiral Courtney knew that two Chinese boomers loaded with ASBMs had been sunk by U.S. *Virginia* class hunter-killer submarines. Courtney did not know whether there were any more boomers in the theatre of operations, but he knew that none had been detected by the hunter-killer subs attached to the six Carrier Strike Groups of the northern and southern Expeditionary Strike Forces.

But Admiral Courtney knew for sure that his forces were in grave danger from Chinese truck launched ASBMs if he strayed too close to the coastline of Brazil. A Marine Corps Force Recon commando team operating covertly in the Porto Alegre area had confirmed earlier that week that there was a force of truck-launched ASBMs at Porto Alegre, and that they were DF-21s. The Admiral Courtney knew that the DF-21 had a maximum range of 1500 nautical miles, and that his force was sitting just 50 miles outside a 1500 mile nautical ring centered on Porto Alegre. For now, his force of carriers, AEGIS destroyers and cruisers, ammunition ships, oilers, amphibious assault ships and troop transports and tens of thousands of sailors and marines was safe. But the admiral knew that until he took out those ASBMs, he had to keep his ships, sailors and marines at least 1500 nautical miles away from Porto Alegre and the invasion beaches or the situation could rapidly turn into a world-class clusterfuck.

Courtney was starting to crack under the pressure. He had risen to his rank in a peace time Navy fighting in a few skirmishes with unsophisticated terrorists and other assorted thugs. But this was the real Magilla – a no-shit super power armed to the teeth with better weapons than he had at his disposal.

The U.S. had no real, proven defense to the ASBMs. Admiral Courtney could not be sure the AEGIS cruisers with their RIM-161 Standard Missile 3 interceptors could intercept and destroy a hypersonic ASBM warhead in its death dive terminal phase. Studies at the Naval Postgraduate School in Monterrey indicated it was possible, but not a slam dunk. And no actual intercept tests had ever been conducted, because the U.S. did not have anything like the ASBM in its arsenal against which actual tests could be run.

A new directed energy laser weapon had just been deployed on his carriers, but it too had not been tested against the Chinese ASBM missiles, and had never been used in combat against any missile. It had shot down a few drones in tests, but a hypersonic warhead screaming down vertically from the edge of space at mach 10 was an entirely different story.

Further, the Chinese were known to have hundreds of land and carrier-based Su-27 and Su-30MK2 Flankers, J-10s and other older jets in the theatre including J-20 stealth jets. The Su-30MK2 Flankers were known to have thrust vectoring, lower wing loading than his F/A-18s and greater thrust than his F/A-18s. All these factors made it possible for the Flankers to turn faster than his fighters and do impossible maneuvers such as the Pugachev Cobra and the complete somersault to defeat missiles and cause pursuing fighters to overshoot. His F/A-18s did not have thrust vectoring.

Nevertheless, Admiral Courtney had orders to take out those ASBMs so that the process of achieving air superiority over Brazil could start. There could be no invasion until air superiority had been achieved – a lesson learned the hard way in previous battles throughout history.

The problem was that a 1500 nautical mile airstrike through airspace controlled by the Chinese was a logistical nightmare and posed great dangers to all crews involved. Many tankers would have to be used, and the large Air Force tankers would have to fly down from bases in Florida so that his carrier-based KS-3 Viking tankers could top up from them. The KS-3 tankers would then have to be spread out along the ingress and egress routes for the strike package jets.

To make matters worse, Admiral Courtney did not know that the Chinese had navalized their J-20 stealth jets. To compound the problem, there were also other significant things the Admiral did not know about the Chinese defenses at Porto Alegre.

It was a prickly problem for Courtney, and he wished he did not have his job at the moment. Admiral Courtney knew that if he screwed this operation up, it would result in the deaths of many, many brave men and women and would most definitely be the end of his career.

"Well gentlemen, what do you think? How do we take out those ASBMs?" Admiral Courtney asked the assembled group. Present were the CAGs of the three Carrier Air Wings embarked on the three carriers under Courtney's command, their intelligence officers and their operations officers.

Captain Mike "Hanna" Montana, Commander of the Carrier Air Wing aboard the USS Ronald Reagan spoke first. "Well sir, that is a very long range air strike, and it is going to take a lot of tankers to carry it out. Other than that, I don't see any abnormal issues. I say we put together an Alpha Strike Package of four attack elements and a combat air patrol element. An element of F-35C HARM shooters will go in first and destroy any Surface to Air missile battery radars or radar guided anti-aircraft guns with High Anti-Radiation Missiles and jam any other enemy radar and communications with their AESA radars and Electronic Warfare Packages. Second and third LGB elements of F/A-18s loaded with laser guided bombs will go in second and third to take out the missiles and their launchers. Finally, a fourth element of F/A-18s will go in and drop cluster bombs to take out ground defenders. Tanking will be provided by eight S-3s who will shuttle from four Air Force KC-10s stationed over the carriers and half way along the ingress and egress routes. A combat air patrol of F/A-18s on MIGSWEEP over the target will be loaded for air-to-air combat against any defending MIGS. If I have missed anything or anybody else has a better idea, let me hear about it."

"What about getting some F-22 Raptors involved for the CAP?" asked Colonel William "Spud" Boise, Commander of the Third Marine Air Wing out of Fightertown and embarked aboard the USS Carl Vinson.

"I already asked the Air Force about that." Admiral Courtney replied. "They said they would have to fly their Raptors all the way down from Tyndall Air Force base in Florida and it is too dangerous since the large number of tankers needed for the mission would almost all be flying in Chinese controlled airspace. The tankers would almost certainly all be shot down even if they had CAP protection since there are so many Chinese fighters in Brazil right now. The Chinese fighters would simply overwhelm the CAP, and, even if they could not shoot down the Raptors, which they most assuredly could not, they could kill them all indirectly by taking out their tankers. They said there are so few F-22s that they cannot risk losing all of them on a mission like this, so they were ordered by the Joint Chiefs to sit this one out. So we are on our own."

"Hmmm. Fucking Air Farce. We should have navalized the F-22. Sounds like a political charade kept that from happening. The Air Force hated that they had to fly the F-4 because it was a Navy plane. Maybe keeping the world's most premier fighter off the carriers was their payback." Spud Boise opined as he spit out his chewing tobacco juice into a styrofoam coffee cup. "Ok well I don't have any other ideas, so lets just go with Hanna's suggested Alpha Strike Package."

The rest of the group concurred, and a briefing was set for 0530 the next morning to go over the package squadron assignments, transponder squawks, lost-communication procedures, bingo fuel requirements and bingo fields, navigation reference points, code words, weapon loads, search and rescue contingencies and set strike package and section leaders. Launch was set for 0800 the following day.

"Did you hear?" Nailgun was assigned as the strike package leader on the Alpha Strike tomorrow to go take out the ASBMs." Ricky had a disappointed look on his face when he said it. He was itching for some action, and was tired of sitting on the boat. Neither Ricky, JJ nor Carmen was assigned to go on the raid.

"No kidding? Well, if anybody can handle it, he can. He is good leader and a great stick." JJ replied.

"It pisses me off that we are not going on this raid. If I have to endure one more sexist wisecrack or put down from a squid pilot, I am going to scream." Carmen said with disgust. "I agree with JJ that Neil is a good choice for the job. I like Neil, but he is still a squid." Carmen was good natured normally, but the Navy pilots never got over Tailhook and resented female aviators and treated them like lepers. Carmen had reached her limit, and was ready to get off the boat and flame some Chinese Communist douchebags.

The S-3 tankers were first off the cats the next morning. SEAD F-35s rigged for Electronic Countermeasures and suppression of enemy air defenses were next off the cats, followed by the F-35 HARM shooters. All aircraft in the first two elements headed straight for the tanker orbiting over the carrier to top off before starting the inbound trip to the target.

The HARM shooters were critical to the success of the raid. The AGM-88 HARM missile is Mach 2 air-to-ground missile that homed in on radiation from emitting radar antennas and destroyed the radar site. As soon as an enemy radar site lit up in a frequency range the HARM seeker head was designed for, the radar installation would find a 150 pound warhead streaking toward it at 1420 miles per hour.

The Combat Air Patrol F/A-18s took off after the HARM shooters, and they also headed straight for the tankers to top off their tanks for the inbound trip to their CAP stations over the target area.

Finally, Nailgun's strike package F/A-18 elements, loaded with laser guided bombs and cluster bombs launched and headed for the tanker overhead.

Neil's raid gets decimated but Neil shoots down five

The raid was an unmitigated disaster. Not a single plane returned. Taco and Tequila Tim were shot down and killed. Neil and Squishy were shot down after downing five Flankers, but were rescued at sea by a SEAL team that had been scouting the target area.

The crushing defeat was for reasons which were not the fault of the aviators flying the raid. Lack of proper intelligence about the Chinese defenses doomed the mission from the start. Although the Force Recon and SEAL teams had found the ASBMs hiding place, they had been unprepared for and not properly equipped or trained to determine the type of Chinese air defense systems that had been set up. Nobody had seen this type of defensive system before. The Chinese had purchased from Russia truck-mounted Almaz-Antey/NNIIRT 55Zh6ME Nebo VHF-band radar systems and S-300P anti-aircraft surface-to-air missile systems. These radar systems and accompanying SAMS were designed to detect and shoot down stealth and low visibility aircraft such as the F-35 HARM shooters.

The Chinese were also using bistatic passive radar systems to detect the presence of the F-35 stealth jets and the F/A-18s without the F-35s or the Hornets even knowing they were being detected. After detecting the approach of stealth jets with the passive systems, they rolled the truck-mounted Nebo VHF target acquisition radars and truck-mounted S-Band SAM guidance radars and truck-mounted SAMs out of hidden positions in warehouses. The combination of systems decimated the raiding planes. Any American jet that made it through the SAM barrage had to deal with a swarm of Su-30MK2 Flankers that came up to intercept them. It was a bloodbath.

The Chinese were actually using two different types of passive detector systems to detect the presence of stealth jets. The first type was called a Czech-designed Vera-E passive sensor system. The type of system depends upon the differences in times of arrival of radio emissions from the stealth planes. If a stealth plane emitted RF pulses of any type, it could be located.

A stealth plane sometimes emits pulses such as from digital communications systems such as data links between planes or pulsed jamming signals. They can also emit SSR or IFF transponder signals, airborne search radar pulses or weather radar pulses. Also, TACAN transponders or even DME beacons can emit signals that can be detected. If any such pulses are detected, then the time difference of arrival of the pulses at each of a two or more side Vera-A receiver sites can be calculated from the known propagation delays of the pulses from the side sites to a central site along a point-to-point microwave link from the side site to the central site. Each Time Delay Of Arrival at a side site locates the stealth plane which emitted the pulse somewhere along a hyperboloid. Three intersecting hyperboloids locates the plane exactly in 3D space without ever having emitted a search radar pulse from the ground.

The Vera-E defensive system did not work. The American jets on the raid were all exercising complete electromagnetic blackout discipline and did not emit any detectable radiation.

But the other more ingenious passive stealth plane detection system the Chinese had deployed did work. It involved use of the existing radio, cell phone and TV towers transmitting broadcast programming and cell phone signals in the Porto Alegre area. When a stealth plane flies through the chatter of thousands of cell phone tower signals, and hundreds of radio and TV broadcast transmissions, it absorbs and reflects energy leaves a disturbance in the normal electromagnetic spectrum in the form of a shadow. This shadow can be detected, and alerts the defenders to the presence of a stealth plane. Once presence of the stealth jets was detected, the Chinese rolled out their Nebo VHF target acquisition radars. These VHF radars emitted radar pulses that were in a frequency range the stealth jets were not designed to evade. The VHF radars found the exact positions of the American jets and sent this position, course and speed data to the SAM S-band targeting radars. Knowing exactly where the stealth jets were allowed the S-band radars to lock on to the tiny returns they received and provide an initial point to which the SAM could fly. The initial intercept point to which the SAMs flew after launch was close enough to the stealth jet that the terminal phase targeting radars in the SAM nose cone could lock on and guide the SAM to its victim. If an S-band radar is close enough to a stealth jet, its returns are strong enough to be usable since strength of a radar return falls off with the square of the distance.

The second Chinese passive system was undetectable to the Force Recon and SEAL teams in the area, because it used almost nothing but the existing radio, TV and cell towers already there. The receiver antennas that detected the disturbances in the electromagnetic spectrum were too innocuous for the recon teams to notice. In addition, they were hidden by the Chinese. This passive "shadow detection" system did not tell the Chinese exactly where the American jets were, but it did tell them they were there.

The Chinese had modified the VHF AESA and Big Bird radars to use 10 megahertz up-chirp radar pulses such that the frequency of each pulse changed by 10 megahertz from start to finish of the pulse which was only a few microseconds in length. This effectively spread the energy of the radar search pulse so widely throughout the electromagnetic spectrum that the HARM anti-radiation missiles could not lock on to these radars and destroy them. Furthermore, the Radar Warning Receivers of the F-35s and F/A-18s were not designed to detect this type of chirp pulse in the spectrum below 500 megahertz.

The SAMs decimated the F-35 HARM shooters. This left the incoming F/A-18s of the Combat Air Patrol and the Hornets armed with laser guided bombs who were supposed to destroy the ASBMs exposed to the SAMs. The Hornets that were not shot down by the SAMs were mopped up by the Flankers.

Neil and Squishy were jumped by 7 Flankers in a furious dogfight. Neil flew a smart fight by turning and burning and getting the Flankers to use their thrust vectoring to try to get a firing solution on him and then going ballistic as soon as he saw the vapor on the tops of their wings indicating they were turning too sharply and wasting their kinetic energy. After achieving the energy advantage in this way, he was able to fly straight up to a point where a pursuing Flanker could not go for lack of energy. This gave him enough vertical separation to do a rudder reversal and fly straight back down on the Chicom pilot who too low on kinetic energy to escape. Neil nailed five of them that way in Sidewinder and guns kills.

But the sixth and seventh Flankers finally got him in a high-low tag team with the high seventh Flanker coming down out of the sun and taking a guns shot when Neil did his rudder reversal at the top of his ballistic climb and was diving back down on the sixth Flanker. The guns shot crippled Neil's jet causing him to lose fuel and hydraulic power.

Nailgun and Squishy made it out to sea a couple of miles before they had lost too much altitude and had to eject. A SEAL team on the ground that was painting the target with a laser witnessed the dogfight and saw Neil and Squishy escape out to sea. The SEALS radioed Nailgun's approximate location upon ejection to the MARSOC commander in charge of the Marine Force Recon and SEAL teams operating in the area. The MARSOC commander relayed their position to a U.S. attack submarine with embarked SEALS that was nearby, and passed word to Nailgun via his AN/PRC-90 survival radio to lay low until darkness.

Neil and Squishy floated and treaded water all afternoon and swam away from their die markers. It was later afternoon with low light in the southern hemisphere, and the seas were stormy with high winds and big waves. Flying conditions for the Chinese helicopters searching for them were not ideal. Nailgun and Squishy heard a Chinese helicopter coming, so they stripped off their floatation versts and left them on the surface and swam underwater about 50 yards from their actual positions to make the Chinese think they had drowned. Whenever they heard a plane or helicopter coming, they ducked underwater, and stayed down as long as they could while swimming away from their vests. They swam back to their floatation vests after the helicopters passed. Luckily the light was low and the seas were rough, so the Chinese could not see them underwater. Finally, the Chinese gave up looking for them. Under cover of darkness, the SEALs disembarked from the submarine and sped on the surface in their F-470 Zodiac to the last known position for Neil and Squishy's. A quick call on the PRC-90 and a short lighting of their rescue lights was all it to to get them picked them up and brought back to the submerged submarine. A quick course in the SEAL LAR-V re-breather and a shallow dive to the submarine brought a grateful Nailgun and Squishy back to the civilized world.

CHAPTER 8

SPECTRUM

"**G**eez Neil, you look like shit." Carmen said walking into sick bay.

"Ya think? You try swimming all day while dodging Chinese helicopters wise ass. Squishy looks worse than me. He is starting to question his choice of career." Neil said laconically.

"What the hell happened Nailgun?" Ricky said as he and J.J. walked in.

"I don't know man. They saw us coming. Taco and Tequila ate it in the first wave of SAMS. The Surface-to-Air-Missiles wiped us out and we could not knock out their radars with the HARM anti-radiation missiles. They all refused to lock on and went stupid. Our targeting radar libraries could not even tell what kind of radars they were using. They saw the F-35s in the Suppression of Enemy Air Defenses element coming and shot them down with SAMs, and then they shot down the Combat Air Patrol element with the SAMs targeted by the radars the HARMs did not knock out. Then they sent up Flankers to jump our bombing elements. I got in a big furball with seven of them."

"We know. Taco and Tequila were good men. Tequila and I had some good times at Top Gun." Carmen said. "We will miss them. What do you say boys. Lets get these Chicom pricks back."

"Damn straight." Ricky said. "I have some ideas."

"Congratulations by the way Nailgun. You know you are an ace now." J.J. said.

"Really?"

"Yeah, you shot down five of them against all odds. The sixth and seventh ones got you. Nice flying. CAG has put you in for the Navy Cross."

"No shit? I was so busy flying my ass off trying to stay alive, I did not have any time to watch what happened with all my missiles. I wish he would have sent us in with better intelligence and a better plan instead."

"Yup. Radar tracks confirmed it and a few of the other pilots that were downed and saved by the SEALs and Force Recon teams backed it up." Ricky said. "By the way. I concur. The intelligence was incomplete, and that plan was a clusterfuck."

"So what is CAG going to do?"

"We don't know yet." J.J. said.

"Feel better Neil. We will be back in a day or so to check in on you." Ricky said.

Ricky and Carmen investigate what happened

Out in the passageway, Ricky looked at Carmen and J.J. and said, "We have some investigation to do. It is very bizarre that a raid goes this badly. Every plane was lost — are you kidding me? When has that every happened?"

"Never." J.J. and Carmen said simultaneously.

Here is what I think we should do, because we almost certainly will be called by the brass to go on another raid to the same target.

Carmen, you go figure out why the HARMs were not locking on, and J.J. and I will figure out how the Chicoms figured out the F-35s were coming. I want to know what is going on with their radars and SAMs that they knew the F-35 SEAD elements were coming and were able to shoot them all down. I have some ideas that I need to verify. I read an article about anti-stealth defensive systems in Popular Mechanics a few years back, and there is stuff I have seen on Air Power Australia about Russian designed anti-stealth radar systems. I want to see if that is what the Chicoms have set up."

"OK roger that." Carmen said. "Got any ideas where to start?"

"Yes. Go to Surface Plot in the Carrier Air Traffic Control Center and go over the tapes of the pilot-to-pilot exchanges on the squadron tactical frequencies and see if you learn anything there."

"In fact, that is where Ricky and I will be headed first. Lets all go together and listen." J.J. advised. "I know also that the spooks in the bat cave over on the Carrier Battle Group command ship record the entire RF spectrum to make sure nobody violates the emissions blackout orders. They will have recordings of the radar frequencies in the spectrum. Maybe we can find something out about what went on from data recorded over there. I will make a few calls and tell them what we are looking for so that they can tee it up for us."

The three made their way to Surface Plot in CATCC the next morning, and settled in to listen to the tapes.

"Good morning. We have been expecting you." Lieutenant Brad Keenan said to Ricky, J.J. and Carmen. "Follow me. We have you set up at one of our workstations with tapes of all the relevant squadron tactical frequencies for the time slice starting 15 minutes before the SEAD elements reached the target area until the raid was over. It is pretty gruesome. You might not want to listen."

Ricky, J.J. and Carmen looked at each other with grim resolve. "Ok thanks Lieutenant. We are going to get started right away. Do you guys tape any other frequencies other than the back channel squadron tactical comm frequencies and the AWACs strike frequency?" Ricky said.

"Yes, we also taped the Chinese comm frequencies and the SEAL and Force Recon team tactical frequencies. And the spooks over on the *Lake Champlain* have tapes of the entire electromagnetic spectrum including the VHF and UHF radar bands garnered from a *SIGINT* (signals intelligence) satellite launched last week from Vandenberg AFB in geosynchronous orbit over the southern Atlantic. They told me that they have some interesting information for you." Lt. Keenan said referring to the Carrier Strike Group command ship, the Aegis cruiser U.S.S *Lake Champlain*.

"Good, that will be our next stop."

Over the next two hours, the group listened intently to the pilot-to-pilot and AWACs communications that took place during the raid. It was hard to listen to the panicked calls of their friends and brothers-in-arms as they tried in vain to escape swarms of Chinese SAMs and air-to-air missiles from the horde of Flankers that came up to meet them. At one point, they had to stop while Carmen broke down into tears. Ricky and J.J. were more stoic about it, but they were in shock. It was a sobering experience. They had had so many good times with Taco and Tequila Tim, that to hear their last moments of life was excruciating.

After listening to the Chinese communication frequencies, it became immediately apparent that the Chinese knew the F-35s were coming before they got there. The F-35 stealth did not work. Carmen translated the Chinese chatter in Mandarin. She said the Chinese knew the F-35s were coming while they were still 100 miles away —something that should not have happened given the extremely small radar cross-section of the F-35. The Chinese had set up an air defense radar and surface-to-air missile system that could not be penetrated by stealth aircraft. It was far superior to and different from any ever seen by

U.S. combat forces in the past. It also was painfully apparent that the American pilots did not know they were flying right into it.

When the Harm missile bearing F-35s charged with destroying Chinese air defense radar systems were still 100 miles from the target, the Chinese chatter picked up. What was amazing was that not a single pilot of an F-35 or an F/A-18 announced he was "spiked", i.e., being painted by enemy search radar. That means the radar warning receivers in the American jets were not picking up whatever radar pulses the Chinese early warning radars were emitting. It was not until the American jets were within 20 miles of the target that the radar warning receivers picked up any radar pulses.

About 10 minutes later, the SEAL teams and Force Recon teams that had the target and surrounding area under observation and were painting the target with a laser designator for the laser guided bombs reported that the Chinese had rolled out some weird looking truck mounted radar or communications facility from warehouses where they had been hiding them. They reported that the radar trucks had huge radar arrays mounted on them that looked sort of like giant mattress springs.

"There it is!" Ricky exclaimed. "I know what those were. They were old World War II low frequency VHF band radars that the Russians re-fitted with digital front ends. They work at a frequency that is so low that our stealth jets are not invisible to them. Our stealth jets are only invisible to X-band radars which work at a much higher frequency."

Carmen and J.J. both looked at Ricky in amazement. Finally, J.J. said, "What the fuck Ricky? How could you possibly have known that?"

"What? I read Popular Mechanics. You should try it. You can learn all manner of things useful. They had an article on stealth busting technologies back in 2013 that I read. Unfortunately, DOD did not read it, and they kept on developing the F-35 for some reason known only to them. It certainly was not apparent to me. Lets go back to the tapes and see what else happened. They could not have targeted those SAMs with VHF radars."

Going back to the tapes of the Force Recon tactical frequencies, they learned that after the Chicoms had moved the first set of trucks out with the massive radar arrays, they rolled out another truck with what the Force Recon Marines knew was an S-band radar. That was followed by rollout of multiple trucks with SAM missiles mounted on them.

"Aah, I see what they were doing. They used the VHF radars to learn that there were stealth jets inbound and to get an approximate range and bearing. Then, when the F-35s got close enough to be detectable on S-band radars, they lit them up with S-band pulses to determine initial points for the SAMs which would be close enough that the SAM nosecone radar could see them and take over for terminal phase guidance. Brilliant." J.J. said. "Lets go back to the tapes and see if I am right."

They turned their attention back to the tapes of Force Recon tactical communications. About ten minutes after all the S-band radar truck was reported as rolled out by the Force Recon teams, the pilot-to-pilot and pilot-to-AWACs chatter indicated that the inbound jets were spiked. "The S-band targeting radars must have been painting them." Carmen said.

They continued listening and learned that shortly after the spiking reports by the pilots, the SAM missiles were launched in waves.

Then the pilot chatter turned gruesome. It was unbearable to listen to their fellow pilots die, and they stopped. The group fell silent for a moment. After some reflection, they looked at each other puzzled. How did the Chinese know to roll out the VHF radars when they did?

Ricky hesitantly took a shot at a hypothesis.

"I have read about some exotic anti-stealth radars in an Air Power Australia report other than the VHF radar I just told you about. I believe that the Chinese were using either some kind of passive radar system that was detecting the F-35s or they were using a radar frequency or pulse type that was not being detected by the radar warning receivers of either the F-35s or the F/A-18s.

The Russians developed a bistatic early warning radar to detect stealth planes like an early warning tripwire, and the Chinese have copied it. They call it the NNIRT Barrier E radar. It is a low power radar operating continuously at 1-3 watts and at low frequencies from 390 to 430 megahertz. At frequencies below 500 megahertz, our radar warning receivers are blind to continuous wave signals.

The Barrier E acts like a picket fence or tripwire for early warning against inbound stealth aircraft. Typically they deploy a chain of stations about 30 nautical miles apart that produce individual coverage zones between stations. The transmit signal is modulated with datalink or other communications data so that it does not sound like a radar but sounds like a communication link instead. The data is actually digitized radar return data that gets linked back to a central processing station. That is how I think they figured out the F-35s were coming. We need to verify that to see if I am right.

The antennas are mounted on masts which have guy wires and they are pretty tall so Force Recon or the SEALs should be able to see them. The chain of tripwire stations typically spans 300 nautical miles and provides coverage up to about 23,000 feet.

The timing of the Chinese chatter and the timing of the rolling out of the trucks reported by Force Recon along with the reports of what those trucks looked like suggests to me that when the F-35 hit the tripwire signals, the Chinese rolled out the VHF anti-stealth radar system.

The Russians designed a mobile VHF band electronically steerable AESA radar mounted on trucks. The only thing WW II about it is the frequency at which it operates. I know the Chinese have bought some and copied the design with their own versions. Shortly after the VHF radar truck was rolled out, another truck with what they think was an S-band radar was rolled out. That had to be either an S-band or L-band targeting radar that could get a more precise fix after the stealth jets got closer since they knew exactly where to look for them since the VHF radar gave them rough fix. Shortly after that happened, the F-35s and F/A-18s reported being spiked. An L-band radar operates at 40 to 60 gigahertz so the radar warning receivers cannot see it. The F/A-18 AN/ALR-67V radar warning receiver operates from 0.5 gigahertz up to 20 Ghz so it cannot see an L-band radar. An S-band radar operates at 2 to 4 gigahertz, so the radar warning receivers could see it. That second radar truck must have been an S-band radar truck.

So putting all that together, I believe the Chicoms used VHF AESA radars to get an initial fix on the inbound F-35s and sent that data to the mobile S-band targeting radar for the SAMs which lit them up causing the reports of being spiked.

The AN/ALR-67(V)3 radar warning receivers used in the Super Hornets and the F-35s only detect PULSED signals below 500 megahertz. Any continuous wave or pulsed VHF surveillance or targeting radar down in the VHF megahertz band would escape the radar warning receiver undetected. The stealth features of the F-35 airframe would be ineffective against these low frequency VHF radar waves since they are designed for stealth only at higher X-band radar frequencies from 8 to 12 gigahertz. F-35s are less stealthy against lower frequency S-Band and L-Band radars, and the lower the frequency goes, the less stealthy they are. I know that Russians have designed some anti-stealth VHF radars operating in the 30 to 300 megahertz range, and I know that they have exported them to China. I think that is exactly the buzzsaw the F-35 flew into.

To make matters worse, I read on Air Power Australia that the Russians have developed an L-Band AESA radar that can be retrofitted into the leading edges of Flanker wings which can detect F-35s. The feature size and shaping of the F-35's airframe is not designed to defeat an L-band radar wavelength of 0.24 meters, especially when the radar is close. The same article said the F-22 Raptor is much less detectable in the L-Band, but we don't have any of those and won't be able to get any since they are not navalized to operate off carriers."

"This is a travesty." J.J. said. "The Joint Strike Fighter task force buried their heads in the sand and locked down the specifications of the F-35 while being completely oblivious to the developments in other parts of the world. How could they not have taken the developments like the VHF AESA radars and the leading edge L-Band AESA radars for Flankers into account when designing the F-35. What makes it completely incomprehensible is the fact that L-Band AESA radars were first developed in the U.S. for our Wedgetail AWACs back about 30 years ago. The fact that this technology would be picked up by the Russians was missed or ignored apparently."

"That is seriously messed up." Carmen said. "But we have to play the hand we are dealt so let's get busy and figure out some way to beat these bastards. Let's go check out the tapes of the electromagnetic spectrum the spooks recorded to see if Ricky is right."

And with that, they were off on a helicopter to the USS *Lake Champlain.*

The shapely brunette Lieutenant Monica Chambers met the three officers at the helipad on the USS *Lake Champlain* with a warm smile. Her gaze lingered just a tad too long when it settled on J.J. J.J. extended his hand and introduced the group. He held her hand just a tad too long, and dragged his index finder along the inside of her palmed as he released her hand. Carmen just rolled her eyes and laughed. Monica flushed slightly and then composed herself as she turned and led the group to the SCIF.

The secure communication facility SCIF on the USS *Lake Champlain* had impressive security. Lt. Chambers first examined their ID cards and then placed each of their index fingers on an electronic fingerprint reader. The machine took just a couple of minutes to access its databases and verify their identities. She then took digital photos of their faces, and imported them into a facial pattern recognition software application which compared their facial features to faces in a database which included faces of all U.S. military, KGB, NATO and Chinese Intelligence personnel as well as the FBI and Interpol databases of face shots. After the machine recognized their faces and said they were who they said they were, Lt. Chambers was satisfied.

As they were escorted into the SCIF, they noticed banks of servers and RAID disk arrays as well as banks of reel-to-reel tape recorders. "Have you carbon-14 dated those reel-to-reels to see if they came from the Jurassic period?" Ricky asked with tongue in cheek.

"Shut up wise ass. That turns out to be the most cost-effective way of recording the radio chatter on the various tactical and strike frequencies of us and the Chinese." Chambers ribbed. "Besides with the budget cuts forced upon the Navy by the Obamacare and the eight wealth-transfer years of his administration, that is all we can afford. It is the same reason why you guys are still flying Hornets instead of the navalized F-22s you are going to need when you go up against the Su-30MK2s and the Sino Flanker copies."

"What is your educational background Lt. Chambers?" Carmen asked.

"PhD from MIT in electrical engineering with an emphasis on radar systems."

"Oh. I see now why they gave you this job. How do you know about the Flankers?"

"Precisely, and I read comparisons of the Flankers to the Super Hornets on Air Power Australia. There is not much to do over here when I am not on duty. My doctoral thesis was on stealth-defeating VHF radar systems. And that is why I have some interesting things to show you. After you told me what you were interested in reviewing and gave me your working theory, I did some analysis of my own on our spectrum recordings. Sit down over here and I will show you what I am talking about."

Chambers pointed to a workstation with a spectrum analyzer on it which was coupled to a disk drive. The group sat down in the four chairs around the workstation.

"When I heard what happened on the raid, I became suspicious about what kind of defensive system the Chinese had set up. No raid should go that badly. When I got your message about your visit and your working theory, I extracted the VHF, S-band and L-band spectrum recordings we had for the interval spanning the raid. I looked at each of the spectrums on the spectrum analyzer with particular attention to the VHF spectrum at the time the F-35 SEAD elements were about 100 miles away from the target area. I found something interesting which I think proves your theory. Look at this replay of the VHF spectrum recording on the spectrum analyzer from 0915 to 0930. At that time, the F-35s were about 100 nautical miles away from the target. Let me pause the replay right here. Do you see the peak slightly above the noise at 100 megahertz right here? If you look closely, you will see numerous peaks poking just above the average noise level spread out over an extremely wide bandwidth encompassing the 100 megahertz frequency. I suspected those were Fourier components of Chinese VHF radar pulses, so I did some further analysis."

Ricky knew what Fourier components were, but he was not too sure whether Carmen and J.J. did. "Hold the phone there Miss Chambers. Would you please explain Fourier components to my esteemed colleagues in case they were partying that day instead of studying."

"Certainly. Every electronic signal of any shape, frequency and amplitude can be broken down by a mathematical Fourier analysis into a fundamental frequency sinusoid and a number of Fourier components which are pure sinusoids of different frequencies and amplitudes. When you add all the components together with the fundamental, you get a signal which has the shape, frequency and amplitude of the signal you started with."

"You knew that Ricky?" Carmen asked.

"Yeah, I was a bigtime egghead in college."

"Impressive, because that is pretty non linear. It is not intuitive at all."

"I know. Neither was the theory of relativity."

"Nice Ricky. I will use that as a party trick." J.J. said.

"Shut up you idiots. This is serious shit. We need to hand these Chinese pricks their heads on a platter." Ricky scolded, and the group got serious again.

"So what I did was a reverse Fourier analysis on the components I found in the spectrum starting just about the time when the F-35s were about 100 nautical miles out. I had to guess at the amplitudes, but I had the frequencies. When you do that analysis, guess what you get? A 100 megahertz VHF search radar pulse with a 25 megahertz up chirp that was about 1.5 milliseconds long."

"What is an up chirp." J.J. asked not being afraid to look stupid.

"It means the Chinese search radars were emitting VHF search radar pulses each of which started out at 100 megahertz in frequency but which is FM modulated to change its frequency upwards by 25 megahertz over the course of its 1.5 millisecond pulse duration. That change in frequency causes each pulse to have a shape which splatters the VHF band with Fourier components over a wide bandwidth. These components are so far down in the noise that they can only be picked up by a radar receiver with a signal processing and filtering software which is programmed to know what it is looking for. The Chinese VHF pulse doppler radar receivers use a correlation process where sampling of received VHF spectrum energy at the frequency of each Fourier component happens during the quiescent period between emitted pulses. Only the Chinese radar receiver software knows what the frequencies are of the Fourier components that it is looking for, because they know the base frequency and the amount of up-chirp so they know the pulse shape and its Fourier spectrum. The Chinese VHF radar receivers use that information to determine which frequencies to sample and integrate. Banks of filters are used to determine range. There is one set of software filters for each possible range, each filter in the set having a passband at the frequency of one of the Fourier components. The filters are opened up and coupled to the receiver to do their passband integration at the time at which pulses would be returning if there was a target at the range assigned to that bank of filters. In other words, there is a set of filters which generate outputs for targets at 10 mile range, another set for 11 mile range, etc.

The inbound American jets never knew they were being painted, because their radar warning receivers were not designed to look below 500 megahertz. Even if they had been, they were not designed to detect spread spectrum pulses like these. To do that, they would have to know base frequency and the pulse characteristics such as its duration and the amount of up chirp. Since they were not designed to detect these types of spead spectrum pulses in the VHF range, the pulses were invisible to them.

That is all a long winded way of saying the F-35 pilots suppression of enemy air defenses pilots walked right into a trap.

It looks like the pulse repetition rate was such that the pulses were spaced out about 3.9 milliseconds between them. A radar mile, or the time it takes a radar pulse to fly one nautical mile is 12 microseconds, so it looks like the Chinese set the system up for detection at about 100 nautical miles. Time for a 200 mile round trip to a target at 100 nautical miles would be 2.4 milliseconds plus a pulse duration of 1.5 milliseconds gives me the pulse repetition frequency at 3.9 millisecond spacing.

The F-35 is not invisible to these VHF pulses, because it was designed to have a low radar cross section at X-band which is up around 6200 to 10,900 megahertz. The Chinese knew we would not see these pulses, and that we would not be able to lock onto them with HARM anti-radiation missiles. The HARM is also blind to targeting or search radars operating below 500 megahertz. It was a perfect trap."

"Is that everything?" Ricky asked.

"No, there is more. We listened to recordings of the communications on the Seal Team and Force Recon special operations team tactical frequencies too, and found out something interesting. About the time, the inbound F-35s and F/A-18s were only 60 miles out, the recon teams reported a big truck with a radar array was rolled out of a warehouse where the Chinese were hiding it. Then they reported multiple mobile SAM launchers rolled out from the same warehouse. They said the warehouse was right next to the warehouse where they found the ASBMs. About 6 minutes later, the S-band spectrum came alive with targeting pulses, and the recon teams reported seeing SAM launches from the truck mounted launchers. Then they reported the trucks were rolled back into the warehouse, all in the space of about 12 minutes. It was a pop up SAM defense. Recordings of the pilot-to-pilot communications indicated their radar warning receivers went off at the same time the S-band spectrum lit up. Several magnum calls were heard indicating HARMs were launched, but the pilots reported the missiles went stupid. That happened at the same time the S-band spectrum went quiet, and at the same time the force recon teams reported the truck with the radar array was moved back into the warehouse. The Chinese obviously shut off their S-band targeting radars after the HARMs were launched, so the HARMs lost guidance with no signals to home on. My guess is that the Chinese must have been listening to the SEAD element strike frequency. They knew HARMs had left the rails, so they shut their radars down. They already had sufficient position, course, speed and range data to program an initial point into the SAM guidance systems to get the SAMs close enough to the inbound jets. Once the SAMs got that close, their on-board S-band terminal guidance radars could get sufficient return to guide the missile to impact.

It was a very clever defense designed to surprise the American jets and destroy them with SAMs without suffering any losses to the HARMs. Cagey little bastards.

Ricky smiled, and said, "But now we know what they are doing and where and when to look for their radar signals and in what frequency ranges. Armed with this information, we can jam the VHF search radars using modified electronic countermeasures pods and drones. We can also home some HARMS modified to see the VHF Doppler radar pulses in on their VHF antenna arrays and blow them into Buddha's backyard before they can send our positions to the S-band SAM targeting radars." Ricky laughed. "Oh we got this now. We are going to rip those guys a new asshole. Great work Lt. Chambers. I am going to buy you dinner when this is all over."

Carmen glared at him, and then smiled at Lt. Chambers. "Outstanding work Miss Chambers. You probably just saved our lives."

"Go kick their teeth in tiger." Chambers said to Carmen. Carmen smiled.

J.J. piped in, "We will coordinate with you as we plan our next raid to make sure we get a good plan together."

"I look forward to helping in every way I can." Chambers said as she gave J.J. a devilish grin. J.J. winked at her.

CHAPTER 9

UCMJ

A sharp knock on his stateroom door startled Ricky out of his contemplation. "Enter."

A young seamen from Ricky's squadron stuck his head in the door. "The skipper wants to see you Captain. Right away."

"Thank you Gibbs. I am on my way."

Ricky knocked on his squadron commander's stateroom door and waited for a response.

"Enter."

Ricky entered Commander Sebring's stateroom and came to attention. "Captain Magnusson reporting as ordered sir."

Lt. Colonel Sebring, CO of the Black Knights of VMFA(AW)-314 was sitting at his desk with his operations officer. "Captain Magnusson, we have planned another raid on the Chinese ASBM launch site at Porto Alegre. You are our best stick. I want you to lead the raid."

"Thank you sir. Have you told Scud you think I am the best stick in the squadron?" Ricky said with a smile.

Lt. Colonel Sebring laughed.

"Sir, may I inquire as to the makeup and plan for the raid?"

"Yes. The raid will have the same basic plan as the last raid, but with more planes, and we will be going at night."

Ricky was incredulous. He was silent for a moment while he composed his answer. "C'mon Ricky, what would Jack Bauer do?" he thought to himself. "Nah, Jack would shoot him in the knee caps and start cutting off his fingers one by one until he caved in." Ricky mused as he waited for his internal anger to cool slightly.

"Permission to speak freely sir?"

"Granted."

"I will not lead that raid sir."

Incredulous, Lt. Colonel Sebring glared at Ricky. The silence was deafening. Finally, Sebring spoke. "Why not Captain Magnusson?"

"Permission to speak freely sir?"

"Granted."

"Because it is dumber than a sake-soaked Bonzai charge. It is insanity to do the same thing over and over again and expect different results. This is a suicide mission, and I would rather be doing a dime at Fort Leavenworth Military Prison than pushing up daisies. I will lead the raid sir, but only if you allow me to re-plan it. Scud, Swat and I have done some investigating, and we have a pretty good idea of what the Chinese are doing to defend Porto Alegre. This raid as currently planned, will not work."

Now with his intelligence insulted and his command authority flaunted, Lt. Colonel Sebring was beyond logic. "You shitbird. I will have your bars for this. You are restricted to quarters until further notice. I will be convening a court martial most ricky tick Captain, and you can expect to be dealt with harshly. Dismissed."

"Aye, aye Sir." Ricky saluted, turned smartly about face and marched out of the room and returned to his stateroom.

As word of the incident spread throughout the squadron, morale started to take a nosedive. J.J. and Swat were the first to visit Ricky that evening.

"Way to go dumbass, now you have pissed off the skipper and we are all going to take it in the shorts for your sins." J.J. ribbed.

"This would be funny if it were not so serious." Carmen said.

"I know. I am in deep shit. The old man says he is going to court martial me."

"For what?" Carmen asked.

"I don't know exactly. Insubordination, mutiny, who knows. He was really pissed. His veins were popping out on his neck and his eyes were bulging. If looks could kill, I would have a one foot diameter exit wound on my back."

"Holy shit. What were you thinking?" Carmen asked.

"I don't know. The 60's were hard on me." Ricky cracked.

"The 60s were hard on all of us dude. What are you going to do?" J.J. asked.

"Nothing. Just stand my ground and hope that common sense prevails."

"Bad plan. This is the United States Marine Corps." Carmen cracked.

Carmen and J.J. left shortly thereafter, heartbroken and discouraged, but determined to subtly spread the word of what a hose job Ricky was being subjected to.

As the course of several days passed, Ricky's phone rang several times with calls from his other buddies in the squadron. To a man, they were behind him and told him that he was a good officer, and that they would testify as character witnesses at his court martial if needed. Neil sent him an email message from sick bay encouraging him to stand his ground. It read, "I heard you were in hack. I always knew you were no good. Seriously though dude, I agree with you. To do the exact same mission profile would be suicide. Stand your ground." Word of the incident had spread throughout the squadrons of the Southern Expeditionary Force.

Lt. Colonel Sebring stewed for several days as he tried to figure out what to do next. He knew morale in his squadron was suffering, but he did not want to escalate the matter for fear of damaging his career if CAG developed the opinion that he was incompetent for planning to do exactly the same thing that got so many crews killed and planes lost on the last raid. On the other hand, if he had to court martial Captain Magnusson, CAG would think he was a bad leader for not being able to inspire confidence in the officers under his command.

While he was deliberating, a sharp knock on his stateroom door startled him.

"Enter."

It was Captain Tom Baker, USN, commander of the air group aboard the U.S.S. *Carl Vinson*. Word of the incident had reached him, and he had come to investigate.

"Good morning CAG. What can I do for you?

"I am just trying to get to the bottom of this flap with Captain Magnusson? What is going on?

"Well sir, I asked him to lead the second raid on the ASBM launch site at Porto Alegre, and he refused."

"Why?"

"He said, and I am quoting, 'Because it is dumber than a sake-soaked Bonzai charge. It is insanity to do the same thing over and over again and expect different results. This is a suicide mission, and I would rather be doing a dime at Fort Leavenworth Military Prison than pushing up daisies.' He did say that he would lead the raid if I allowed him to re-plan it though."

"What did you do?"

"I put him in hack and told him I was going to court martial him."

"Did you ask him why he wanted to re-plan the raid or what he would do differently?"

"No."

"Why not?"

"I did not want to appear weak in front of my operations officer by not punishing an insubordinate junior officer who has insulted my intelligence and flaunted my command authority."

"I see. Not a good enough reason. Call Captain Magnusson back in here. I want to hear what he has to say." CAG ordered.

Lt. Colonel Sebring picked up the phone and called Ricky. "Captain Magnusson, this is Lt. Colonel Sebring. CAG wants to talk to you. Report to my stateroom on the double."

"Aye, aye sir."

A few minutes later, Ricky knocked on Lt. Colonel Sebring's door and entered.

"Good morning Captain Magnusson. I have been briefed on what happened here a couple of days ago, and I want to hear your explanation for your refusal to lead the raid and how you would plan it differently if you were allowed to do so." CAG inquired.

"Yes sir. First let me apologize for appearing to be insubordinate. I just believed that the order was illegal and that I was not obligated to follow it. I and some colleagues have investigated what happened on the first raid, and I know that given what we found out about the Chicom defenses, that exactly the same thing would happen on the second raid if it were to be carried out in the manner planned. But we have some ideas about what to do to overcome the Chinese defenses, and I will explain what we found out to you if you want to hear it."

"I do. Proceed."

Ricky then laid out all the information he, Carmen and J.J. had discovered about what the Chinese were doing.

After he was done, CAG was silent for a moment, then spoke. "Good job Woody. I believe you have a valid point and that we should re-plan this raid. Get together with Scud and SWAT and make a plan and bring it to me most ricky tick. Dismissed."

"Aye, aye sir, and thank you." Ricky said and turned about face and left the room.

"Lt. Colonel Sebring, you are hereby relieved of your command. Your XO will assume your duties immediately. Report to me tomorrow for re-assignment."

"Aye, aye sir."

CHAPTER 10

RICKY'S PLAN

"**S**cud, call Carmen and get to my stateroom on the double. We have some work to do. CAG overruled Sebring and ordered me to re-plan the upcoming raid. We have some work to do."

"Right. Let me find her, and we will be right there."

Five minutes later, J.J. and Carmen showed up at Ricky's door. "Good. Have a seat and let's plan a raid. Got any ideas Carmen? J.J., ideas?" Ricky inquired.

"Yes." Carmen said.

"Me too." from J.J.

Ricky picked up the phone. "Yeoman Anderson, Captain Magnusson. Would you please bring us a carafe of coffee please."

"Aye, aye sir. Right away." It was 9 PM and the ship was steaming in pitch blackness of the icy southern Atlantic.

"What do you have so far Carmen?"

"First, I think we are going to need some modified HARMs to see and lock those VHF chirp pulses and home in on their radar transmitters. Fortunately, I know a guy at Eglin AFB in Florida where I did my RAG training on the F-35 who has some experimental HARMs they have been evaluating to handle this type of situation. Those

HARMs were designed to counter the VHF radar threats the Russians have been developing. That guy was hitting on me the whole time I was there. If I have to, I will take one for the team to get him to give us some of those. It pains me to say that. It flies in the face of my central being. My Mom taught me never to use my beauty or body to manipulate men. She insisted I earn whatever I get by hard work and perserverence. I would just be using Captain Baker. I have taken that advice very seriously, and have never done it. Till now. Oh what the fuck. He will probably enjoy it, and we can sure use those missiles. Forgive me Mom for I am about to sin."

Ricky and J.J. looked at the pained expression on her face, and then looked at each other in silence. Their respect for this woman grew a little bit in that instant. After a moment, Ricky spoke. "Thank you Carmen. Once we get this plan organized, and the CAG buys into it, I want you on the next COD out of here and headed for Eglin. Bring back those missiles."

"I am with Ricky." J.J. chimed in. "I hate to see you have to do this, but if it were me, I would do the same thing."

Carmen looked at him with amusement, but did not say what she was thinking. "Consider it done."

Ricky floated an idea. "The Chinese used a J-20 stealth jet to take out the AWACs in Neil's raid. Information is king, so whoever still has an AWACs up with the other side blind is in the money. I think we should get an XB-47 drone and trick it out with an electronics package to give it the electronic signature of an AWACs. Then we give it a HAVCAP patrol of a few F/A-18s and an F-35 to fool the Chinese into thinking it is a real AWACs so they send their stealth jets after it. In Neil's raid, they apparently used a long range R-37 air-to-air missile, and shot his AWACs down from 150 nautical miles. I say we let them shoot down the XB-47 drone and think they got our AWACS, and then send up the real AWACs to join the HAVCAP patrol after they tank."

"How are you going to protect the real AWACs?" J.J. asked.

"When they shoot down the XB-47, they will give away the location of their J-20 base, and their *modus operandi*. I am guessing they will also send some Su-30MK2 Flankers from a Brazilian airbase near the town of Porto Alegre to engage the HAVCAP patrol while the stealth jet sneaks up on the AWACs undetected. I say we contact the Air Force and get them in this fight. I say we ask the Air Force to sneak about 12 F-22s down the western side of South America through Columbia, Peru and Chile. They can come over the Andes when they reach the latitude of Northern Argentina and land at a secret airbase we share with the Argentinians at Paso de los Libre. It is at almost the same latitude as Porto Alegre and only about 300 miles west of it. They can hide their F-22s there and sneak up on any Chinese planes taking off from the Porto Alegre area. The F-22s can take out any J-20 attacking the real AWACs if the Chinese figure it out, and they can help take out the Flankers. The Andes are very high and will provide a natural barrier to Chinese radar. They can fly the F-22s and their tankers below the peaks of the Andes all the way down from Tyndall AFB or maybe Holloman AFB and never be seen. The Chinese pilots won't be expecting to be attacked from behind them, and their VHF radars will all be pointed out to sea to detect the carrier-based elements. What do you think J.J.?"

"I like it. I would say that if we get the brass to order the Air Force to bring some F-22s down, they should bring some Bones down too for a low level, terrain following attack from the West under the radar. They have a cool terrain following system that is made for deep penetration into hostile air space at high speed under the radar."

J.J. was referring to the B1B supersonic bomber designed during the Cold War to penetrate deep into Soviet airspace while hugging the nap of the earth. It was referred to affectionately as the Bone.

"I love it. I knew there was a reason you are my best friend." Ricky said with a big smile.

"Yeah I know. I am so smart, I scare myself sometimes."

Ricky noticed a hurt look on Carmen's face. "Oh don't be such a crybaby Carmen. You are my best female friend. You are the coolest girl I have ever met."

Carmen's face lit up with a huge smile. "Thank you stud. You are not too bad yourself. Oh and I am not a girl – I am a full blown woman now."

J.J interjected. "Oh get a room you two." Ricky and Carmen cracked up.

Ricky pulled out his laptop and pulled up a file. "I have some satellite photos that show the Chinese have about two battalions of troops on the ground around Porto Alegre and armor. Apparently they are ready for a ground assault also. I think we use the Bones to drop cluster bombs on the troop positions and CBU-105 cluster bombs with submunitions on the armor."

"What is a CBU-105?" Carmen said.

"It's a tank killer." Ricky replied. "I read about them in an article in the Economist about the Iraq war. A small Force Recon team was happened upon by a column of Iraqi tanks and ground troops that far outnumbered the team. They called in an airstrike, and a pair of CBU-105's were dropped on the column. Each bomb opened while falling and released ten submunitions which were slowed by parachutes. Each munition was then spun by a mini-rocket and ejected four disks outward which were the size of hockey pucks. Now the air was full of 80 falling hockey pucks which were scanning the ground with lasers and infrared sensors to find armored vehicles. When an armored vehicle was found, the puck exploded in mid air several meters above the tank which fired a tangerine sized slug of copper down into the tank. The resulting impact and shrapnel destroyed the tank. The rest of the column was so shocked to see all their tanks blown up simultaneously, they surrendered without a fight."

"Would not want to be in one of those tanks. J.J.'s face turned inquisitive. "How do we know the F-22 Raptors will be able to see the J-20 stealth?"

"Good point. First, remember Ice Pick's lecture at Top Gun. The J-20 is not stealthy from behind. The CIA salted the F-35 design files the Chinese stole from the contractors with bad designs. The design of the tail is not as stealthy as the Chinese think it is." Ricky said.

"Oh right. I remember that now. But what if a J-20 get an R-37 missile off the rail before the Raptors get him?"

Ricky thought for a moment about J.J.'s question. "I think what we want to do is send up an F-35 with the HAVCAP Super Hornets protecting the AWACs. The F-35 can see the heat signature of the inbound R-37 missile on its DAS Infrared Search and Track system. If a J-20 gets a shot off, we can use the F-35 to try to shoot the R-37 down with an AMRAAM or a Sidewinder."

"Good idea. I would suggest one more thing though." Carmen said. "Lets send up an XB-47 drone with the HAVCAP element, and have it tow a decoy. The decoy can be activated to try to jam the targeting radar of the R-37, and to switch to projecting the heat signature and radar cross-section of the AWACs if the jamming does not work."

"I like it." Ricky said. "We can use one of the spare towed decoys the Super Hornets use."

"What about protecting the SEAD F-35s leading the attacking elements in?" J.J. asked.

"Got any ideas?" Ricky said.

"Yes. I suggest we don't use any F-35s at all for the Suppression of Enemy Air Defenses element. Instead of F-35s, we trick out some XB-47 drones with VHF up chirp-pulse doppler transponders. The transponders echo the Chinese VHF up-chirp pulses back to the VHF search radar, and are set up to emulate the radar cross-section of an F-35. The Chinese think it is another wave of F-35 SEAD jets, but we load the XB-47s with the modified HARMs Carmen brings back. When the XB-47s get in range, they launch the HARMS and wipe out the VHF radars."

"OK that is a good idea." Ricky said. "I have an idea to take care of the L-band radars and SAMs. What we do is send in a swarm of Predator C Avenger drones under the XB-47s but flying at the wavetops. The Predators are loaded with Hellfire missiles. We have some MARSOC teams watch for the rollout of the L-band radar trucks and the SAM mobile launchers. When the MARSOC teams report the trucks have been rolled out, they start painting them with laser designators. Then we have the Predator C's pop up into a swarm attack formation and fire their Hellfires. Even if the MARSOC teams get eliminated, the Predators can self-designate with their own laser designators. If the SAMs get off, they will only shoot down XB-47s. The Super Hornet attack elements come in behind the XB-47s and drop 2000 pound GBU-24 laser-guided bombs on the ASBM launchers in the warehouses. The MARSOC teams or the Predators can paint the warehouses with laser designators. We will have two CAP elements to fly high cover to protect the Predators and the attack elements from Su-27MK2 Flankers. One is comprised of Super Hornets with one F-35. The other CAP is comprised of F-22 Raptors and an F-35. The F-35s can act as infrared AWACs and link their DAS pictures to the Super Hornets and the Raptors. That will prevent any J-20 stealth jets or air-to-air missiles from arriving undetected. The DAS will pick up their heat signatures. Our regular AWACs can provide advance warning of any inbound Flankers that show up on radar. Just to make sure we got all the ASBMs, I think we should jump two battalions of the 75th Airborne Ranger regiment and some more MARSOC teams into the area after the raid to mop up."

"I love it Ricky. You are bona fide evil genius." Carmen said as she came over and planted a big wet kiss right on his lips. Somewhat taken back by the adulation, Ricky actually looked embarrassed for the first time since they had known him.

"Can I get some of that? I thought up some good stuff too." J.J. said with a smile to Carmen.

"Maybe later if you prove you are worth it." Carmen laughed. "I have an improvement to the plan that provides additional protection for the attack elements. I say we use a sucker fight. We send in some

XB-47s behind the SEAD elements programmed to emit the radar signature of F/A-18s. We have them fly the same altitudes and route of the attack profile the F/A-18s flew on the first raid. We send the actual attack element F/A-18s in on the deck under the XB-47s. About 100 miles ahead of the attack elements, we send a swarm of carrier-launched XB-47s armed with AMRAAMs and Sidewinder Xs. They fly on the deck far south of Porto Alegre and then turn north to fly to the west side of the airfield from which the Chinese launched their Flankers last time. When the Flankers launch to attack what they think are the inbound F/A-18 attack elements, we fly the XB-47 drones in behind them and shoot them down with AAMRAMS and Sidewinders right as they are taking off. We have an F-22 CAP element flying high perch to cover the drones. The VHF radar antennas will not be pointed in the direction of the XB-47s or the F-22s on the west side of the field since the last attack came from the East from the carriers. The Flankers are much faster than the drones, so the F-22s finish off any Flankers that escape the drones. The XB-47 is a flying wing stealth drone and has very low visibility to X-band radar. So does the F-22. The rearward looking X-band radar in the Flankers will never see either the XB-47s or the F-22s."

J.J. and Ricky looked at each other in amazement and then looked at Carmen. "How can you be so smart and so beautiful and so deadly at the same time?"

"Ha, if you dirtbags weren't such man-whores, you would probably get more work done."

At that, Ricky and J.J. broke into a gale of laughter.

"I hate to be Ms. Buzzkill, but what about the tankers. They are going to need protection too. I say we have the tankers fly down in the weeds with the attack elements of F/A-18s so maybe the Chinese will not even see them. The refueling will have to be at low levels, something nobody has practiced, but in principle, it ought to be the same. We keep an F-35 and two Super Hornets on HAVCAP with each tanker. The F-35 can use its DAS to watch for inbound missiles and bogeys and shoot them down. The F/A-18s can engage inbound bogeys that escape the F-35's missiles."

"Won't the F-35 and F/A-18s orbiting over an empty space on the radar tip off the Chinese that something is amiss?" Ricky asked.

"Yes, I think Ricky is right. I say we put the tankers up high where they normally are and assign a Raptor and an F-35 to each one." J.J. said. "I see no reason to increase the risk of tanking by doing it low where nobody has practiced it."

"I think that will ruin the surprise element of sending in the Super Hornets of the attack elements at the wavetops. They will have to pop up high to tank. They will be seen on radar then, and that will give away that they are coming in low because before they popped up, they had been invisible. That will tell the Chinese they are coming in low." Carmen pointed out.

"Good point. I say we put the F-22 and F-35 HAVCAP down low with the tanker and tank low. The tanker pilot can concentrate and not flying into the water, and the refueling jets just have to concentrate on the basket." J.J. said.

"OK we have a plan." Ricky said after a moment of final deliberation. "It has a lot of moving parts, and is not like anything the Navy or Marine Corps has ever done before, but this is a war we have never fought before. People are going to get killed, but if I may quote double Medal of Honor winner Gunnery Sergeant Dan Daley, 'Come on, you sons of bitches, do you want to live forever?'"

"Ooh Rah!" they all said in unison.

"Well done Marines." Ricky said smiling. "Let's run it by CAG and get him to sign off on it."

Eglin AFB, Two Days Later, 1830

Carmen knocked lightly on Captain Baker's door.

"Enter"

Carmen opened the door slowly and then stood in the doorway with the shortest, sexiest little black cocktail dress on that Captain Baker had ever seen.

"Dinner?"

"Alright Marines, here is the deal." Ricky was ignoring the fact that Neil "Nailgun" McAble, a Navy pilot was amoung the CAP pilots he had assembled for the HavCAP briefing on the night before the big raid was among them. Nailgun had attained honorary Marine status for a number of reasons.

"On Nailgun's raid, the Chinese came in with a stealth jet and knocked down the AWACs with an R-37 long range air-to-air missile. They fired it from 150 nautical miles in cruise glide profile, so the CAP jets never saw it coming and never saw the stealth jet the fired it. Neil's AWACs CAP was all F/A-18s so nobody had infrared capabilities like the F-35 to see the missile coming. The AWACs was down before anybody knew what was happening. They followed up with an 8-ship formation of Su-30 MKII Flankers, and took out the CAP Hornets who were outclassed by the superior Flanker high speed turn and supersonic maneuver performance along with its superior thrust-to-weight ratio and radar aperture. The Flankers the Chinese are flying have the AL-41F engines with 40,000 pounds of thrust with thrust vectoring which gives them the raw agility of the F-22. Hopefully, our F-22s hiding behind the Chinese airbases on the Andes side will take the Flankers by surprise and wipe them out. But just in case, they don't, here is what we are going to do in the AWACs CAP on this raid.

Ricky spent the next hour explaining the Doppler notch stealth flanking maneuver he had in mind, the detection ranges of the Flanker and J-20 stealth radars and the limits of their radar apertures in the forward and reverse directions and the plan for the fight.

CHAPTER 11

CHINA MEETS THE UNITED STATES MARINE CORPS

Ricky slipped into his torso harness and G-suit at 0430 on raid day. As he checked his survival radio and strapped put his pearl handled .45 into its chest holster, he thought about how long and hard he had worked to prepare for this day. Then he thought about all the good times he and J.J. and Carmen had had together as they struggled to overcome one challenge after another in their training. Their training as fighter pilots had taken almost 4 years. It was like being pumped by a pressure washer through a series of filters, each with smaller holes than the previous one. They had lost many colleagues and friends along the way to academic failure, physical injury, inability to meet physical or performance standards, failure to pass carrier qualification and fatal training accidents. It was a bonding experience like no other. Ricky stopped a moment to focus on his feelings. What he scared? Damn skippy. Would he fight? Without a doubt. Ricky's mind shifted for a moment to thoughts about the brave Marines who fought and died before him at Belleau Woods, Guadacanal, Tarawa, Iwo Jima, the frozen Chosin and Hue city. He had a feeling he was about to take part in another historic battle that would pass into Marine Corps legend.

At this point, Ricky had no delusions about God and country. He was going to fight and possibly die for his buddies. It was as simple as that.

Their plan had been approved by CAG, and the Air Force had done their part. Twenty four magnificent F-22 Raptors and four B1B Bones two of which were missile trucks had been snuck along the back side of the Andes and flown in the dead of night into the secret base in Argentina. The MARSOC teams had been listening in on Chinese radio communications, and the Chinese were unaware.

Carmen had performed her mission to Eglin flawlessly and came back with 6 modified HARMs and 12 VHF up-chirp radar transponders for the XB-47s. Feverish around the clock preparations were carried out to swap out electronics modules on the drones for the jamming and HARM SEAD mission. It was decided to not alter the XB-47 drones that were to emulate the F/A-18 attack elements, but simply to have them tow the same decoy the Super Hornet towed and lock it into emulation mode to simulate the heat signature and radar cross section of a Super Hornet. The modified HARMs were loaded on the SEAD element drones, and a towed decoy from an E2-C Hawkeye AWACs was incorporated into the XB-47 that would emulate the AWACs. Hellfire missiles were loaded onto the Predator C Avenger drones, and air-to-air AMRAAMs and Sidewinders were loaded onto the XB-47s that would carry out the sucker fight attack on the Flankers and J-20s from the West as they took off. All was ready.

. . .

"Cheetah 1, Aspen, sixteen bandits inbound, bullseye 084 at 45, angels 32, nose hot, 960 knots closure, Corvette, weapons free. Snap vector 290, buster, take angels 36. " the AWACS controller called warning Ricky and his Cheetah flight of the presence of enemy fighters inbound. The AWACs call told Ricky that the bandits were located on the 084 radial from Bullseye for 45 miles. Bullseye for this mission was the target warehouse about 10 miles from the Cheetah CAP's patrol position. The AWACs controller knew the position of bullsey would be entered in the Inertial Navigation System of the F/A-18s, and that the Hornet's mission computers would quickly calculate the offset and point their airborne radars toward the inbound bogeys. Her Corvette call was the day's brevity code and confirmed the radar signature of the inbound bandits confirmed them to be Chinese Su-30MK2 Flankers. Her "weapons free" call freed the Cheetahs to go weapons hot. "Snap vector 290, buster, take angels 36." meant she was vectoring the Cheetahs to a heading of two niner zero and she wanted them to go full afterburner and climb to 36,000 feet for the intercept.

The data from the AWACs was linked to the Cheetahs via the Link 16 Data Link, and showed up on their left DDI screens and in their HUDs. A compass rose with the scale picked by the AWACs to show the range to the bandits appeared in their HUDs. The snap vector heading was indicated by a double chevron next to the 290 heading number on the rose.

The real AWACS had joined them now that the attack on the XB-47 decoy had been attempted by the Chinese. This attack on the decoy gave away the position of their base of operations for the Stealth jets, which was one of the main objectives they were trying to accomplish. Not having an AWACs in the air now would put them at a serious disadvantage since information is king in air combat.

The Chinese were true to form. Just like in Neil's raid, they followed up the stealth jet attack on the AWACs with a flight of Flankers to take out the HAVCAP element. And they were screaming in supersonic in full burner.

All the pilots of Cheetah flight, upon receiving the AWACs call, simultaneously switched their APG-79 radars to air-to-air mode with a flick of their fingers on the HOTAS.

An ES-3 ELINT electronics intelligence jet monitoring the known Chinese tactical frequencies picked up chatter in Chinese that a mandarin speaking officer on the ES-3 translated. The Chinese knew that the attack on the AWACs had not yet been completed, and they had figured out that there were either two AWACs operating in the area or one of them was a decoy. They were vectoring the 16 Flankers toward the Cheetah HAVCAP. It was the job of these Flankers to wipe out Cheetah flight so the J-20 Stealth could finish off the AWACs. This information was linked on the encrypted Link 16 datalink to the AWACs and the Cheetahs who saw it on their DDI displays.

"Shit, they know they did not get the AWACs and are sending the Flankers in to take us out first." J.J. transmitted to nobody in particular.

"Stay tactical." Captain Ricky "Woody" Magnusson replied. He knew the Chinese were listening on their tactical strike frequencies and he did not want anybody giving them any valuable information.

"Roger that." J.J. transmitted and then dictated a text message and sent it to the Cheetahs over the encrypted data link. "I thought the Air Force Raptors were supposed to take out any Flankers from behind just after they took off."

"I thought so too. At least that was the plan. The Air Force must have screwed up. Wouldn't be the first time." Ricky texted dryly. "Combat spread, come left to 290, gate." Ricky transmitted. The Cheetahs spread out to about a mile apart, except for SWATs F-35 who remained in a very tight formation with Woody's Hornet. Each wingman dropped down 1500 feet from his section leader for mutual visual support allowing each pilot to check his wingman's six. All five planes turned to a heading of 290 and slammed their throttles into afterburner. What Woody did not know was that the Chinese had moved their Flankers during the night before the raid to a different airfield, so they did not take off on their mission to attack the AWACs from the field the Air Force Raptors assigned to take out the Flankers were watching.

Cheetah flight protecting the AWACS, having escaped a sneak attack by a Chinese J-20 stealth jet, now faced an even bigger challenge —a force of sixteen aerodynamically superior Chinese Su-30MK2 Flankers armed with long-range, radar-guided AA-10 Alamo missiles, AMRAAMskis, heat seekers and 30 millimeter cannons were inbound and intent on killing them. To further complicate the situation, the J-20 Stealth was still out there and still inbound. The XB-47 decoy plan was a good one, but things rarely go as planned in war. Their AWACs was still vulnerable if the Chinese could guess which radar return was the real AWACs.

. . .

(From the Mandarin.) "Rabbit one has four bogeys, 240 degrees, 67 kilometers, 10,600 meters, 814 kilometers per hour closure. Flight of four in combat spread." the Chinese leader of the sixteen Su-30MK2 Flankers of Rabbit flight called.

"Two concurs." the confidence of the Chinese pilots was now brimming. It was sixteen to four and they were in jets that were far more powerful and maneuverable than the outdated Super Hornets they were about to kill.

. . .

Two minutes that seemed like two seconds passed. The Hornets passive ALR-67 RHAW radar warning receivers were chirping now. The Flankers air-to-air radars were painting them. The Hornet air-to-air radars were also painting the Flankers, and the Chinese radar warning receivers were going off in the Chinese cockpits. The fight was on.

Woody centered his radar search on the vector indicated by the radar warning receiver. Contact. Ricky saw 16 blips show up on his right DDI display right where the AWACs said they would be. He made a mental note of their altitude, speed and heading. "Dash 2, search wide low and high. Dash 3, look for trailers." Ricky ordered.

"2"

"3"

"Nineteen miles. Action now." Woody called ordering the Cheetah Hornets to commence their plan. The Flankers were still out of visual range.

All four Hornets broke hard right to put the inbound Flankers on their 9 o'clock beam and dispensed a cloud of chaff and flares. SWAT rolled her F-35 inverted and pulled back on the stick to nose over into a vertical dive toward the ocean below. As she did so, she chopped her throttle to idle to reduce her heat signature. She was pulling a "Woody" to stay off the Chinese air-to-air search radars and get below their radar horizons.

WOODY EXPLAINED AS IMPROVED HAWK DIVE INTO DOPPLER NOTCH

A "Woody" was a tactic improved by Captain Ricky "Woody" Magnusson on a move first developed by Naval Aviator Lieutenant Commander John Monroe Smith, call sign "Hawk". Hawk's move was to dive vertically downward into the Doppler notch out of a very tight two-ship formation that looked like one target to the search radar of an inbound bogey. The search radars of the inbound Chinese Flankers would be operating in pulse Doppler mode so as to obtain the best radar picture for an intercept. Pulse Doppler mode also gave the least cluttered picture when the radar antenna was pointed below the horizon in a look-down, shoot-down fight. When the radar beam pointed toward the ground or the ocean, it picked up "ground" returns of stationary or slow objects such as rocks, cars, ships, etc. Because of the way the Pulse Doppler radar's filtering software works, all the ground returns are filtered out. But so were the returns of targets with the same relative velocity to the search radar host platform as stationary objects. That absence of returns where the stationary objects and zero relative velocity objects would have been is called the Doppler Notch.

Hawk's move was a clever ploy to exploit this weakness. A Hawk move set a trap for the inbound bogey by diving into his Doppler notch from a tight two-ship formation while still out of visual range of the bogey. This causes one ship to gain separation from the inbound bogey without being seen. It also sets a trap because the target the inbound bogey's is watching on his radar display does not disappear. The other ship of the two-ship was "bait". Since the Hawk move is commenced while still out of visual range, the inbound bogey has no idea there were two enemy fighters where he sees only one.

The Hawk move required a dive straight down toward the ocean floor or ground or a notch right or notch left turn at the same altitude as the inbound bandit or ballistic climb in the vertical to achieve zero relative velocity. The preferred move with a vertical dive toward the ocean. Climbing, or going left or right, provides an opportunity for the bandit pilot to see the jet executing the Hawk move. A vertical dive puts the jet into the bandit's visual blind spot below his nose and below the lower limits of the inbound bandit's radar aperture, called the radar horizon.

When the diving jet was far enough below the inbound bogey to be below the radar horizon, he levels off and flies toward the underside and rear of the inbound bandit. The radar horizon occurs because their are travel limits of the bogey search radar's mechanically moved antenna or the limits of an AESA radars electronic scanning of the radar beam. In other words, the search radar can only look down to a certain maximum angle. Once the stalking jet has climbed up to a position at close range behind and below the inbound bandit, the stalking jet lights up the bandit and he is toast.

The "Hawk" move worked well against older fighters like the F-14, F-16 and F-15 and even the older F/A-18s without IRST, but it needed updating against more modern fighters that have forward looking infrared systems.

To bring the Hawk move up to date, Ricky had studied the modern jets like the Chinese J-20 stealth jet and Su-30MK2 Flankers in great detail. These Chinese jets had passive electronically scanned array search radars which were electronically steered. The Russian radars the Chinese were flying have greater angles of coverage in both the horizontal and vertical planes than their mechanical predecessors. In addition, the Russian-designed SU-30MK2 Flankers have side looking radar and rearward looking radar, but, for some reason, the Chinese did not implement the rearward looking radar of the Russian Flankers they bought nor the Sino Flankers they built under manufacturing license from the Russians.

Both the Russian and Sino Flankers (J-11s) also have forward looking infrared search and track systems. Ricky knew that the Chinese-designed J-20 stealth jet had radar and IRST copied in large part from the Su-30MK2 Flankers China had purchased from Russia. That meant its IRST was forward looking only, and its forward and side looking radars had limits on how far down they could see —specifically the Russian radars had a 110 degrees vertical up scan and minus 55 degrees down scan. The forward-looking Flanker IRST was even worse. It could only look down minus 15 degrees. That meant there were big infrared and radar blind spots below and behind a Chinese Flanker and the J-20.

A "Woody" was a Hawk move which was modified in two ways. First, the bait jets dispensed a cloud of chaff and flares at the moment of departure of the ambush jet, and, second, the ambush jet lowered its heat signature by chopping its throttles to idle during the vertical dive in the Doppler notch. Key to the success of a Woody was for the jet assigned to carry out the ambush to dive out of a tight two-ship formation and out of the cloud of chaff and flares into the Doppler notch. This tactic meant the ambush jet would have never been seen by the approaching enemy because their radars were not good enough to distinguish the ambush jet from the bait jet to which it was flying very close. Diving into the Doppler notch kept the ambush jet off the enemy radar till it reached a point below the lower radar and IRST horizon with throttles chopped to idle so as to not be detected by the forward looking IRST or the Doppler radar. Woody's fellow pilots liked his modification of the Hawk move so much, they named it the "Woody".

. . .

(From the Mandarin) "The Hornets are breaking right. I show four targets. Rabbits 2 through 8 stay on me. Rabbits 9 through 16 break right and come up behind them. Rabbits 1 through 8 will shoot them in the face." Captain Chin Woo radioed on the Chinese tactical frequency. The individual pilots of Rabbit flight acknowledged the order. What they did not know was that SWAT was listening on her standby radio and could speak Chinese.

SWAT continued her screaming dive toward the ocean until she reached 6000 feet and then leveled off and located the Rabbit flight on her helmet mounted display from infrared DAS inputs. She was below the radar horizon now and in their radar and IRST blind spots. She was not worried that her stealth was compromised by her load of AIM-9X off-boresight sidewinders and Slammers on her external hard points. She had ten missiles to play with between her internal weapons bays and the external hard points. It was going to be a turkey shoot. She dictated a text message into her radio communications system and transmitted it on the encrypted data link to the Hornets describing the Chinese plan. She told Cheetah flight she was going to come up under Rabbits 9-16 and take them out, and received an acknowledgement by text.

The text message system via the Link 16 encrypted datalink was a new wrinkle developed after the Woody tactic became widely used in the Navy and Marine Corps to allow communications with the ambush jet without it being detected by any enemy operator listening on the U.S. jet's tactical frequency.

Carmen did some quick mental intercept calculations. She banked her F-35 over to an heading to intercept Rabbits 9-16 where they would be in two minutes. She cruised for a minute on that heading and then went to zone 5 afterburner and pulled her nose up into a ballistic climb headed for a point in front of her prey. As she climbed up underneath the 8 Flankers of the enveloping element of Rabbit flight, she went weapons hot and selected the first of her first eight AIM-120 AAMRAM slammers mounted on the external hard points. She slaved its seeker head to her DAS. As she reached 25,000 feet, SWAT designated each of Rabbits 9 through 16 in her helmet mounted display and selected, slaved and fired the first eight of her AAMRAMs in rapid succession. Carmen was a little less than 10,000 feet below the Flankers now, and the AIM-120 slammers took off like coyotes in a petting zoo. They were salivating for a kill and screaming up under the Flankers at Mach 4.

Never having used any on-board radar on her F-35, the Chinese pilots had no idea what was happening until the slammer's on-board radars went active and locked them up. Since a mach 4 AIM-120 covers 10,000 feet in 2.2 seconds, the Chinese pilots never knew what hit them. All eight of them erupted in massive fireballs. Carmen had to reef her jet over hard into a vertical dive to avoid sucking the debris into her engine. She was now an instant ace. It was time for her to execute a "shoot and scoot" before the other Flankers found her. She rolled inverted and did a split S to dive toward the ocean at a steep angle on a heading toward the rear of Rabbits 1-8. She was about 8 miles away from Rabbits 1-8, so it was doubtful they could see her. She chopped her throttle to idle and prayed they could neither see her nor pick her up on radar or IRST.

. . .

(From the Mandarin) "What the fuck just happened. Rabbits 9 through 16 just disappeared from my radar. Anybody else have them?" Captain Woo transmitted.

"Negative." came the replies.

"Anybody see what happened?"

"Negative. The Hornets did not fire upon them."

"Rabbits 7 and 8 go find whatever killed them." Captain Woo ordered.

"7, roger that."

. . .

"Cheetah 1, Aspen, the remaining bandits are splitting up. Two bandits breaking left, 250 for 15, nose cold. Six bandits 270 for 15, nose hot, closure 940 knots now, Cheetahs are weapons free." the AWACs controller called. There was about a minute to the merge.

"Nailgun, chase those two splitters down and take them out." Ricky transmitted. He knew SWAT was listening on the tactical frequency and knew that the two splitters were after her and that Woody had dispatched Neil "Nailgun" McAble to help her. "Cheetahs 2 and 3, come left to 270 and go weapons hot." Ricky commanded. It was now six Flankers versus three Hornets. SWAT had substantially improved the odds.

"2." Scud replied.

"3." Captain Tim "Tequila" Randall replied.

Nailgun broke left to go after the two splitters. As he broke, Nailgun transmitted "4 on it. Delta Bravo." He knew SWAT was listening, knew where he was and his heading and would know he wanted to do a "drag and bag".

SWAT transmitted an encrypted text message to Neil, "SWAT copies drag and bag. Be my hero." She could see the two Flankers had found her and were on an intercept course at 10 miles and that Nailgun was below and at their 3 o'clock. She broke hard left to put her on a heading that would drag them right in front of Nailgun and put him on their six.

Nailgun slammed the throttles of his F/A-18F Super Hornet into full afterburner and uncaged his first AMRAAM. His back seater, Lt. Tom "Squishy" Moore reported contacts for both Flankers on the APG-79 radar display. "The Flankers are turning to show us their sixes. They are fixated on SWAT and do not know we are here. 280 for 8 now. Come slightly right for the intercept." Squishy stated matter-of-factly over the intercom.

Suddenly, Squishy yelled into the radio, "We are being jammed!. It must be that J-20 Stealth. Negative contact." He knew SWAT was listening and might have the J-20 on her DAS infrared search and track system.

"305 for 20 Squishy." SWAT radioed finally breaking her radio silence.

"Roger that. Found him." Squishy transmitted.

"Shoot the Tailend Charlie Flanker as soon as you can get burn through." Nailgun said over the intercom.

At five miles, Squishy achieved burn through the jamming signal on the Hornet's radar. The powerful Hornet APG-79, with its huge Power Aperture Product, had defeated the Chinese Stealth jet's jamming and achieved lock on the trailing Flanker. Squishy selected an AAMRAAM , uncaged it and slaved its seeker head to the APG-79's target designation. As soon at the shoot indication appeared on the HUD, Nailgun fired. The missile jumped off the rail and streaked ahead to the Flanker. "Fox 3 Yippee Kay Yay. Greetings from the US of A motherfucker."

The panicked Chinese pilot was in a hard 7G turn and vapor clouds were roiling above his wings. Too late. He was in the zone of no escape. The missile warhead detonated right over his cockpit and cut his jet in half. The Chinese pilot was killed instantly.

The other Flanker, seeing his wingman disappear in a fireball, broke hard left then inverted and dove straight for the ocean below. He was giving up on bagging SWAT and was bugging out to save his own skin. "Your six is clear. Nailgun out."

"Ooohrah." Carmen yelled into her oxygen mask mike. "Lets go help Woody and the boys. 095 for 10, gate."

"Roger that. You have the lead. Cheetahs, Nailgun and SWAT are inbound buster." Nailgun transmitted on the mission tactical frequency as he slammed his Hornet into full afterburner.

"Roger that. We are in a world of hurt." Woody grunted as he squeezed his leg and butt muscles in the anti-G exercise. He was obviously in a high-g turn.

Ricky's flight of three were all in hard break turns trying to evade a salvo of AA-12 Adder affectionately known in the business AMRAAMskis fired by the inbound Flankers. Chaff clouds were puffing out of each jet as each new break turn was executed. The hard turns from 550 knots brought them quickly down to corner speed of 360 knots. That is exactly where they wanted to be for this fight. Even though the Flankers were aerodynamically superior in all respects, a Hornet at its corner speed of 360 knots is no slouch and turns well.

The situation was desperate. Ricky, J.J. and Tequila Tim were outnumbered two to one, already on the defensive and spending down their energy fast. "Use your Xray heaters to shoot down the Adders." Ricky grunted. It was a difficult decision. The Hornets did not carry as many missiles as the Flankers and the Sidewinders were precious. All three pilots looked at the inbound AMRAAM'skis with their helmet mounted sites, designated them for off-boresight shots and pickeled off a salvo of AIM-9X heat seeking Sidewinders. The focal plane array seeker heads of the Sidewinders immediately saw and locked the rocket motors of the inbound Adders and blew them out of the sky.

The Flankers were just outside 6 miles now. "Shoot them in the face with slammers." Ricky commanded.

The three Cheetah pilots all broke back hard onto a heading facing the inbound Flankers, flicked a finger on their sticks to select AMRAAMs, and flicked another finger on their HOTAS to put their radars in Raid Assessment Mode. Each radar automatically began seeking a lock on two of the Flankers while tracking the remainder. Each target's speed, altitude, range and heading were displayed on their HUDs. Dynamic missile launch zone and snapshot gunnery solutions are also computed and displayed by their mission computers. In seconds, all their radars locked, draw target indicator box in the HUD to show the pilots where to look, and all their radars flashed a "SHOOT" message in the HUD.

"Woody has the two southern bandits. Fox one." Ricky flicked the weapons select button and selected another slammer. "Fox one." The brilliant white-yellow plumes of flame of the rocket motors of his two AMRAAMs as they lept off the rails and streaked ahead at mach 4 lit the morning sky.

"Scud has the two northern bandits. Fox one. Fox one." J.J. said as he launched two slammers in quick succession.

"Tequila has the two in the middle." Two AMRAAMs lept off Tequila's rails.

The Flanker formation immediately scattered. Two of the Flankers broke in the same direction and collided in a fireball that could be seen even at 5 miles. "There they are Woody. 11 o'clock low." Scud called.

"Gate." Woody called. One more fireball erupted as one of the slammers connected.

The three Hornets all slammed their throttles into full afterburner, covered the remaining 5 miles in seconds, and dove into the scattering Flankers. The situation immediately turned into a wild furball with jets everywhere heading in all directions. Ricky took a Flanker up into the vertical in a rolling scissors hoping to outturn him with the superior low speed flight characteristics of the Hornet as both jets lost airspeed in the climb. The Flanker was outturning him in the scissors though, so Ricky flicked a finger on the stick to select another AIM-9X Sidewinder, looked at the Flanker 45 degrees off his nose, selected him and got good tone right away. He pressed his fire button and the heater jumped off the rail and streaked in a perfect lead pursuit arc toward the Flanker. The Flanker thrust vectored over into a vertical dive, but the drastic maneuver squandered all his energy and the Sidewinder flew right up one of his tailpipes and blew the tail off his jet. "Splash four." There were just two Flankers left now, but the Chinese J-20 stealth jet was still out there somewhere.

Ricky was startled out of his fascination with watching the Flanker disintegrate and the Chinese pilot eject by the screaming of his radar warning receiver. Somebody had a lock on him. Ricky immediately did a rudder reversal from his ballistic climb and saw a heat-seeking A-11 Archer fly by his canopy seconds later. The Chinese missile had mistakenly locked onto the sun when Ricky turned his exhaust skyward with the rudder reversal. But now he was faced with a Flanker in full burner screaming up at him. "One is spiked."

To his amazement, the Flanker screaming up at him disappeared in a fireball. "Splash five." Scud transmitted with cool aplomb. J.J. "Scud" Saleen was in a wild horizontal scissors with Flanker #6 2000 feet below Flanker number 5 who was climbing after Ricky. While so engaged, he had somehow managed to glance at the ballistic Flanker in burner, uncage an AIM-9X Sidewinder, get tone and fire an off-boresight heater shot. His amazing flying had taken out the ballistic Flanker and saved Ricky.

But now Ricky could see J.J. was in deep shit. The Flanker was outturning Scud and, in a couple more turns, the Flanker would be in the envelope for a shot at J.J. Ricky lit his burner and screamed straight down toward the Flanker with which Scud was engaged. Closing to guns range, Ricky transmitted, "Break out left Scud and drag this guy in front of me. I will take him out with my 20 mike mike."

"Breaking left."

Ricky's mission computer gave him a guns solution and he pressed the guns trigger on his stick. A short burst of 20 millimeter cannon shells arced gracefully through the sky and crashed through the Flanker canopy. The inside of the canopy turned red as the Chinese jet blew up in a huge yellow and white fireball. Ricky jinked hard right to avoid sucking fragments of the Flanker into his intakes. "Splash six." Ricky transmitted.

Just as the word six came out of his mouth, Ricky saw some tracers fly by his canopy. He spun his head around to see another Flanker drop into his six at 6000 feet. He was moving his nose around for another guns solution. "Fuck" Ricky screamed. It was the runner. He had re-engaged. Ricky only had seconds to live.

Instinctively, Ricky yanked the stick back into his lap, kicked full left rudder and slammed the stick over into full left aileron and flicked the speed brakes button. Instantly, his Hornet snapped into a high G barrel roll and shed a massive amount of airspeed while flying a longer path than the Flanker. The surprised Chinese pilot saw he was going to overshoot, and pulled up into a Pugashev Cobra attempting to slam the brakes on. But he was too late. His Flanker shot out in front of Ricky's jet just as it pulled up into the Cobra. The Flanker pilot, having blown all his kinetic energy in the Cobra, hung suspended momentarily in space right under Ricky's pipper. The Chinese pilot looked up through the top of his canopy with fear in his eyes just in time to see Ricky's 20 mm shells crash through his canopy and explode inside him. "Splash seven."

"Cheetah 1, Aspen, four new bandits inbound, 290 for 10, angels 25, nose hot, take angels 28, snap vector 110, buster, missiles in the air." the AWACs controller announced. Ricky looked around for Scud and Tequila and found them at 2 o'clock low. A second later, Tequila's jet exploded in a massive fireball as a Chinese AMRAAM'ski connected.

"SWAT and Nailgun, say status. We have four new bandits." Ricky and J.J. both notched vertically and dispensed chaff and flares as they rolled inverted, did a split S and dove vertically for the land below trying to avoid the inbound missiles. Ricky grunted as he pulled maximum G. Both Ricky and J.J. dove down to 28,000 where they pulled out on the 110 intercept heading. "Tequila is down."

"Cheetah 1, Nailgun and SWAT inbound, we will be there in two mikes. Do you want us to call the rescue helo?" Carmen transmitted.

"Negative, no chute. Call Chisel SWAT." Ricky transmitted. He was telling Carmen that Tequila had not survived and that Chisel, the B1B missile truck had arrived on station.

"Roger that. Missiles signatures are Adder, now five miles." Carmen acknowleged.

"Great, four more AMRAAM-skis inbound." Ricky thought to himself.

"Two is spiked." J.J. transmitted.

Ricky snapped his head around and saw a Flanker two miles behind and below J.J.'s jet. Worse, he saw another Flanker in guns range on his six. The Chinese were flying a sucker fight. "We've got two trailers Scud. The 4 new bandits are a decoy. Missile in the air! Notch right. I have your six." Tracers flew by Ricky's canopy to the right. "Woody engaged with one of the trailers." Ricky grunted as he broke hard left and punched the chaff and flares button on his HOTAS. The Flanker on his six followed easily. Ricky immediately broke hard right at 7 Gs. Ricky looked out the top of his canopy and saw J.J. break hard right in a cloud of chaff and flare. The communist missile's guidance system of the closest missile went stupid in the cloud of chaff and flares and flew by J.J's jet. Ricky saw that the Flanker on J.J.'s six had turned with J.J. That was a big mistake. The Flanker's big afterburners were glowing white hot against the cool sky, and J.J.'s pursuer was only 6000 feet away from Ricky's jet now. Ricky selected an AIM-9X and stared at the burners in his helmet mounted display to select it as the target as he uncaged the sidewinders's seeker head. The AIM-9X gave him tone right away, and he pulled the trigger. The heater streaked off the rail and flew right up the Flanker's right tailpipe 2 seconds later. The Chinese jet exploded in a massive fireball as both AL-41F turbofans disintegrated and ignited the fuel tanks.

Chunk, chunk, chunk…. Ricky looked out at his right wingtip and noticed it had been shredded by his pursuer's 30 mm cannons. He snapped his head around and saw that the Flanker was only 2000 feet behind him now. Instantly, he flicked his fly-by-wire system override on, pulled the stick back into his gut, banked slightly right and kicked full bottom rudder. Ricky's canopy was filled with sky then earth as his Hornet pitched up violently then nosed down in a half cartwheel. The violent maneuver threw the Hornet's entire planform into the slip stream to act as a massive speed brake. The Hornet shed 300 knots of airspeed almost instantaneously and probably overstressed itself in the process. Ricky neutralized the stick to stop the cartwheel, and sat in awe as his jet hung in the air momentarily at almost zero airspeed then began plunging toward the earth in full burner to regain flying speed. The startled Flanker pilot, completely unprepared for this violent maneuver, flew right by him. Ricky pulled up his nose after he had lost 5000 feet but gained his energy back. He did a chandelle in the direction he last saw the Flanker flying.

Ricky had just re-acquired the Flanker when he saw tracers coming from its left impacting the Flanker amidships. It blew up spectacularly. Ricky looked left and saw J.J. doing a victory roll.

"Splash seven."

"Cheetah-1, Aspen, two Ghosts inbound, 240 at 4." The Air Force had finally showed up. Ghost was the brevity code for Air Force F-22s.

Boom! Boom! Boom! Boom! The four inbound AMRAAM-skis blew up two miles from their position as four AIM-9Xs from a flight of two Air Force F-22 Raptors intercepted them.

"Cheetahs, Dusty-1, we have Aspen. You take care of those Flankers." the Air Force flight leader called.

"Dusty-1, thanks for the help." Ricky replied.

Chunk, chunk, chunk, chunk. Ricky looked out the right side of his canopy just in time to see his right wing fold in half after taking four 30 mm cannon rounds. His Hornet started a violent roll to the right and began to cartwheel and dive for the earth picking up speed every second. Ricky struggled to reach the eject handle in the high G load of the wildly spinning jet. He could see the sun flashing by his canopy then the dense green of the terrain below and then the sun again. It was all he could do, but finally he got both hands on the eject handle and pulled.

The rocket motor in his ejection seat erupted, and he smashed through the canopy into the 550 knot slipstream. His head, which had been bobbing around like a bobble head doll in the violent gyrations of the jet, smashed back against the seat and his helmet shattered and pieces of it blew away. He felt an intense pain in his skull, and his legs, which also had been flopping around the cockpit, were now broken as were two of his ribs. He passed out from the pain only to come back to consciousness a minute later. He looked up and saw a beautiful chute. The ejection seat had worked as advertised. He passed out again.

"Nailgun, Woody must have been hit. He just disappeared off my DAS picture." Carmen transmitted to Neil.

"Looking." Neil transmitted back indicating he was looking for a parachute indicating Ricky had safely ejected. They were still out of visual range of where Ricky's jet had been hit. They flew on for a couple of minutes.

"Good chute! Woody may be alive. I am transmitting the grid to SAR." Carmen transmitted indicating she was transmitting Ricky's position to the Search and Rescue forces that were orbiting off-shore.

When Ricky woke up, he was hung up in a tree with his mangled legs dangling 3 feet off the ground and useless. He head throbbed like there was a Led Zeppelin concert going on inside his skull. Slowly his eyes came into focus, and he saw the nose section of a crashed Flanker about 75 yards away from his tree. There was a red dragon painted on it. Then he noticed a Chinese pilot walking toward him with a knife in his hand. It was Captain Woo, PLAAF. He was going to kill Ricky.

Ricky felt for his chest holster. It was still there, and his pearl handled .45 service revolver was still in it. He furtively flicked the safey off and unsnapped the hold down. The Chinese pilot was still 50 yards away now. "Holy fucking shit, this is not the way I want to go out." Ricky thought to himself. He still had unfinished business. He thought about his rough childhood growing up in Michigan and all the struggles he had gone through to make it through college, OCS, the Basic School, Pensacola, the jet pipeline and F/A-18 finishing school. Nope, this motherfucker was not going to take him out. The Chinese pilot was only 15 yards away now and sprinting toward him brandishing his knife wide-eyed with a twisted look of rage on his face. Like a Cobra, Ricky pulled his pistol from his chest holster, steadied it for a second and then shot Captain Woo right in the face. Woo's brains exploded out the back of his head as the big .45 caliber slug crashed into his forehead and disintegrated his skull both going in and coming out the other side.

CARMEN'S FURBALL

"Cheetah-5 is spiked!" Carmen yelled into her radio. Her radar warning receiver was shrieking. Nothing on my radar yet."

"Cheetah-6 is spiked. No joy." Neil transmitted as his radar warning receiver also went off. Neil also had no return on his radar.

"Anybody have a visual?" Carmen's voice was tense. This wasn't Top Gun any more. It was real. A Chinese stealth fighter had her jet and Neil's jet locked up on his radar and was about to kill both of them. The fear was evident in her voice.

"Negative, no joy." J.J. acknowledged.

"Nailgun has your six. I am going to stay and take out these new guys." J.J. transmitted.

"Roger that." Carmen acknowledged. They were on their own.

"Found him." Carmen exclaimed as the stealth jet popped up on her DAS picture. "J-20 is Bulleye for 15 at 320, mach 1.3 closure, angels 24." They were over land now south of the target area, and the Chinese stealth jet was about 10 miles from their position. It was a perfect setup. Carmen and Neil knew that the Chinese jet's radar was not good enough to paint them individually from that distance since they were in a tight two-ship. To the Chinese jet, they looked like one target.

"Woody time." Neil texted Carmen in case the Chinese were listening on their tactical frequeny.

"Roger Woody." Carmen dictated a text back.

CARMEN DEFEATS J-20 WITH A
VERTICAL ROLLING SCISSORS

The Chinese J-20 stealth was a huge airplane tipping the scales at 80,000 pounds. It had a long combat range and very low radar cross section having been designed with stolen F-22 Raptor and F-35 technology. The Chinese liked to use it to sneak up on high value targets like AWACs and tankers and shoot them down since these targets were indispensable components of any air superiority fight. But first, it had to get past the HAVCAP patrol to get to the AWACs. But at 80,000 pounds, it could not turn and burn with a Hornet or even an F-35. Stealth was its only advantage. It was not a dogfighter.

Neil still had no return on his radar, but he was receiving targeting information via Link 16 from Carmen's DAS system. Neil designated the stealth jet in his helmet mounted sighting system, flicked a finger to select an AMRAAM and pickeled it off the rail to give the Chinese stealth pilot something to think about. "Fox 3." Nailgun transmitted to let SWAT know he had just launched a radar guided missile. By designating it on his helmet mounted sight, he had downloaded Carmen's infrared target return into the AMRAAMs guidance computer as its

Initial Point. When the missile got to this IP, its own radar would activate and may even lock up the J-20 since even stealth jets have radar returns when the radar is close enough to them.

RUSSIAN RADAR ANTENNA ELEVATION LIMITS

The inbound Chinese stealth jet was about 6 miles now. When Nailgun launched his missile, the J-20 broke hard into the missile's Doppler notch and dispensed a cloud of chaff and flares. Carmen knew that he could not see her yet visually. She also knew that with an F-35 radar cross section the size of a metal golf ball, with his Russian-designed NIIP N-011M BARS hybrid passive electronically scanned array radar operating in pulse Doppler mode, he would not be able to paint her when she dived into the Doppler notch.

Carmen looked over at Nailgun, gave him the kiss off sign, rolled her jet inverted, chopped the throttle to idle to reduce her infrared signature and pulled the stick back into her lap to commence a vertical dive toward Brazil below. The jet picked up speed fast as it plunged at 10,000 feet per minute. She knew the Chinese phased array main lobe radar beam could only be steered negative 55 degrees in elevation, and it would be searching high since the AWACs and its HAVCAP element had all been higher than the J-20. When she was at 2,000 feet, 20,000 feet below the inbound Chinese stealth jet, she leveled off, slammed the throttle up to zone 5 burner, and went into an almost ballistic climb toward the J-20's control zone on his rear quarter.

STOLEN F-35 FILES SALTED WITH BAD DOPE TO MAKE TAIL NOT STEALTHY

"Ok you communist prick, I've got your balls in my nutcracker now." Carmen thought to herself. She watched him on her Distributed Aperture System as he flew toward and above her still unaware of her presence. He had successfully dodged the AMRAAM, but now he was hunting for her. She knew that the J-20 was not radar stealthy from the rear quarter. The NSA knew the Chinese were stealing design files of the F-35 and had set a trap for them.

The files specifying the F-35 tail design the Chinese had stolen from the F-35 contractors had been salted with bad dope by the NSA. The files looked like a legitimate design, but the Chinese did not know the design was not stealthy to the L-band radars that had secretly been installed in the leading edges of the F-35's wings. Most fighter's radars were X-band. But the stolen tail design for the J-20 was highly visible to the super-secret leading edge L-band radar incorporated into the later versions of the F-35 one of which Carmen was flying. The Chinese pilot might as well have fired off a starburst flare to the L-band radar.

Carmen knew she would be able to get a good lock on the Chicom pilot with a radar-guided AMRAAM with a rear quarter shot if she needed it, but she did not want to light up her radar and give away her position. She wanted to make a stealthy approach using only her DAS.

She continued to climb and close the distance to the J-20 with her radar off. She knew that the initial position to which the AMRAAM flew before it turned on its own terminal guidance radar could be supplied by her infrared search and track DAS system, so she did not need her radar anyway since she had a good target display on her DAS.

This was going to be a complete stealth intercept. The idea in modern air combat is not to get in a fair fight. The main operating principle is to get in as unfair a fight as possible and kill the enemy pilot quickly before he is even aware of your presence. Modern aerial combat is like a knife fight in a phone booth. With stealth jets, it is like a knife fight at night in a blacked out phone booth. However, the Communist was the only one who was blind in this fight. Carmen knew right where he was.

When Carmen approached minimum range for an AMRAAM shot, she stared at the J-20 target in her helmet mounted display and selected the J-20 as the target. She immediately selected an AMRAAM as the weapon of choice which caused her on-board computer to feed the J-20's position on her DAS into the AMRAAM as the initial point to which it would fly.

Carmen continued her climb. When she was about 5000 feet below the Chinese J-20 Stealth jet and in heater range, she selected an AIM-9X heat seeking Sidewinder and uncaged the focal plane infrared seeker head. She immediately got tone with the Sidewinder growling in her helmet having locked on to the J-20's hot exhaust. She punched the fire button and called "Fox two" on the radio indicating she had just unleashed a heat seeking missile. Carmen then re-selected the AIM-120 AMRAAM. She put it into visual range dogfight mode to activate its on-board terminal guidance radar immediately. She saw that it had locked on so she pickled it and watched if leap off the rail and streak ahead.

"Fox Three."

She knew that the AMRAAM terminal guidance radar would set off the J-20 radar warning receiver. The Chinese pilot would shit his pants when he heard that. He would be too preoccupied to launch any missiles of his own while trying to evade the inbound missiles. From 5000 feet, the missiles would take less than two seconds to send him to hell.

Suddenly, the Communist pilot did a split-S and dove vertically down toward her, punched off a cloud of chaff and flares and fired two heat seekers of his own. The Communist heat seekers locked on the AMRAAM and AIM-9X immediately and blew them up just as the J-20 flashed by her cockpit.

Carmen immediately did a rudder reversal and dove after the J-20. They dove together for 10,000 feet with the communist pilot breaking hard left and then right to keep her from getting a guns solution. She was Winchester on missiles now, so guns were the only thing she had left to fight with.

The airspeed was building rapidly and the jets plunged toward earth in full afterburner. The communist pilot could not get her off his tail. Just as she was closing on him to get within guns range, he pulled up into a ballistic climb pulling a massive amount of g's. Carmen followed suit and the fight turned into a rolling vertical scissors.

The communist pilot had made a major mental error. At 80,000 pounds and higher wing loading than the much lighter F-35, the communist could neither turn and burn with Carmen nor outclimb her. He would run out of energy in the climb and stall before Carmen's F-35 did. At every rolling turn in the vertical scissors Carmen gained some angle on the communist. She could see he was about to run out of energy and stall, when suddenly he nosed over and started another vertical dive. Huge mistake. Carmen slammed full left rudder, nosed over and lined him up in her HUD gunsight. She selected guns, and when the HUD gave her the shoot signal, she squeezed the trigger. The armor-piercing, incendiary 25 mike mike shells from her Equalizer cannon ripped into the communist pilot's red hot engines. He blew up like a bottle rocket.

"Splash 7. Adios you communist prick. Greetings from the U.S. of Fucking-A." Captain Carmen "SWAT" Nicoise, USMC radioed.

FOUR FLANKERS INBOUND

"Cheetahs, Aspen. Pop up targets! Four bandits, nose hot, Bullseye 090 for 21, angels 24, Corvette. Weapons free. Snap vector 080."

"Roger that Aspen." J.J. radioed.

"Cheetahs, 080, arm them up. Gate." Captain "Scud" Saleen called. The Cheetah flight Super Hornets and the F-35 were all data linked to the AWACs radar, and, after a slight pause, what the AWACs controller was seeing on her radar showed up in the radar displays of Cheetah flight. They all turned to the intercept course and went to zone 5 burner.

"Three has them. 4 o'clock low, 20 miles." "Batboy" radioed.

"Five."

"Six."

"Papa John. Three on me, Five and Six break right. Cheetah-5, shoot-and-scoot. We have your six. Scud out.". Captain Saleen's radioed instructions called for a pincer attack with himself and Cheetah-3, Batboy Anderson, breaking left and SWAT and Nailgun, to break right. He was also ordering Cheetah–5, Captain Carmen SWAT Nicoise to blow straight through the fight and take out as many Flankers as she could with off-boresight AMRAAM missile shots and then get out of town on full afterburner.

"Five is Winchester. Missile truck." Carmen radioed. Indicating she was out of missiles and would engage the on-call B1B bomber carrying a boatload of AMRAAMs to fire missiles at targets she selected.

"Hammer-1, Cheetah-2, standby for engagement. Link to Cheetah-5."

"Hammer-1 roger that." the bone pilot acknowledged.

The pincers attack would force the enemy force to divide. If all four Flankers broke after one of the pincer elements, they would be exposing their hot tailpipes to the infrared heat seeking missiles of the other element of the pincers attack.

"Cheetah-3, Scud. Go to combat spread. Come left to 350." Scud ordered. He wanted to put the Flankers on his right wingtip to steer into their doppler notch and reduce Cheetah flights closing velocity toward the Flankers to the speed of the Flankers themselves. This would reduce the returns the Flanker's pulse doppler search radars would generate."

"Three."

"Cheetah-5 has visual. Chinese Mike Kilo 2 Flankers. 4 o'clock low, 6 miles now." Carmen was looking at a magnified infrared video display of the Flankers taken by one of the infrared cameras in her

DAS system. "They know we are here. They just came right a little bit for the intercept."

"Cheetah flight, break now." J.J. radioed to start the pincers attack. Cheetah flight broke into two pincer elements to envelope the six inbound Flankers.

The Flankers immediately responded by breaking into two segments, each segment setting a course for high aspect intercepts with the pincer segment of Super Hornets on their side of the formation.

"Cheetah-5 has them at 4 miles now. Cover my six Nailgun, or I won't let you play golf with Ricky anymore."

"Roger that. He cheats anyway." replied Neil.

Carmen chuckled under her oxygen mask as she designated the two Flankers inbound toward her element as targets for two AMRAAM missiles from the Bone. "Hammer-1, Cheetah-5, linking two targets now. Shoot when acquired.

"Hammer-1, Fox Three." Two slammers were in the air.

"Groovy. Nailgun, combat spread. Give them some heaters to think about when they are in the envelope." Swat advised Nailgun who immediately backed off in trail in a loose deuce out two miles and 1500 feet above Carmen's jet. The two-mile trailing position insured Nailgun himself would not become a target for the for the AMRAAMs.

The two inbound Flankers broke hard and ejected chaff and flares when they detected the inbound slammers. Their wingtip mounted Sorbtsiya-S mid/high band defensive radar jammers also automatically lit up their steerable wideband phased arrays in an attempt to provide cross-eye jamming of the AMRAAM terminal guidance radars.

SWAT and Nailgun intercepted the two Flanker from the Flanker's 9 o'clock position. When the Flankers broke into them and away from the slammers, Carmen and Neil pulled up slightly, rolled in the opposite direction to the Flankers turn, put their lift vectors on the fleeing Flankers and pulled hard in a classic displacement roll attack to put them on the Flanker's tails.

The barrel roll attack put them right on the Flanker's tails. With their jets pointed downhill, SWAT and Nailgun gained fast on the Flankers who had been dissipating energy fast in their hard break turns. The slammers went stupid when they got hit by the cross-eye jamming and missed.

At a mile and a half behind the Flankers, Nailgun went to work designating his targets, selecting his Sidewinders and uncaging their infrared seeker heads. Neil got tone on one heater right away, and mashed the pickle button to launch it. The Sidewinder jumped off the rail and took off like a hound in heat. "Fox 2." Nailgun sounded excited. Maybe one of these commies was the one who shot him down earlier.

Neil got tone in the other Sidewinder at 5000 feet and pickled it. "Fox 2." Both SWAT and Nailgun rolled inverted and did a split-S to extend. Carmen designated the two Flankers again and linked the data to the Bone missile trucks fire control computers. "Hammer, Cheetah-5, standby to receive two more targets. Fire at will."

"Fox 3, salvo of two." the Bone Weapons System Officer radioed.

The two Flankers were now maneuvering violently to evade the inbound Sidewinders and the inbound AMRAAMs. The sky was festive with hot burning flares and tinsel chaff as each Flanker launched its countermeasures while jinking wildly. Carmen's systems indicated the Flanker electronic countermeasure jamming transmissions were now in panic mode.

Carmen strained to look up through the top of her cockpit bubble while pulling up from the split-S. Just as she located one of the Flankers, it was blown to bits as one of Neil's sidewinders crashed through the hot sunlight glint coming off the Flanker's canopy. The Sidewinder had locked onto the hot sun reflection from the Flanker canopy, and flew right through it.

Carmen also saw one or the Bone's AMRAAMs fly into the air intake of the second Flanker causing it to erupt in a brilliant fireball as the AMRAAM fragmentation warhead exploded inside one of the Flanker's massive engines.

Just then Neil noticed two launch plumes from another Flanker that had snuck into the fight. He designated it in his helmet mounted sight and uncaged a Sidewinder and got tone. He pickeled it off and pressed his mike button.

"SWAT, we have a trailer. Missiles in the air. Fox two."

"Roger that."

Nailgun's Sidewinder missed. Carmen thought he must have done something extraordinary to evade it.

She was right. What had actually happened was the Flanker had performed a Somersault to suddenly bleed off all his airspeed and stop his forward motion just as the Sidewinder got close. That was a maneuver only the super maneuverability of the Flanker enabled. The sudden loss in airspeed and the Flanker's change in position from where the Sidewinder guidance system had calculated it would be at intercept exceeded the Sidewinder's ability to correct and caused the missile to overshoot.

Meanwhile, the AN/ASQ-239 Barracuda electronic warfare suite on Carmen's F-35 merged the infrared and RF sensor data and analyzed the heat signatures of the two inbound Chinese missiles and identified them. The Barracuda automatically launched flare and chaff countermeasures and started jamming transmissions to spoof the inbound missiles. The Barracuda system indicated one missile was an R-77 Adder AMRAAM-ski radar-guided missile and the other was an R-73 Archer heat seeker. "The guys must have been trained by the Russians." Carmen thought to herself. It was a typical Russian tactic to launch multiple missiles with different types of seeker heads in a dogfight. This made it much harder for the target to maneuver to escape.

"One Adder, one Archer. Notch vertical. Decoys out." Carmen transmitted to Neil.

Carmen and Neil both immediately rolled inverted and pulled the stick back to commence a vertical dive into the doppler notch of the Adder and cut their engines to idle to reduce her heat signature while gaining as much energy as possible in the circumstances. Carmen's Barracuda system automatically deployed her ALE-55 towed decoy which began emitting spoof radar pulses to trick the AMRAAM-ski into thinking she was someplace she was not. The combination of the strong signals from the towed decoy plus the weakened signal from Carmen's stealthy F-35 flying vertically downward in the doppler notch caused the AMRAAM-ski to lock onto the decoy and destroy it.

Just then she noticed J.J.'s Super Hornet flash into the fight supersonic on full burner and go ballistic right up into the sun. She saw the inbound Archer heat seeking missile lock onto his afterburner and turn upward about 10,000 feet behind him.

"The Archer is locked on you now Scud. Ricky Ricardo." Carmen was referring to the rudder reversal move they had learned in RAG training. This deadly move was an energy fighter's best friend. It was loosely attributed to "Hawk" Smith. But Hawk admitted in his biography, which J.J. had read during RAG training, that the rudder reversal was actually invented by Vietnam era tactics designers who were trying to invent tactics for the F-4 Phantom to be used against the aerodynamically superior MIG-21.

"Roger that. Way ahead of you." J.J., seeing that he had a significant separation from the climbing heater, immediately yanked his throttles back to idle and did a rudder reversal by deflecting his rudder full right. This flipped the Super Hornet end-for-end and put the hot end up and away from the heat seeker. The Archer now could only see the blazing sun and J.J.'s cold nose in its liquid-nitrogen-cooled thermal eye. It locked onto the hot sun, and went stupid as it continued its ballistic flight upward past J.J. till its rocket motor burned out.

Carmen went to full afterburner as soon as she saw the Archer turn upward. She was still flying straight down and building kinetic energy fast. Her IRST now showed that the Flanker that had not been destroyed by Neil's Sidewinder was now diving to intercept her. Fortunately, for Carmen, the Flanker had expended all his kinetic energy in the Somersault he used to evade her Sidewinder, so he was at an energy disadvantage. SWAT quickly built airspeed and kinetic energy in her dive, but the Flanker was building energy too. Luckily, she had a good head start on him. SWAT pulled up to level out at the wavetops and attempted to extend away from the pursuing Flanker. She was outside his infrared missile and guns range now, and he was having trouble locking up her stealthy F-35 with his radar to enable a radar-guided missile shot. But the Flanker had a better thrust-to-weight ratio than her jet, and was closing the gap fast for a guns kill

Just then she saw J.J.'s jet scream by her in the opposite direction headed right for the Flanker and about 1000 feet above him. "J.J., you magnificent bastard. I know exactly what you are doing. I read your book." Carmen transmitted to nobody in particular.

J.J. was supersonic now. The Flanker was still trying to re-build its energy lost in the Somersault. As they closed on the merge, J.J. noticed the Chinese pilot begin a lead turn pull up to try to get a guns snapshot at the merge. J.J. observed that the Chinese pilot had waited too long and that he would not be able to obtain enough lead for the snapshot. Now confident, J.J. pulled up into the vertical zoom climb at a sustained G just as he got close to guns range. J.J. looked out the side of his canopy to see if the Chinese communist pilot had taken the bait. He had.

The Flanker pilot had decided to break off his pursuit of Swat and pulled up into the vertical to chase J.J. "Thank you very much Captain Dong. That is exactly what I thought you would do. Going ballistic is going to be your last mistake." J.J. thought to himself. Carmen's attitude had rubbed off on him.

J.J. continued to gain altitude and lose airspeed in his climb, while he watched the Flanker pursue him upward. The mistake the Flanker pilot had made is that he failed to assess J.J.'s energy state and his own before he pulled up into the vertical. Since J.J. had substantially more airspeed and a 1000 foot altitude advantage, the Flanker had not only less kinetic energy to start the climb, but also had to make a sharper pull up for the guns snapshot when he realized he was late. That is why J.J. chose to come to the merge with a slight altitude advantage. The Flanker's higher G pull up into the vertical bled even more energy off. Despite the Flanker's thrust-to-weight ratio advantage over the Super Hornet, the Flanker was going to run out of energy before J.J. did in the ballistic climb.

As J.J. continued his zoom climb, he pulled his nose slightly past the vertical and flew to a position almost directly above the Flanker. J.J. had enough vertical separation to be out of guns range of the Flanker. J.J. kicked is rudder to put the Flanker on his right wingtip. This presented the Flanker with a profile view which made it harder for the Flanker to see J.J.'s jet. J.J. continued to look down through his canopy. Then he saw the sight he had been waiting for. The Flanker had lost most of its airspeed and was in danger of departing controlled flight. The Flanker did a rudder reversal to a vertical dive out of a near stall. "There he goes." J.J. thought to himself as the Flanker's nose started to fall through the horizon.

J.J. quickly kicked his rudder to complete the rudder reversal and pull his nose down toward the Flanker. He lit the afterburner, selected guns and checked the range to the Flanker quickly. The Flanker started to fill his windscreen. J.J. put the guns pipper just ahead of the Flanker's nose and pulled the trigger as he walked the pipper back across the Flanker's entire fuselage. BRRRAAAAAAP. The 20 mm canon shells erupted from the gatling gun in his nose and raked the Flanker. When they hit the canopy, the Chinese pilot's body exploded into a molten mass of protoplasm and coated the inside of the plexiglass in bright red blood. "Splash whatever."

"Aspen, Cheetahs five and six are bingo. Say picture."

"Cheetahs five and six, Aspen. Two bandits 060 for 10 engaged with Cheetah 3. Cheetah-2, snap vector 060. Ghosts inbound. Texaco 095 for 40."

Scud rolled his jet to 060 and went to zone 5 burner. It was a two v. one engagement between Batboy Anderson and the remaining two Flankers. Batboy was in deep shit.

"SWAT and Nailgun, tank. I have Batboy. Dusty-1, Cheetah-2, say intentions." J.J. transmitted on the strike tactical frequency.

"Cheetah-2, Dusty-1, delta baker. Light them up, then come to 060." the lead F-22 pilot said. He was calling for a drag and bag with Scud as bait.

J.J. got to the furball just in time to see Batboy's Hornet dodge a Vympel R-73 heat seeker, aka Archer with a slick last minute rudder reversal into the missile from a ballistic climb into the sun after deployment of flare countermeasures. Batboy went to full afterburner and unloaded his jet in the dive in a defensive move to extend the distance between his jet and the pursuing Flanker and to rebuild his kinetic energy as soon as possible. The Flanker also did a rudder reversal, lit his afterburner and dove after Batboy trying to close for a guns kill.

"Batboy, Scud. I just got here. He is gaining on you. Highroll him and spit him out." J.J. radioed suggesting to Batboy he do a high G barrel roll underneath to cause the rapidly gaining Flanker to overshoot.

"Roger that. Shoot him in the face to give him something to think about." Batboy suggested. Batboy wanted J.J. to enter the fight on a reciprocal heading and make a high speed merge with the Flanker from head on and shoot a missile at him before the merge.

"Negative. Delta Baker on 060 for Dusty."

"Roger." Batboy pulled a hard turn to 060 and the Flanker followed him.

Batboy waited for the Flanker to close to just outside guns range and for his airspeed to decay in the high G turn to 250 knots. As soon as he hit 250 knots, Batboy pulled big back pressure, put in right aileron and stomped on the bottom rudder and held it at full deflection all the way around the barrel roll. His Hornet shed a major chunk of airspeed and flew a corkscrew path which has less axial displacement than he would have had flying at 250 knots.

The Flanker was caught by surprise, and overshot Batboy. Just then the Flanker pilot noticed J.J.'s Super Hornet bearing down on him from the opposite direction and had a moment of indecision. That was his last mistake. While he was pondering what to do about J.J., Batboy got his pipper on him from the Flanker's six, selected guns and mashed the trigger. BRRRAAAAAP. The 20 mm cannon shells ripped the Flanker's right wing off, and he went into a violent roll.

"Fucking American capitalist dogs. I spit on your mother's grave." the Chinese pilot transmitted in broken English as he spun toward the sea below.

"Blow me you little prick." Batboy transmitted in Mandarin. Who knew.

Batboy watched as the canopy exploded off the Flanker and the Chinese pilot's ejection seat rocketed out of the cockpit.

"Holy shit Batboy. I didn't know you spoke Mandarin."

"Rosetta Stone."

"Fuck! A trailer! 12 o'clock, weeds, 4 miles." J.J. yelled into the radio. Another Flanker had snuck into the fight from out of nowhere down low so as to be under their radars.

"Cheetahs, Dusty-1, we have him. Break hard to 060."

"Standby Dusty-1, Cheetah-2. I got this. Cover me."

"Roger."

J.J. pushed the throttle past the detent into full afterburner and pushed the stick over to unload the jet to zero G and dive down toward the Flanker. With no parasitic drag at zero lift, the Hornet accelerated to 650 knots rapidly and closed the distance to the Flanker in just a few seconds.

"Got him. He's at 610 knots. Say intentions." Batboy called.

"Koufax." J.J. was telling Batboy in code that he was going to do a Pitch Back maneuver referring to one of the best major league pitcher of all time.

"Roger, got your six." Batboy said.

With a slight speed advantage but having squandered his altitude advantage in the dive down to the Flanker, J.J. was going to have to generate more of an energy advantage than he currently had.

J.J. saw the Flanker roll right for a lead turn before the merge, and countered by rolling left and turning into the bogey to spoil his attempt to generate flight-path separation. J.J. then rolled his wings level, slowed to his best climb speed and pushed the throttles past the detent into full afterburner and climbed straight ahead.

The Flanker was still turning at high G and bleeding energy in an attempt to get a lead for a guns kill. The Flanker pilot then made another big mistake. J.J. saw flash clouds forming above the Flanker's wings and his nose coming around in his turn faster than was possible normally. J.J. knew that the Flanker pilot was using his thrust vectoring engine to turn harder than he could with control surfaces alone to get the lead angle he needed for a guns kill. Thrust vectoring squanders a lot of energy.

As soon as J.J. saw the Flanker's nose come around to the point where the turn toward him was completed, J.J. checked his HUD to make sure he had accelerated to a sufficient speed for a zoom climb. J.J. pulled up into a wings level, inverted, sustained-G, zoom climb while watching the Flanker through the top of his canopy. The Flanker, not realizing he was being rope-a-doped, tried to follow J.J. He did not figure out he did not have enough energy until it was too late. When J.J. got to the top of his climb, he was just above stall speed and he was out of guns and heat seeking missile range of the Flanker. J.J. now had a significant energy advantage over the Flanker, and was directly above him.

The Flanker struggled with decaying airspeed and then did a rudder reversal to avoid departing controlled flight.

When J.J. saw the Flanker nose drop off, he rolled his wings to put his lift vector on the Flanker, and pulled the stick back smoothly to begin a boom and zoom attack on the Flanker's rear hemisphere.

When the Flanker pilot saw J.J. nose over into his dive, the Flanker broke into a hard right diving spiral turn.

J.J. started to spiral down in lag pursuit toward the extended six o'clock position of the Flanker. J.J. kept his jet unloaded as much as possible to maximize his acceleration toward the Flanker.

As J.J. closed the distance, the Flanker pilot started to panic and turned even harder in his spiral dive. "Good. He is bleeding off even more of his energy." J.J. thought to himself. "That just makes my job easier."

While the Flanker had been engaged with J.J., Batboy had been maneuvering in for a rear quarter shot on the Flanker, and he was closing in fast. "OK you little communist prick, let's see if you enjoy getting an Sidewinder up your ass." Batboy thought to himself. Captain Batboy Anderson designated the Flanker as the target on his fire control computer's radar display, selected a Sidewinder, got tone and pulled the trigger. The missile burst off the rail and took off like a bat with its hair on fire.

Inside the Flanker, the Chinese pilot looked at the radar display for the Flanker's rearward looking radar, and saw that J.J.'s Hornet was on his six about two miles back flying toward him at 670 knots. "Fucking stupid American capitalist father of a pig. Watch this from your pathetic little Hornet." the Chinese pilot screamed to nobody in particular behind his oxygen mask as he started a Pugachev Cobra manuever to cause J.J.'s Hornet to overshoot. The Chinese pilot pulled the throttle back to 85% power, deployed his speed brakes to slow down to 220 knots and yanked the stick back in his lap with 35 pounds of pressure to overcome the angle of attack limiter. The Flanker reared up like a Cobra to a 120 degrees angle of attack and then blew up in a huge fireball as Batboy's Sidewinder flew up his right engine's exhaust nozzle. The whole airframe had became a speed brake and the Flanker bled off all of his airspeed. Exactly the wrong thing to do with a Sidewinder streaking toward you.

"Splash another commie. I am bingo, lets RTB." Batboy radioed.

"Cheetah-2, roger that. Aspen, say picture."

"Picture is clear Cheetah-2. Texaco is 110 for 20."

"Cheetahs are RTB. Thanks for the help Dusty-1."

"Welcome. Nice shooting. Dusty-1 out."

When they got back to the boat, they got out of their jets and sprinted across the busy flight deck. Six more Hornets and an F-35 had been launched to take over their HavCAP duties protecting the AWACs, so they had a little time to rest.

J.J. walked to his stateroom and collapsed on the bed. Not more than two minutes later, he heard a knock on the door, and the door opened. It was Carmen. Carmen's juices were fully flowing from the excitement of aerial combat, and, more importantly, of not dying in it. She had that look in her eye as she walked up to him.

He stood up to greet her.

"J.J., you magnificent bastard, thank you for saving my life."

"Thank you for spotting that J-20 stealth. You saved all of us."

"Shut up." Carmen said as she threw her arms around J.J. and kissed him with a full mouth open kiss exploring his lips with her tongue. She reached down and stroked his crotch and found he was already fully erect.

She slowly stroked him until his legs started to shake and then grasped the zipper on his flight suit and slowly pulled it down, looking into his eyes with an unblinking stare and a devilish smile on her face.

"What about Alexandra?"

"She's not here, and I am. This is just a one time thing. Shut up."

"OK." He surrendered to her, and she fucked his brains out.

Twenty minutes later, the phone in his stateroom rang. It was the ready room. "There is a war on J.J., get your ass up here. We've got some commies to kill and Woody to rescue. Is Carmen with you?" the skipper said.

"Yes."

"Thought so. Bring her with you."

"Yes sir."

"We gotta go Carmen. The Skipper wants us in the ready room ASAP."

Ricky rescued by Force Recon patrol and evacuated to hospital ship

Ricky awoke with a start. His PRC-112B survival radio, which had somehow survived his ejection and was still in his survival equipment vest was squawking. "Cheetah-1, Viper-6 actual. Do you copy?"

Slowly and painfully Ricky extricated the radio from his vest. The pain from his broken ribs was excruciating to say nothing of his throbbing skull and legs dangling at unnatural angles. He looked down at them and puked involuntarily. "Viper-6 actual, Cheetah-1, I have you 5 by 5. Say grid."

"Nevermind. We are close-by. We have your grid from your encrypted Prick 12. Danger close. Standby."

As he came to his senses a little more, he could hear armor moving. The he saw a column of tanks moving in a column down a dirt road about 3 miles from him. Chinese infantry were spread out on both flanks and some were moving down the road behind the tanks. Their anti-ship ballistic missiles had just been blown up by the American raid, and they knew there was at least one pilot down somewhere in this general area. They were looking for some pay-back.

"Wildcat, Viper-6 actual, fire mission."

"Viper-6 actual, Wildcat, say grid and target type."

"Wildcat, Viper-6. Armored column with troop concentration around it. Do you have 105 clusters aboard?"

"Affirmative."

"Wildcat, Viper-6, give me a Charlie Baker 105 and two troop clusters. We will paint the column. Standby for grid." Captain "Drive-by" Sims, USMC MARSOC read his GPS lat long, took a laser rangefinder azimuth and range sighting on the middle tank in the column and punched it into his pad. He then read off the latitude and longitude coordinates to the BIB Bone cruising overhead at 25,000 feet. Sims was calling for a CBU-105 tank killer cluster bomb to be dropped on the armored column and two troop killer cluster bombs to be dropped on the troops. His little team of 6 recon marines did not have much of a chance against a force this big unless he got some help.

"Roger the grid. Ready." the Bone WSO radioed.

"Paint is on. Fire for effect."

Two CBU-105 tank killers and two troop killer laser guided cluster bombs dropped out of the Bone and whistled down toward their targets below. At 1000 feet above ground, the dispenser skin was severed in each CBU-105 and ten BLU-108 submunitions were dispensed by an airbag from each 105. A short time later, each submunition deployed a parachute so that they were about 100 yards apart in the air. A short time later, all 20 submunitions released their chutes and a rocket motor stopped the descent and spun the submunition to eject 10 hockey-puck sized Skeets at 90 degree intervals in pairs. The 80 Skeets then began scanning the ground below in a 1500 x 500 foot area for a pattern match. Each Skeet was looking for a tank, truck, artillery piece or armored personnel carrier with laser and infrared sensors. The ones that found a target fired a shaped charge to shoot a molten copper slug armor penetrator into the target from the top. It was a wonder to behold.

All the tanks were destroyed, and most of the Chinese troops were killed by the other two cluster bombs.

"Bullseye Wildcat. Viper-6 actual out."

Captain Sims waited for the sun to finish setting and darkness to descend. He then gave a hand signal for his team to move out toward Ricky. They were about 300 yards away hidden in a stand of trees. The team silently ran through the grass of the intervening meadow.

When they got to the tree Ricky was hanging in, all hell broke loose. The surviving Chinese Marines had closed to within 300 yards of them, and they were taking fire from the very tree line where they had just been. Conveniently, Captain Sims now knew their position. He ordered two of his men to cut Ricky's parachute cords and lower him out of the tree which they successfully accomplished. The other three were leapfrogging toward the Chinese left flank. Ricky was lying on the ground firing his .45 at the Chinese Marines as if he could hit anything with a pistol at 300 yards. All he was doing was giving away his position by his muzzle flashes.

"Stop it Ricky. It is not like you are going to actually hit anybody with the thing at 300 yards. We are trying to save your dumbass." Sims barked.

"I though that was you Drive-by when you came over the radio. How is Veronica?"

"We will talk about that later wise ass if we live through this."

Ricky laughed and then groaned as the convulsion of laughter sent an ice pick of pain through his rib cage.

"Badger, Viper-6 actual. We need a gunship ASAP and a SPIE extraction for 7."

Viper-6 actual, Badger, Cobra gunship call sign Viking on the way, 2 mikes. SPIE extraction for seven to follow. Paint the target." Captain Sims was calling for a high speed extraction using a special rope with seven spots on it that the Force Recon Marines could hook their torso harnesses to as well as a torso harness they put on Ricky. The helicopter would come in, hover low enough to dangle the rope on the ground long enough for the commandos to hook up and then take off at high speed in the darkness dragging the rope and the Marine commandos up into the air and away from the danger at 120 knots. Captain Sims heard the Cobra approaching. "Viking, Viper-6 actual painting the target." He pointed his laser designator at the tree line where the Chinese Marines had established a position. The laser designator had a green laser beam that was all but invisible to the naked eye in the dark. Captain Sims pointed the laser at the tree line wherever he could see muzzle flashes originating.

"Viper-6 actual, we have it. Standby ten ticks for low pass." Ten seconds later, the Cobra gunship roared over at 50 feet and lit the tree line up with a 7.62 mm multibarrel M134 minigun, a Gatling style gun that spewed out 6000 rounds per minute. The Cobra co-pilot/gunner was wearing night vision goggles and could see the laser like it was a Christmas Tree. Every time a Chinese Marine would fire, Captain Sims would move the laser to that location and the Cobra pilot would light it up. That quieted the Chinese down, but they were not all killed.

"Viper-6 actual, Sierra-1 with SPIE rope out. Light your extraction point."

Captain Sims cracked a couple of chemical light sticks and threw them out in the meadow about 10 yards from his position. This drew a hail of gunfire from the Chinese Marines, so Sims lit them up with the laser again and the Cobra hosed them down. "Suger Ray, Battle Ax, get back her for extraction." Sims called for his two Marine Commandos to get back to his position.

"Viking, Viper 6 actual, we are preparing for extraction. Need you to hose them good while we hook up and extract."

"Roger that."

"Suger, Battle Ax, Go, go, go take the zoomie with you and hook him up to #1." Sims screamed. Two of his commandos leaped into action dragging Ricky out to the SPIE rope. Ricky was screaming in pain, but there was no other choice. The Cobra was hosing the shit out of the tree line and firing 40 mm grenades into with his grenade launcher in the gun turrent. It was total chaos with the noise of the gunfire, roaring engines, swirling winds, fearless Chinese Marines charging out of the woods and being mowed down by the Cobra and Sim's other commandos who were using their night vision scope equipped MP5 assault rifles to pick off the charging commies one at a time. Sugar Ray and Battle Ax hooked Ricky up to spot 1 on the SPIE rope and hooked themselves into spots 2 and 3. The gave a hand signal to Sims that they were done and pulled up their MP5s and started providing covering fire for Sims and the rest of the team. The rest of the commandos sprinted out and hooked up while Sims laid down more covering fire. Finally Captain Sims sprinted out and hooked himself up and looked up at the door gunner of the extraction helicopter and gave him the hand signal to take off.

With a massive roar, the Huey gunship poured the coal to its engine and the pilot lifted up on the collective and pushed the stick forward to pitch the nose down and stomped on the rudder to spin the bird around to point away from the tree line. The Cobra gunship was firing frantically walking its fire up and down the tree line and lobbing grenades in as fast as the grenade launcher could fire them. The SPIE rope became taught and then with a great whoosh, the whole team was dragged up into the night sky like they were on Santa's Sleigh. They picked up speed, but they could hear the supersonic cracks as Chinese rounds whipped by them.

Finally they were safely away from the Chinese Marines far enough to relax. They were over water now and the extraction was over. They enjoyed the night air as they whooshed along on the way to the hospital ship.

US carriers move in and battle for air supremacy begin

The raid on the ASBMs had been a success. The fearsome missiles had been destroyed with only minor losses to U.S. forces. The three super carriers and the escort ships of the Southern Expeditionary Force were ordered by Admiral Wallace Courtney to proceed north to the Tupi Field to join with the three carriers and escort ships of the Northern Expeditionary Force to do battle with the six Chinese carriers and the rest of the Chinese armada. The battle for air supremacy was crucial to the success of the U.S. rescue plan to wrest the oil of the Tupi Field from Chinese control.

Ricky laid in a medically induced coma in the hospital ship USS Mercy. The doctors had to drill a hole in his skull to relieve the pressure of swelling in his brain. His legs had been put in casts and would recover. His ribs were healing. But the doctors did not know how much damage the swelling had done before they were able to reduce the intracranial pressure. Only time would tell if Ricky had suffered brain damage from his ejection. Carmen, Captain Anderson and J.J. visited him when they could between flight operations, but there was not much they could do other than read to him while they were there. Word of the tactics used during the HAVCAP dogfight got around to the squadrons in the fleet, and the pilots were briefed on how to use them. It became standard operating procedure to deploy a couple of F-35s with each F/A-18 squadron to provide each squadron with infrared DAS capability while simultaneously protecting the F-35s from the vastly aerodynamically superior Su-30MK2 Flankers and J-11 Sino Flankers.

Kilo boats attack carriers with sea skimming anti ship missiles, but carriers transmit kill signals to hidden kill chips and defeat the missiles

COMBAT INFORMATION CENTER: U.S.S. CARL VINSON, 0230 HOURS, MAY 15, 2034, 45 NAUTICAL MILES SOUTH OF THE SOUTHERN EDGE OF THE TUPI FIELD

"Surface contact, 350 degrees for 190 kilometers, high speed sea skimming missile, Sunburn, closure rate 3430 knots, impact 3 minutes, 30 seconds." the CIC watch officer screamed into the interphone to the Sea Whiz Phalanx battery operator. "Whizzer protocol in 2 mikes." The watch officer was referring to a spoof protocol to take advantage of the secret kill switch in the Sunburn missile's guidance system that had been planted by a corrupt Chinese government contractor the CIA had bribed. The CIA had developed a lookalike chip for one of the chips in the missile guidance systems of the Sunburn and Sizzler class of anti-ship missiles. The chip looked like the chip it replaced, but it had circuitry that responded to a secret coded radio signal by causing the missile's guidance signals to the missile's control surfaces to crash it into the ocean. To avoid giving away the fact that the missile had a kill switch in it, the secret, coded radio signal was not transmitted until the missile was within two miles of the ship so that it looked like the Sea Whiz 20 millimeter rotary cannon gatling-gun had shot the missile down. In reality, the closure rate of the Sunburn class of missiles was too fast to be shot down by the Phalanx rotary canon, especially if there was more than one of them inbound. The Sea Whiz could only engage one target at a time, so it could be easily overwhelmed. Since its capabilities were top secret, it was the hope of the CIA that the Chinese and Russians would believe that the Phalanx system had been improved to the point it could engage and destroy a Sunburn class, sea-skimming anti-ship missile.

The Sea Whiz opened up on the inbound missile with a fire hose stream of spent uranium 20 mm shells at two miles to impact. Simultaneously the radio operator in CIC transmitted a radio frequency burst on a special frequency modulated with the encrypted secret kill switch code. The missile continued inbound for another 500 yards and then suddenly plunged into the sea. A cheer went up around the ship. The CIC officer crossed himself and said a little prayer of relief that the chip worked as advertised. The Sunburn class of missiles were known to be armed with 340 kiloton nuclear warheads.

Admiral Wallace Courtney stormed into CIC and bellowed, "Where the fuck did that missile come from? Did we have any surface or aerial targets out in that direction?"

"Negative sir. I checked with the escort ships and CAP patrol. Nothing. No radar returns of any sort sir." the CIC watch officer, Lieutenant David Smith, answered. "Probably a Kilo sub out there somewhere sir. We dispatched a sub hunter helo out there with sono buoys, but no sonar returns sir."

"Lets get some SEALS in the water out there with CAS arrays in tow." Admiral Courtney ordered.

"Yes sir. Right away. Ensign Miller, get team 2 actual up here ASAP."

"Aye sir."

Three minutes later, Lt. Jerry "Ninja" Pattison, Seal Lieutenant and commanding officer of Seal Team 2 appeared in CIC. "Lieutenant Smith, what can we do for you?"

"Lt. Pattison, we need you to get some SEALS out on the water in rubber boats and tow some CAS sonar arrays around and launch some drone subs with CAS arrays. We are looking for one or more Kilo subs out in the general direction from which that Sunburn missile came from. Need it yesterday."

"Roger that. We are on it."

. . .

Fifty minutes later, Lt. Pattison and three SEALS from SEAL Team 2 leaped out of a hovering helicopter into the inky black ocean 200 kilometers north of the *USS Carl Vinson*. The helicopter dropped their CRRC rubber boat into the water, and they quickly attached the towed Continuously Active Sonar array to the boat and established a satellite uplink to the sonar signal processing center on the *USS* .

The SEALS started trolling the waters with their CAS towed sonar array behind them and continuously transmitting data back to the *Halsey* for processing. A P3 Orion sub hunter using an airborne magnetometer had previously recorded a magnetic anomaly in the area the SEALS were patrolling, so they were hopeful the mission would not be a dry hole.

. . .

CHINESE KILO SUBMARINE YUAN ZHEND 65 HAO, DEPTH 400 FEET, 0545, 215 KILOMETERS NORTH OF USS CARL VINSON

"Con, sonar, screws in the water, 095, very close. Sounds like an outboard motor. I think it is a SEAL rubber boat."

"What would they be doing way out here in the middle of the ocean?" Shang Xiao (Captain) Jin-Bao thought to himself. Then it occurred to him. He had read an article that the only way the ASW forces of the United States could detect a Kilo submarine that was not moving pretty fast underwater was to use towed Continuously Active Sonar arrays. Having just fired a Sunburn-class anti-ship missile at a U.S. carrier, he knew that they would be looking for a sub since there were no other airborne or surface contacts in the region he was operating. He quickly put two and two together.

Jin-Bao gathered his resolve and picked up the ship intercom. "Boarding party, be ready for a surface gunfight in two minutes. Prepare to blow tanks. We are going to attack a SEAL team towing a CAS array on the surface above us."

"Aye sir." the boarding party commander replied.

"Sonar, con, where are they now?"

"Right above us sir."

"Blow tanks, emergency surface."

A great whooshing sound filled the sub and compressed air gushed into the ballast tanks and replaced the sea water in them. The small submarine took a very steep angle and rocketed toward the surface.

"LT, we found them. They are blowing tanks right under us and coming up. I could hear the Captain announce an emergency blow and to get ready for a suface gunfight." Petty Office "Gonzo" Gomez yelled above the din of the outboard motor from his hydrophone station. He was listening in to the output of the hydrophone 100 yards back in the towed array.

Ninja Pattison looked down at his GPS and pressed the transmit button on his satellite transceiver. "Honeybadger, Goldilocks 6 actual, target Bullseye 350 for 94, Kilo surfacing. ASROC on my mark."

The Combat Information Center watch officer on the USS Halsey, which was only 14 kilometers away, replied, "Goldilocks 6 actual, Honeybadger, we copy Bullseye 350 for 94. Standby for ASROC. Isn't that your position?"

The ASROC was a torpedo-tipped, ballistic missile used as a standoff weapon against submarines. It had a range of 19 kilometers.

"Affirmative. We are going to duke it out with them. If you do not hear from me in 2 mikes, fire the ASROC."

"Roger that."

The Kilo breached out of the water with its nose at a 60 degree angle. It crashed back down with a tremendous splash 30 meters from the SEALS. "In the water, use the boat as cover. Gonzo, swim underwater to the other side of the sub, pop up and hose them. We will keep them busy. Whizzer and Bo, stay with me."

"Roger LT." Gonzo said as he threw his MP5 over his shoulder on its sling and took off swimming. As soon as he saw the hatch open on the sub, he did a surface dive and began swimming underwater.

The first Chinese sailor popped his head out of the hatch and was rewarded with a 7.62 NATO round through the forehead. It was kind of a miracle shot from 30 meters, using a bobbing boat as a rifle support in the very faint light of an emerging dawn. "Lets see you do that again Whizzer." Ninja Pattison laughed.

"Blow me LT, I can do that all day." Whizzer said with a matter of fact tone that belied the desperation of their situation. Then he laughed.

"OK shut up, they are going to eventually get that guy out of the way and who knows how many of them will come up." Pattison said, all business now.

Thirty seconds later, the sub turned its tail toward them and five more sailors popped out of the hatch using the conning tower as cover.

A fierce gun battle ensued. The SEALS had the advantage because they were about 40 meters away now and were hard to see in the faint light. The boat was the first casualty and multiple rounds penetrated it. The SEALS had abandoned it though and were popping their heads up to shoot a burst, submerging and popping up again at a different position. It was hard to shoot an MP5 while treading water, so they were not doing too well in the marksmanship department.

Then they heard a short burst, and all five Chinese sailors dropped to the deck like sacks of potatoes. They had been lined up along the axis of the hull searching for the SEALS off the starboard rear quarter, when Gonzo popped up at the bow of the sub and hosed them down in enfilade fire with a short burst. It is highly likely that one or more of his MP5 rounds went completely through more than one of the Chinese sailors and took out the next one up the line.

" Honeybadger, Goldilocks 6 actual, fire the ASROC before this thing gets off another shot."

"Lets get out of here boys, they are sending a Mark 46 torpedo by airmail."

They took off swimming as fast as they could, but the ASROC arrived in only a matter of seconds. The shock wave through the water as the Mark 46 torpedo exploded and sunk the Kilo, ruptured their internal organs, and they all drowned. Lt. Jerry "Ninja" Pattison and all three of his SEALs were later awarded the Congressional Medal of Honor posthumously.

Chinese send waves of drones in to fool air defenses, our fighters go winchester on drones

The carrier battle groups of the Southern Expeditionary Force arrived at the Tupi Field the next day and formed a blocking and enveloping force to the Chinese carriers and their escort ships. For the Chinese to escape the attacks from the Northern Expeditionary Force, they would have to first go through the Southern Expeditionary Force.

A fierce air battle ensued for air supremacy over Brazil's coastal waters. The Chinese sent a wave of armed drones first which caused the F/A-18 Hornets to expend all their missiles to shoot down to protect their carriers. The wave of drones was followed by a wave of Su-30MK2 Flankers and Sino Flankers.

The American carriers sent up a second wave of Hornets to take out the Flankers and Sino Flankers, but the losses were very heavy since the Flankers were aerodynamically and numerically superior and each plane carried more missiles than the American jets.

Just as the battle appeared to be lost, three Russian super carriers sailed into the battle. The Russians brought multiple squadrons of their own Flankers and two squadrons of their Fifth Generation PAK-FA stealth fighter. The Russians were pissed off at the Chinese who had breached their manufacturing agreement with the Russians. The Chinese had stolen all the Russian technology, exceeded the limits on numbers of Flankers that could be manufactured under the terms of the manufacturing license and cheated the Russians out of billions of dollars in royalty payments. The Russians were out for blood.

To make matters worse for the Chinese, the Air Force finally got off the dime and got all their F-22 squadrons down from the U.S. bases and up from Porto Alegre.

It was a Flanker bloodbath for the Chinese. The Russian pilots knew how to fly their Flankers better than the Chinese, and the PAK-FA and F-22 stealth jets had a field day sneaking up on unsuspecting Chinese pilots and hosing them with Sidewinders, AMRAAMs, Alamos and Archers.

Three Chinese carriers and their escort ships were sunk the first day of the battle. Two U.S. carriers and a Russian carrier were also sunk by a combination of Kilo submarines, air attacks from Chinese Flankers and anti-ship missiles fired from the Chinese cruisers and destroyers.

The other three Chinese carriers turned to run for home.

As soon as air supremacy had been achieved, six divisions of United States Marines invaded the beaches of Brazil from Rio and southward. Fierce fighting on the ground ensued. The Army parachuted in the Screaming Eagles of the 101st Airborne division and the 75th Ranger Regiment consisting of six battalions of Ranger Commandos.

The Chinese were no pushovers. They had eight divisions of highly trained Marines and commandos ensconced in fortified positions at strategic locations throughout Brazil. Over the next two weeks, the fighting was fierce and bloody.

Brazilian resistance forces armed themselves from captured Chinese weapons and joined the fray. Their ambushes of Chinese columns and sabotage of Chinese installations and heavy equipment helped immensely. They had suffered greatly under Chinese occupation, and were able to get payback in some small measure.

Finally, after suffering 35% casualties the Marines, Army paratroopers and Rangers prevailed. The refineries, ports, drilling rigs, Rio and Brasilia were wrested from Chinese control. Hundreds of thousands of Chinese Marines surrendered when their command structures were destroyed and they no longer were receiving orders from their commanders.

. . .

The phone rang in Carmen's stateroom on the *USS Carl Vinson*. Carmen picked up the phone having been awoken from slumber. "SWAT get up the ready room like yesterday." It was J.J.

"Why what's up."

"Just get up here on the double."

"Be right there."

A few minutes later, Carmen walked into the ready room. CAG Tom Baker and Admiral Courtney were there as were J.J. and Nailgun.

"Captain Carmen Nicoise, reporting as ordered sir." Carmen said to the Admiral.

"Thanks for your excellent service SWAT. We need you again. I understand you speak Chinese is that correct?"

"Yes sir."

Admiral Courtney started the conversation. "An extraordinary opportunity has arisen. A Force Recon team scouting the Porto Alegre area has found three mobile ASBM launchers complete with missiles hidden in the woods outside Porto Alegre. They apparently were moved to avoid our raid. The Chinese must have a spy in the fleet somewhere that found out about the raid. In any event, the crews abandoned them, and now we have them with three Chinese carriers attempting to flee southward away from the Tupi Field. They are going to sail right by Porto Alegre and we are going to let them. We want you to sink them with those ASBMs."

Carmen's eyes widened. "Yes sir. Why me?"

"Because you speak Chinese, have a degree in Aeronautical Engineering. The weapons are complete with operations manuals and all the switches and gauges are labeled, but it is all in Chinese. They are solid fuel boosters, are full of propellant and are ready to fire. We want you to see if you can figure out how to load the necessary data in them and launch them. Your flight leaves in ten minutes. Get a move on. Nailgun will be flying you down there in his Hornet."

"Roger that sir. I will do my best." Carmen was elated. This was a golden opportunity to kill a bunch of communists all at once. Her thoughts drifted briefly back to that day in Shanghai when she was a little girl and communist thugs machine gunned her father to death right in front of her.

. . .

Nailgun gave the thumbs up sign to the catapult officer after wiping out his controls and finishing his cat launch checklist. A second later, the cat stroke came like a huge kick in the pants and accelerated them to 130 knots in about 3 seconds. "It never gets old." Carmen said to Neil over the intercom.

"I know. It is more fun than actually having an orgasm."

Carmen laughed. "Can I fly this thing?"

"I doubt it, but your airplane."

Carmen immediately snapped it into a high G barrel roll even though they were only about 2000 feet off the deck.

"Holy shit, give this thing back to me before you kill us all."

"Ha, what a pussy." Carmen said with a smile. She loved to give Nailgun shit.

An hour and a half later, they touched down at the airfield outside Porto Alegre that the Chinese used to fly their Flankers out of. Captain Adam "Drive-by" Sims USMC rolled up to the jet in a world war II Jeep flying a MARSOC Raider Battalion flag, got out and gave Carmen a snappy salute. "I will be your personal driver today M'aam."

"Sims, how is Veronica?"

"Blow me Carmen. I still owe you one. You better hope the Chinese don't attack us while you play girl scientist with a giant solid fuel rocket bomb."

"Thank you. I feel much better now." Carmen said with a laugh. "Lets go Sims, we are burning daylight."

Carmen hopped into the jeep and they sped off at breakneck speed.

A half an hour later, they arrived at the missile site and Carmen was awed by the size of the missiles and their launch trucks. "We have a company of Marines surrounding us in a defensive perimeter. There is no organized force still operating down here, but there are rogue elements operating independently. Better get to work."

"Thanks Adam. Where are the ops manuals." Adam Sims went to the cab of one of the launch trucks and got them for her.

"We have a satellite uplink established for communications and data downloads if you need it."

"Roger that." Carmen dug into the manuals. They were beautifully written and illustrated. Her Chinese came back to her fast even though it had been quite some time since she had read Chinese. She zoomed through the manual in about an hour and then looked up. Sims was napping nearby. "Drive by, wake up. I need to talk to the Chairman of the Joint Chiefs."

"Roger that he said sleepily." He went over to the satellite uplink radio and made a short call asking for a patch into the Pentagon. He motioned her over and handed her the handset. "Admiral Picket is on the line."

"Good morning sir. Captain Carmen Nicoise here."

"Hello SWAT, what can we do for you?"

"Sir, I need three data files, one for each missile. Each data file has to be a Synthetic Aperture Radar image of one of the fleeing Chinese carriers taken from the edge of space. I also need each carrier's latitude and longitude, course and speed at a time just before I launch so I can program that data into the missile's guidance system along with the SAR image."

"Roger that Carmen. We have a Misty spy satellite still in operation that can get the SAR images for you and some cube sats that can provide you with position, course and speed information. I will send the Aurora down to get backup SAR images from 90 miles up. Expect that data in about 2 hours."

"Thank you sir. Call us on this link when you are ready to download and I will set up a computer to this link to receive the data and upload it into the missiles".

Carmen busied herself setting up a computer to talk to each of the three missile's guidance systems at the satellite uplink radio's data demodulator by a Gigabit Ethernet local area network.

True to his word, about 2 hours later, Admiral Picket called on the sat phone and told Carmen he had the SAR images ready for download. "What is the source of the images?"

"The are from the Aurora spy plane."

"Good. That is about the altitude these things fly at while they are in hunting mode. Wait one while I set up the computer." She set up the computer to receive the images and told the Admiral she was ready. He started the download. Each SAR image had header data as to the name of the carrier of which it was an image, the carrier's position, course and speed and the time the image was taken in Zulu time.

"Got them. Excellent work sir. Give me 30 minutes to upload this data into the missile's guidance systems and then provide an update on each of the carrier's positions, course and speed please."

"You got it young lady." Picket had re-tasked the Misty stealth spy satellite to make a pass over the southern Atlantic just about the time Carmen needed the data. He had also commandeered a commercial weather satellite in geosynchronous orbit over the southern Atlantic so that he could watch the movements of the Chinese carriers. The carriers were about 1150 kilometers from Carmen's missiles at that moment and moving closer by the minute as they fled south toward the tip of South America.

Carmen logged into each missile's guidance system in turn. The Chinese missile battery officer had been kind enough to write his username and password for each missile in the manuals. She uploaded the SAR image of the target carrier into the pattern matching module of missile 1 and then loaded that carriers last known position, course and speed into the guidance system module. She repeated the process for missile's 2 and 3. Then she called Admiral Picket again and said she was ready for a position update. He gave her each carrier's current position, course and speed and wished her luck.

She thanked him for his help and updated each missile's guidance system target IP parameters. Each missile would fly to the IP in a horizontal flight path at the edge of space and then begin a target search by turning on its downward looking Synthetic Aperture Radar. Each missile would compare the images returned by its SAR to the image in its pattern matching memory. When it found its target, it would start a vertical death dive toward the target, and, more specifically, the spot on the target which had been designated in the image. Carmen had designated a spot amidships, right in the middle of the flight deck of each carrier. She armed the 30 kiloton nuclear warheads and set their fuses to detonate when they penetrated the hanger decks.

When all was ready, she started the automated countdown and made sure everybody was clear.

Five minutes later, the missiles took off in unison with a deafening roar and a spectacular light show. All three missiles climbed ferociously and curved gently eastward. When they reached the edge of space on their calculated headings to the intercept points, they leveled off and flew horizontally parallel to the surface of the ocean and turned on their Synthetic Aperture Radars and began searching the surface of the ocean below. First missile 1 found its target, then missile 2 and then missile 3. All three missiles arched over into a vertical death dive and screamed downward at mach 10 out of the noonday sun. The Chinese carriers never saw them coming.

Forty two seconds later, all three Chinese carriers were vaporized.

EPILOGUE

- -

CARMEN TAKES LEAVE TO BE WITH RICKY IN HOSPITAL AND THEN WHEN LEAVE EXHAUSTED, GOES AWOL

It was two in the morning. Carmen was dozing in the chair next to Ricky's bed where she had been sleeping the last four weeks. She had been sitting by his bedside in a round-the-clock vigil, reading to him, singing to him, stroking his hair and telling him how she felt, and pleading with him to come back to her.

Ricky's eyes fluttered, and he stirred in bed. Carmen was instantly awaked. "Ricky? Ricky baby are you back?" A minute of silence dragged by.

Ricky was starting to be aware of activity and lights in the hallway outside his hospital room. He felt a warm and loving presence close by. He could see a hazy face in the distance in his mind's eye, but he could not make out who it was. Then in a rush of consciousness flooding back in, his eyes slowly opened and he could see Carmen's smiling face looking down at him in the faint glow of blue light bathing the room from a night light Carmen had bought him.

"Carmen?"

"Yes baby it is me. I have been waiting for you. Welcome back. I have missed you so much."

"Oh my God Carmen was that you I could feel close by while I was out?"

"Yes it was me here by your side the whole time you were out."

"How long was I out?"

"You were gone for a month."

"Holy shit. What happened to me?

"You fractured your skull, broke a rib and fractured both of your legs in the ejection. The swelling in your brain was dangerous, so they drilled a hole in your skull to relieve the pressure and put you in a medically induced coma."

"Just what I need. Another hole in my head." Ricky chortled.

"You have so many now what's one more? How do you feel?"

"I feel like I have been bitch slapped by Shiva, the eight-armed Hindu Goddess."

Carmen burst into laughter. Still giggling, she finally said "Shiva is a male God you nitwit, and he has 23 arms."

After she finally stopped laughing, Ricky asked, "Duly noted. You have been here a month? In that chair?"

"Yes."

"How does your Skipper feel about that?"

"Well when I ran out of leave, I went AWOL. But they know where I am, and have not come to arrest me yet, so I am hoping they do not court martial me and just put me in hack for a year." She was only half kidding. If she was not a genuine war hero and a woman to boot, they would have run her up the mizzen mast and then drummed her out of the corp. Instead, they gave her the Navy Cross and some leeway. It was not like the old corps.

"Thank you baby Jesus for bring me somebody who loves me." Ricky said with a smile.

"I do love you Ricky." She was not kidding. She had had a lot of time to think while she was standing her vigil and had made up her mind. He was the one.

"No shit? I cannot believe my luck. You are kidding right?"

"No you dumbass, I am not kidding. And the proper response would have been, 'Oh Carmen, you are the love of my life. I cannot live without you. Will you marry me?'"

"Yeah, what you said." Ricky said with a sly smile. He was sticking the needle in deep now.

"Oh my God, I cannot believe I have fallen in love with such a douchebag."

"I am what I am."

"That what Popeye the sailor man always used to say."

"What you see is what you get." Ricky said.

The next week they were married, and Ricky was awarded the Silver Star. His whole squadron attended.

THE END

www.ingramcontent.com/pod-product-compliance
Lightning Source LLC
Chambersburg PA
CBHW020622110726
47899CB00002B/606